"I TOLD YOU THAT I MARRIED YOU FOR BETTER OR WORSE. FOREVER."

Callie felt a wave of shame wash over her. Chandler didn't want her. He wanted to punish her for running out on him, to show her that she was his to do with as he wished. Her eyes defiantly met his and she stiffened. But before she could escape him, Chandler grabbed her and pulled her roughly back to crush her against his chest. "You'll come back, Callie, and on my terms."

Then his lips lowered ever so slowly to hers. Callie tensed in his arms, trying to pretend cold indifference, but she relived a thousand other kisses that Chandler had given her, and knew she must escape—before it was too late.

BITTER VINES

Megan Lane

A CANDLELIGHT ECSTASY ROMANCE ™

Published by
Dell Publishing Co., Inc.
1 Dag Hammarskjold Plaza
New York, New York 10017

Copyright © 1982 by Brenda Himrod

All rights reserved. No part of this book may be
reproduced or transmitted in any form or by any
means, electronic or mechanical, including photocopying,
recording or by any information storage
and retrieval system, without the written permission
of the Publisher, except where permitted by law.

Dell ® TM 681510, Dell Publishing Co., Inc.

Candlelight Ecstasy Romance™ is a trademark of
Dell Publishing Co., Inc., New York, New York.

ISBN: 0-440-10825-X

Printed in the United States of America
First printing—May 1982

Dear Reader:

In response to your continued enthusiasm for Candlelight Ecstasy Romances™, we are increasing the number of new titles from four to six per month.

We are delighted to present sensuous novels set in America, depicting modern American men and women as they confront the provocative problems of modern relationships.

Throughout the history of the Candlelight line, Dell has tried to maintain a high standard of excellence to give you the finest in reading enjoyment. That is and will remain our most ardent ambition.

Anne Gisonny
Editor
Candlelight Romances

CHAPTER ONE

Callie glanced worriedly at her stepfather as she drove through the heart of the agricultural country, swirls of dust dancing at the side of the narrow road as the car raced along on the sunny June day.

"Are you all right, Logan?"

His smile was one of false cheerfulness as he reached out to pat her shoulder reassuringly. "Yes, of course I am. Stop worrying about me. I'll be fine." Pale gray eyes studied her as a frown knitted his forehead. "Callie, I'm sorry I've lived to burden you. You don't owe me anything and your mother wouldn't want you to be saddled with such a sad responsibility."

"Don't talk foolishness," she said, forcing a broad smile to her full lips. She tugged lightly at the Peter Pan collar of her simple biscuit-colored dress, then gripped the wheel more tightly with long, slender fingers. "Mother loved you, and I am worried about you. I certainly don't have any intentions of abandoning you in your hour of need," she teased lightly. Her eyes searched his face tenderly. "I don't know what I would have done without you these past few years, and I'm glad I can return the favor."

He issued a low grunt as he ran a frail hand through short, thick gray hair. "You would have done a hell of a lot better, honey. I should have insisted that you leave a long time ago."

"I enjoyed working at the mine, Logan," she interjected. "I'm an adult. It wasn't your responsibility to tell me when to come and go."

He shook his head. "I had no right to ask you to help me. I've never been anything but trouble to you. I took your mother away during your most vulnerable years, and I left you to be raised by your aunt. I was never around when you needed someone, and I had no right to lean so heavily on you when things got bad at the copper mine. Now I've put you in the position of returning to this place. I really wish it didn't have to be this way."

"Don't be silly," she chided softly, glancing at him with big brown eyes. "It was my idea to return to the Salinas Valley." She looked at the leafy lettuce crop neatly lining the sides of the road, then her gaze shifted to the orderly rows of bright green grapevines flourishing on the gently sloping hills of the surrounding countryside, the smooth flow of jade broken only by a few isolated houses. The rays of the sun spilled bright gold across the ground and the houses from a brilliantly blue sky. Despite the uncertainty of her homecoming, Callie felt excitement brewing inside her. She loved this part of California; the rich earth with its proliferation of growing things and scarcity of population gave her sustenance. She had been glad to leave the desolation of Montana behind.

"This is home to me, Logan," she said with feeling. "It's the only place I've ever really felt I belonged. When you get to know this country, you'll love it as I do."

"Do you love it, Callie?" he asked, regarding her intently. "Can you live here again? Is the bitterness gone? Have you forgotten about Chandler?" he probed gently.

Callie shifted uncomfortably under his scrutiny and glanced defensively at him with her almond-shaped eyes. They met Logan's pale, close-set gray ones briefly before her gaze returned to the road. "I've long ago forgotten about Chandler Matthews," she said thickly, wondering how she ever coaxed the lie from her lips. "He means nothing to me now."

But she hadn't forgotten about him, of course, no matter how she tried to convince herself of the futility of remembering. In the past four years, he had lived in her dreams, in her mind, and in her heart. She had seen his face on half the men she met, gazed into his eyes a hundred times, and seen his broad back on a dozen of the men who worked the mine. Time had dulled the anger, the heartache, and the humiliation, and a new life had distracted her, but neither had erased the memory of the man. Callie had actually welcomed the chance to come back and face him, for it was the only way she could ever expunge him from her soul.

A thousand memories tumbled free in her mind at just the sound of his name on her lips, and there was no way she could turn the tide that lapped at her consciousness. She had married Chandler the summer she became twenty-one—and such a young, naive twenty-one she had been. Sheltered by a domineering and possessive spinster aunt who was bitter about men in general, cloistered in the tiny local community, surrounded only by people she knew, educated at the junior college in Salinas where she studied secretarial skills at her aunt's insistence, Callie had been totally unprepared for the wealthy, cosmopolitan, dashing Chandler Matthews when he took the neighborhood by storm and purchased the ranch down the road from Aunt Caroline's house. He had come from San Francisco, complete with his flame-haired, sophisticated, sultry mistress, who had moved to the valley along with her parents and grandfather under the pretext of getting away from city pressures. At first the locals had smugly looked on, sure that Chandler Matthews only wanted to play at being a cowboy, but he soon won them all with his charm, his smooth ways, and his knowledge of cattle ranching.

Chandler had arrived in March, and by May his mistress had returned to San Francisco and married another man. Gossip had run rampant in the little community, and even the parents of the bride had confessed that the wedding was abrupt. Chandler and Nadine Harris had grown up together, and though both were in their early thirties, it had been taken for granted that wedding bells would ring for them one day.

A small sigh escaped Callie's parted lips. By June, Chandler had wooed and wed her. The courting had been stormy and intense, with Chandler insisting that he was too old to be satisfied with fondling and kisses, and Callie clinging to her dream of marriage by the sheerest threads of willpower. She hadn't dated much and she hadn't had the experience to rein in the passions of a man like Chandler. Determined and powerful, he had told her bluntly, "I want you, and I don't stop until I get what I want."

She had wanted him to want her, but she also wanted him to marry her. When she told him she was a virgin and would settle for no less than marriage, he had been both surprised and amused that any twenty-one-year-old was so Victorian—but then he hadn't known how much influence Aunt Caroline had wielded.

In the end, he had talked at length with her, telling her that she had best be sure that marriage was really what she wanted because he intended to marry only once. She had been thrilled by his words, for she believed that marriage was sacred and the commitment a lifelong one.

The wedding took place when the warmth of day had cooled into evening, but Callie couldn't forget the fire that Chandler had created inside her that night. She had never imagined the union of a man and a woman held such awesome power or such exquisite pleasure. A vision of Chandler, tall and muscled and so very virile, as he had looked when he drew her into his arms that night, lived again in her mind with vivid clarity. She had trembled with excitement and fear, and Chandler had caressed her nude body until the trembling turned into shivers of desire. His kisses had grown more passionate and his caresses more hungry, and when he had guided Callie's hands over his own hard, throbbing body, she had forgotten all about her anxieties. He had aroused her past all point of reason and she had known only that her body was aching deep down inside for him, her mind crying out to him.

There had been only ecstasy when Chandler's body joined with hers, and to this day what Callie recalled most clearly about her initiation into love was the spiraling joy rising in her mind and the hot, eager warmth rippling throughout her loins as Chandler moved inside her with increasing ardor, causing her to gasp breathlessly with pleasure.

The summer had been filled with breakfasts in bed, horseback rides, picnics under tall trees, late evening swims, midnight frolics, and unforgettable nights—long, thrilling nights, made up of a thousand wonders and a hundred pleasures, as Chandler introduced her to the rapture of lovemaking and showed her ways to heighten the joy for them both.

A darkness spilled into her mind like an ugly, creeping red stain, obscuring the glorious memories of the summer. By the end of October, Nadine had returned to the valley with a quickie divorce and a ferocious desire to reclaim Chandler. The winter had been long and cold, with increasing dissension between Chandler and Callie as Nadine became a part of their lives again. By the spring roundup, the red-headed witch had accomplished her goals.

"Callie."

Startled from her reverie, Callie turned to look at Logan. "I'm sorry. Did you say something?"

He smiled wanly. "I asked why you didn't put the house

up for sale through an agent. We didn't need to come back here to live."

"The doctor said you needed a warm climate, Logan," she commented. "You know he mentioned California in particular, and this area, with its warm summer days and cool evenings, will be ideal." Her eyes skimmed over his thin frame, taking in the beige jumpsuit that called attention to his pallor, and she felt a rush of protectiveness toward him. When she had gone to him, her heart breaking, her mind hurting, sure that her life was over at the tender age of almost twenty-two, he had held her until the tears stopped, then tossed her into the middle of his dream. The floundering copper mine in a barren part of Montana had occupied her days and helped her get through the darkness of her heartache and humiliation, and as she began to know Logan better, she had wanted to help him with his impossible dream. He was like a little boy building castles in the air, and though they both struggled to keep his enterprise alive, Callie had known it was doomed to failure.

"But California's a big state," Logan said, penetrating her thoughts.

"We can get on our feet here, Logan," she said with no hint of accusation for the state of their affairs. She felt that they both had failed in the copper business, with the result that they were nearly without funds now. She didn't like the feeling, and she wanted to give them some measure of security. Their positions were reversed now; Logan needed to lean on her until he could get back on his feet, and she was glad she could repay the favor.

"I'm grateful for the house Aunt Caroline left me. With real estate prices so darned high, it's a blessing to have a place to live—and we do have to set up housekeeping somewhere and get a regular income. The job offer to work in the winery was a gift, Logan." She didn't need to remind him that his health prevented him from working or that jobs were scarce or impossible in the community, or to mention that she needed to be close by him until he grew stronger. "I'm sure you'll love it here," she reiterated, her eyes sweeping over the beauty of the hills. She reveled in the nuturing quietness and the rural peacefulness of the verdant valley.

Logan smiled again and fell silent as he stared out the window, causing Callie to wonder if she was being transparent. He had been in Montana when she decided to marry Chandler, and because her mother had died the year before, he felt it was his duty to advise her. Both he and Aunt Caroline had vehemently opposed the wedding, objecting to Chandler being twelve years Callie's senior, their brief acquaintance, and the haste of the proposed union. Callie had wanted Chandler too much to listen to anyone's advice, and she had discounted the rumors that he was marrying her on the rebound. Disappointed especially with Logan's stand, Callie hadn't told Chandler anything about having a stepfather.

Callie's father had died when she was four. She had been thirteen when her mother left her with her aunt to go off with Logan to start a copper mine, and she hadn't understood how anyone could pursue a single dream to the exclusion of all else. It wasn't until she had wanted Chandler so all-consumingly that she had understood. She and Logan were alike in their compulsions; he had given up all he had, including his health, to bring to life the dream that had burned so passionately within him, and he had failed. Callie clenched the wheel tighter; she had alienated her aunt, ignored gossip, endured embarrassment, given herself totally to Chandler in her desire for him; and she had failed. Logan had been right about him. Chandler had seen her as a temporary diversion whom he impulsively married in order to have his way with her. And he *had* apparently married her on the rebound. One had only to see Chandler and Nadine together to realize how well they knew each other and how much they meant to each other. Callie had been a young fool to think she could chase Nadine from Chandler's mind—or his bed.

When Nadine returned, Chandler had welcomed her, empathizing with her over her unfortunate marriage, and inviting her to all the functions at the ranch as though they were still a twosome. Callie had tried to fight her growing jealousy, but she didn't know how to cope, and she had nowhere to turn for help. Nadine had a thousand excuses to call or see Chandler, ranging from car trouble to a shoulder to cry on, and when Callie protested that it wasn't Chandler's place to be at the woman's beck and call, he had teased her unmercifully about her possessiveness.

She had been desperately afraid of not being able to hold his love—an insecurity, she realized much later, that was the result of her mother relegating her to Aunt Caroline's care in her first, vulnerable teen-age year—and the more frantic she grew, the worse the situation became. She had known well what Nadine was doing, but she hadn't known how to put an end to it. All their friends were friends of the Harrises, and she had suffered in silence or cried alone at night after Chandler had gone to sleep. And more and more she had felt that she was losing Chandler, despite the passions that flamed so hotly when they were in each other's arms. She had begun to suspect that Chandler's primary attraction to her was sexual, and that had increased her fears. Without love to build on, she had known that neither she nor the marriage had a chance.

Chandler had turned on her angrily when she had once used the close moments of their loving to ask him not to invite Nadine to ranch happenings. He had declared that he wouldn't commit such an open and obvious snub and he had reminded Callie that Nadine was her friend as well as his. Hurt and embarrassed because Chandler thought she was such a fool that she didn't know what was going on between him and Nadine, Callie had never mentioned it again.

She fought down the memory rising in her mind. She had known Nadine despised her, for the woman had subtly, and on occasion openly, needled Callie about her inexperience and her absurdity in believing she could hold Chandler. Callie had found out how much of a friend Nadine was the night she caught her with Chandler.

She tried to blot the vision from her mind, but to her consternation and chagrin, she found herself struggling with conflicting emotions and a flood of hurtful memories. She had crept away, pained and humiliated, instead of confronting the couple then and there. Nadine had won, and Callie had accepted defeat.

A sigh escaped her lips. She hoped that the ensuing years had braced her for this return. She knew that she needed the confrontation with Chandler to purge herself of him once and for all. It had been one thing to brood over him from afar and to despise him at a distance, but she hoped she had gone beyond those damaging emotions; she hoped she could look at the handsome, sun-burned giant of a man who had sparked passion's wildest fires with subtle skill and quenched them with experienced seduction, and realize that he was out of her blood at last. She needed this chance to test herself. She wanted to put the past behind her and start life anew. She had surely learned to handle her earlier heartache. She was almost twenty-six now, and away from the overpowering influence of her aunt and the overwhelming presence of her husband, she had matured.

She had dated two men in the past four years, but she hadn't been able to get past the friendship stage with them. She knew that it was because of Chandler's memory burning so brightly in her mind. She had to rid herself of him once and for all, and the only way to do it was to face him again.

"Callie?" Logan murmured in a quiet voice. "Honey, we don't have to do this."

Callie struggled to erase the emotions that had twisted her facial features into a mask of unhappiness. She hadn't wanted Logan to see her distress, and she told herself sharply that she was simply experiencing the shock of returning to the scene of her shattered dreams. Of course, living here would require some adjustment on her part.

"I'm fine, Logan. It's just—it's the dust. And it's rather warm, don't you think?" She laughed softly. "My goodness, what am I complaining about? Things are working out wonderfully. I was so surprised to get the job offer to work at the winery. It had to be fate. Of course, Roy has known me since I was thirteen and he taught me what I know about wine. I used to hang around the winery and the vines asking all kinds of questions, and I worked there giving tours the year before my marriage." A frown marred the smooth skin of her forehead. "Isn't it odd that a vacancy came up just when the house was left to me?" she mused as she turned onto the road leading to her aunt's house.

Logan nodded distractedly, lost in his own reflections. "If I were any kind of man, I would have been more careful with my business. We wouldn't have wound up back here. It's this damn illness, you know. It ate up so much of my money so rapidly." He sighed wearily. "Some business tycoon I was. I don't even have adequate insurance for a major illness. All I've got left of the copper mine is a wasted piece of land and bankrupt dreams."

Callie patted his hand. "It doesn't matter." She was glad that she could help him now; she felt indebted to him, and she wanted to repay his kindness. She experienced her own agitation as her eyes swept over the Dumontt Winery, then focused on the sprawling white ranch house up the road. The house, surrounded by a rose-covered split-rail fence, sat a short distance from the road.

"Well, there it is," she said with feigned indifference, her frantic heart pounding erratically. "There's Chandler's house—where I lived for a year as the wife of one of the richest men in Monterey county." She suddenly wished fervently that there was another way to reach her aunt's house, but it sat at the end of the only road into and out of the vineyards. To get there, it was necessary to pass Chandler's house.

"It's lovely," Logan said appreciatively. "I'm sorry you weren't happy, sweetheart, but I didn't see how you could have been under the circumstances. You were too young for such a man, and so very unsophisticated. Those whirlwind romances don't often last."

Smiling at him too brightly, Callie hoped he couldn't see the vulnerability in her soft brown eyes. Her palms felt moist as she tucked a pin tighter into her golden blond bun, though it hadn't come loose. "Have I changed, Logan? Do I have the polish of maturity now?" she asked.

"Yes," he agreed quietly. "You have the polish of maturity, Callie, but you have a hardness, too. You're very beautiful, but that hardness isn't attractive in a woman."

"No?" She laughed briefly, and sitting a little straighter against the seat back, she murmured, "Perhaps not, but you can bet that it's useful." She had no intention of repeating her painful lesson, but she wondered what Logan would say if he could see how surface the hardness was; she had too much pride to let anyone know that she had spent four long years unable to forget a man who preferred another woman. She needed the hard surface shell to protect her wounded heart, her shattered pride, her damaged dignity. She knew only too well that life didn't always yield what one hoped for. Some dreams had to be set aside or abandoned so that room could be made for new ones. Her marriage to Chandler had been one of those impossible dreams.

Now she wanted to put it—and the man—completely

behind her so that she could live her life to the fullest. She still had other dreams to pursue: someone to love her for herself, a family of her own, a home that would be filled with happy voices and warmth, a career—perhaps a small business. She loved to work with plants and she was very good at making things grow. Although she hadn't been able to keep Logan's copper mine from succumbing to lack of capital, she knew that she could make a business work, given the right opportunity. She had learned a lot about management, and she had finally appreciated those skills she had learned in college.

Logan looked at her intently for a moment, but he made no comment before his gaze moved across the scenery in front of them. As unobtrusively as possible, Callie glanced back at Chandler's house.

A barely noticeable gasp rose in her throat and she forced it back down. Chandler was standing out on the lawn, looking toward the road. Callie couldn't control the breathless way she felt when she looked at him: seeing him again was more difficult than she had imagined. Her eyes drank in the tantalizing sight; even in jeans and a madras shirt, he was aristocratic and commanding, and so very tall. Her gaze traveled over the sun-bronzed length of him as he stood there with a cowboy hat pushed up on his forehead, a few of his black curly locks visible beneath the brim.

He was more handsome than she had remembered, and she was alarmed by the wild beating of her heart. She felt as if her throat had constricted, and she was annoyed by her physical reaction to him. Her eyes seemed to rest on him for an eternity, but it was really only seconds before she imagined that he had seen her with those laughing blue eyes of his, and she looked away. She had actually thought she had been able to see the little wrinkles at the corners of his eyes and his well-shaped lips.

It was ridiculous, of course; she was too far away to see

such details. She focused on the road, determined to keep her mind on her driving, and she realized that she had unconsciously slowed down. She placed her foot more firmly on the pedal, wanting to escape the sight of Chandler, but she couldn't run from her memories. Seeing him again stirred longings in her which had been repressed all these years. After all the long months, and not so much as a single glimpse of Chandler Matthews, her breath had caught in her throat the moment she had seen him. She felt flushed and warm all over, and she experienced the most absurd desire to run to him and throw her arms around him. She fought to control her emotions; surely she was immune to those old feelings Chandler had been able to arouse in that twenty-one-year-old girl.

Involuntarily glancing back in the rearview mirror, she felt an old familiar burning in the pit of her stomach. A woman had joined Chandler on the lawn, and even at this distance, Callie could tell by the height and the flame of red hair that the woman was Nadine. Chandler had probably married her by now, and Callie couldn't understand why her heart rebelled at the thought. She had known that it was likely; she had never received divorce papers, but she had been told that it was possible to give notice in primary newspapers and, after a reasonable time, divorce the mate who had deserted. A smile twisted her lips. The mate who had deserted—that was she, even though she was the one who had found her husband in the arms of another woman.

Callie couldn't keep the memory of that fatal night from her mind. There had been a barbecue at the ranch and Chandler had invited Nadine, of course.

Callie could still hear Nadine's husky whisper: "This will be such a shock to your wife." The picture of the two of them lived on in her mind in vivid detail: Chandler had been standing there in Nadine's arms in the bedroom.

After all these years, Callie's face still paled at the

remembrance, and she could feel the erratic beat of her pulse. Chandler had told her to meet him so that he could tell her something privately. She hadn't needed to hear what he had to say. She could still visualize the rich brown leather suitcases lying open on the forest green bedspread —one filled with Chandler's clothes, and the other with Nadine's. The sight of all those beautiful clothes had lingered in her mind in colorful detail. They had looked new, and they had been gorgeous: frilly pink nightgowns, a long shimmering teal blue evening gown, flowered shirts in silk and velour, camel slacks, a rich brown sweater, and other articles that had been obscured from her sight.

"Isn't that the house your aunt lived in?" Logan asked, breaking into her whirling thoughts and bringing her sharply back to reality.

"That's it." Callie pointed to a Victorian farmhouse, dark green in color, trimmed in peeling white paint, and ornately decorated with gables, cupolas, and pillars. She had forgotten how old it was, and how haphazardly the rooms had been added on. Had it always been so ramshackle? Or had she just failed to notice? The building was almost a monstrosity, but she gazed at it fondly. It was home, and she was glad to see it.

"It doesn't look like much from here, and I suspect that it's been neglected since Aunt Caroline's death, but we can clean it up. Besides, we need to fix it up to sell it. I see no need to keep such a large, rambling old place for you and me. It's got thirteen rooms." In truth, she really did want to keep the house, but she knew that it simply wasn't practical now.

"Thirteen?" Logan asked, a surprised look on his face.

Callie smiled gently, glad for any excuse to keep her mind off Chandler. "Yes. Aunt Caroline was eccentric and superstitious, you see. Only she believed just the opposite of what most superstitious people believe. She thought that thirteen was a number sure to be desirable since so many people thought otherwise. And it wasn't unusual to see her go out of her way to walk under ladders or to let black cats cross her path."

"She sounds like she was quite a character, and the place definitely doesn't look like the run-of-the-mill. It has a certain amount of fascination, though."

"Yes," Callie agreed. A small sigh escaped her lips. She did hate the idea of selling the house, but she knew that Logan might need emergency medical care and they had to have ready cash; it was impossible to entertain foolish ideas. His heart was failing, and his token insurance wouldn't be nearly enough to cover a hospital bill should he need treatment. "Let's hope someone else finds it attractive," she said, ignoring the whispers of her heart that reminded her of how much she loved the house.

Logan studied the old building curiously. "It really is too large for two people," he conceded.

Callie turned off the main road onto a gravel lane forming a semicircle in front of the house. "You know," she murmured, "it looks reasonably good, really. I think someone has been caring for it, although I don't know who would have. Aunt Caroline never did much to maintain it because she had so little money."

"It's a shame you and your aunt didn't communicate those last years, Callie," Logan said thoughtfully.

Callie smiled half-heartedly. She had been deeply troubled over her aunt disowning her. She had come to love the old woman dearly, and it had hurt her when her aunt refused to speak to her again and returned her letters unopened. With her mother and father gone, Aunt Caroline had been her only living blood relative.

"I tried, Logan," she murmured reflectively, "but she was old and stubborn and she never forgave me for marrying Chandler. She said I was disobedient and ungrateful and that I would be sorry. Though I experienced a terrible guilt at the time and was torn between my love for her and for Chandler, I had to follow my heart. Then, when I told her I was leaving him to spend some time with you until I could decide what to do with my life, she became furious. She didn't understand that I had to get away from Chandler and the valley. She was bitter and lonely and she hated the world. I realize now that she just didn't want to be left all alone again, but then I was too upset to do anything else."

Callie shook her head. "You know I wrote, even though she never read any letter after the first one. Fortunately, she kept that one, or Ned, the lawyer, and Roy Dumontt, the winery owner, wouldn't have been able to trace me."

Logan stroked his chin absently. "It was such a pity that Caroline was jilted at the altar when she was a young woman. She let it distort the rest of her life."

Callie's brow furrowed. "She was embarrassed in the community," she said with feeling, but she didn't add that she knew how her aunt must have felt. "I wonder if she did leave me a final, personal letter as she told Ned, and if so, what's become of it? It would ease my mind to know that she didn't go to her grave hating me. She was very good to me in her way."

"I'm sure she didn't hate you, Callie, but she was old and forgetful. She may have only thought she wrote a letter to you, and she probably did compose one in her mind a hundred times. I'm sure she loved you very much; otherwise, she wouldn't have been so hurt when you left home." He looked at her carefully. "I wouldn't put much stock in a letter. Just believe that she meant well, and don't you dwell on it."

Callie smiled at him. "I suppose you're right." Still, if there really were a letter, it would salve the aching sadness that surfaced at the mere mention of her aunt. She did feel that she owed her aunt a great deal for the time she had devoted to a young girl who had been left on her doorstep, and she wished desperately that the old woman had spoken to her just one more time. Callie had even flown out to visit, only to have her aunt shut the door in her face and refuse to see her. The old woman had a cold and unforgiving nature when she felt she had been wronged, and she had long ago forgotten how difficult it sometimes was to cope with affairs of the heart.

Stopping the car in front of the steps, Callie put it in park and breathed a sigh of relief that the old vehicle had made the trip. "Here we are." Her voice carried a tiny little thrill. "Home sweet home. For a while, anyway. My goodness," she mused, more to herself than to Logan, "I hope the inside looks as good as the outside. Even the plants have been kept up, and Ned's letter said Aunt Caroline died many weeks ago."

She looked at the tall hedging around the green grass in the front yard. Ignoring the broken stones of the sidewalk, she contemplated the ancient oak tree, her gaze traveling over the long, shady branches, then settling on the red and gold daisies in the circle of stone at the base. She glanced at the other flowers thriving in the faded shadow boxes under oddly shaped windows. She had planted the begonias herself; Aunt Caroline had liked the grounds simple and stark, but Callie delighted in the colorful plants. Eagerly, happiness rising in her, Callie walked up the broken walkway to the creaky steps. She cautioned Logan about them, then unlocked the front door. Holding her breath, she stepped into the hallway. Joy coursed through her; she had made many wonderful memories in the old house, and this really was a homecoming to her. She turned back to see Logan following slowly behind, his face ashen. His appearance tugged at her heartstrings, and she was concerned that the trip had been too much for him.

"Are you all right?"

He waved the question aside. "Stop worrying about me. I'm just getting old." He tried to laugh, but Callie knew it wasn't a joke. He looked much older than his forty-five years, and his body wasn't as healthy as that of a man his age should be. She opened the living room door and went inside.

"It's lovely," she murmured, trying to see everything at once. "It looks better than when I lived here, and it's so tidy. All it needs are some houseplants to brighten the rooms." She had filled the house with indoor plants when she lived here, taking cuttings from whomever would give them to her and taking plants other people had discarded and nurturing them back to health. She had loved working with the plants and she had seen what an addition they could make to the decor. She hurried over to the Victorian sofa and ran her fingers over the pale green of the medallion back, then looked around at the golden yellow matching velvet-seated mahogany chairs.

"You're going to like living here," she said with a burst of enthusiasm, turning back to Logan and impulsively hugging him. He wrapped his arms around her and gently patted her back, smiling slightly at her affectionate gesture and good humor.

Callie hadn't heard anyone enter and she jumped away from Logan when a gruff voice said disdainfully, "Pardon me. I didn't know I would be interrupting anything."

A shiver raced up her spine at the contemptuous words. She instantly recognized the cold tone, and she found herself momentarily reluctant to look at the speaker. Taking herself sharply in hand, she slowly turned around, her heart thudding heavily as she gradually raised long-lashed brown eyes to look up into the face of the man filling the doorway.

Their eyes locked for a moment and time stood still for Callie. A warmth fanned throughout her body as she looked upon Chandler's handsome countenance. It was as if the bitterness and the long separation hadn't come between them. His blue eyes blazed as they glared down into hers, and the sight of him so near stole her breath away. She could feel the tension in the air and the blood rushed to her temples as she stared at him, unable to look aside. If it were possible, he was more dashing than ever, but there was a defiance in the lean, hard stance of his muscled body that Callie didn't remember, and the years had carved character lines into the dark, chiseled-jawed face. And those blue eyes—had they always been so piercing? she wondered, as she tried not to blink under their scrutiny. She wanted desperately to hate this man, but she discovered that a thousand anguished thoughts and four bitter years hadn't erased him from her savagely beating heart.

Chandler broke the spell that held them; he scanned her insolently from head to toe, as though he had the right to visually strip her of every shred of clothing. Callie flinched under the harsh inspection and she stood uneasily before him as he measured her with his icy eyes, his gaze roving down her high breasts, over her shapely hips and long legs, then back up again. At last he regarded her face. Callie pressed her lips firmly together to still their quivering.

For a moment, she imagined that she saw a hungry longing in Chandler's eyes, and she chided herself for her stupidity. Why would he long for her? He had taken what he wanted from her, and when the summer cooled into autumn and his passions were satiated, he had been sorry he had been obliging enough to marry her. Nadine had only to return and beckon, and Chandler had gone back to the woman he really loved. Callie watched as Logan became the target for those cold blue eyes, and she sensed a fury in Chandler that alarmed her.

In the calmest voice she could manage, she made the introductions. "Chandler Matthews—Logan Bartholomew."

Callie watched awkwardly, her voice silenced by Chandler's hateful expression as Logan extended his hand and stepped forward. For a second, it appeared that Chandler would refuse it, then he shook hands brusquely, as though resenting Logan's touch. Logan glanced at Callie, and she started to tell Chandler that Logan was her stepfather, but Chandler turned on her before she could explain. "I will speak to you alone," he commanded.

Callie had to look up into his eyes, although she stood five feet eight inches in her sandals. A rush of color darkened her face and she bristled at his arrogant order. "If you'll excuse us, please, Logan," she requested in a crisp voice that betrayed her agitation.

Logan walked briskly from the room, and he had barely shut the door when Chandler reached up and removed his hat as if suddenly remembering his manners. Callie was dismayed by how tightly his long, strong fingers gripped the brim; she tried not to stare at the slightly mussed curly black hair she had loved to run her fingers through, but she couldn't help but notice the silver strands at Chandler's temples. They hadn't been there four years ago. Her eyes lowered to his vibrant blue eyes, shielded by long black lashes, then to his Roman nose, full lips, and the cleft in his chiseled chin. She felt flustered and ill at ease standing before this man she had once known so intimately, his brooding presence filling the room with oppression.

Chandler conducted his own perusal before he spoke. Startling blue eyes, emphasized by his dark tan, studied Callie's flushed features, appraising her blond hair, large eyes, small, pert nose, and then lingering on her generous mouth. His self-assured, almost belligerent pose disturbed her, and she felt feverish under his disconcerting gaze.

"You look fine, Callie," he murmured too softly, a dangerous glow in his eyes.

"You, too, Chandler," she replied breathlessly.

"Why did you run out on me?" he demanded abruptly, his voice cold. "I tried to find you, but you left no trail. Caroline wouldn't speak to me, let alone help me find you.

It wasn't until she died that Ned contacted me, saying that Caroline had made out a will leaving the house to you and that you would be returning here." His gaze suddenly whipped over her cruelly, and he laughed harshly. "Alone, I thought. As far as I knew, we were still married."

Callie clasped her hands together tightly to still their trembling. He must think her the same young fool he had married. So, he hadn't wed Nadine, but surely he hadn't spent the past four years expecting her to crawl back to him on any terms she could get. She smiled bitterly to herself; apparently he was egotistical enough to think exactly that. Her glance fell to the once plush floral rug beneath her feet, then met Chandler's gaze rebelliously. "I never sought a divorce—" she began, but before she could complete her statement, he growled sarcastically.

"I see. Now you don't insist on the formalities. That was just for the first poor idiot, was it?"

Abruptly, he threw his hat down on the floor, grasped her upper arms, and dragged her against his body, his firm lips swooping down on hers punishingly. His fingers gripped the hair at the nape of her neck, causing the bun to fall free of the tight pins, and her blond mane tumbled down her back. Chandler's lips moved fiercely against hers, and Callie was surprised to hear a groan deep in his throat as the kiss gradually gentled into a hungry caress. Her lips responded warmly to his familiar touch, despite her resolve to remain unmoved. She was breathless and speechless when he pulled away from her.

"Was I that easy to forget?" he murmured softly, an enigmatic look in his eyes that quickly gave way to anger. Reaching down to pick up his hat, he shoved it on his head and turned his back on her to stalk from the room.

Callie was left to stare after him, confused by his behavior and startled by his anger. She could only conclude that she must have damaged his ego very badly when she had

had the nerve to leave him. Fighting back an urge to run after him, she rubbed the back of her hand over her slightly swollen lips and she was troubled by the sense of relief that filled her mind. Chandler had rashly thought that she and Logan were lovers—and he obviously hadn't married his own lover if he hadn't gotten a divorce. Her lips twisted into an unhappy smile and her relief was short-lived. Chandler had learned his lesson well with her; marriage was too confining for a man like him. Besides, since when had he needed a commitment to Nadine to have his way with her?

Shaken by the encounter, Callie brushed at her wayward hair, turned on her heel, and went in search of Logan, determined that he wouldn't know how disturbed she had been by Chandler's sudden appearance. The fact that he hadn't divorced her as she had suspected would only complicate matters, for she would have to seek the divorce herself when she had funds. But she would do it. She had come here to put Chandler and all that he had meant behind her. She would not be swayed from that purpose.

CHAPTER TWO

Struggling to hide her conflicting emotions, Callie called out, "Logan, where are you?"

He stepped into the hall at the same time she did.

"Chandler's gone," she commented with a calmness she was far from feeling.

"I heard the door slam. How do things stand between you two? Did he get the divorce?"

Callie shook her head, but she was suddenly unable to meet Logan's eyes.

Approaching her slowly, he tilted her chin with one finger and gazed into her eyes. "Callie, are you still in love with him?"

Brushing his hand aside, she turned away from his perceptive eyes. "Of course not. Don't be silly." She walked briskly down the hall and looked back evenly over her shoulder. "Come on. I'll show you the house." Her face remained impassive, but a thousand butterflies fluttered in her stomach and she felt a deep, hungry longing somewhere down inside. She *wasn't* still in love with Chandler: she *couldn't* be that big a fool.

While Logan followed, she explored the dining room, trying fervently to put Chandler out of her mind. She had forgotten how charming the ancient house was. Her most treasured years had been spent there with Aunt Caroline, and though the old woman was often sharp and sour, Callie knew that at one time she had really loved the niece who had been thrust upon her by a much younger sister. They had enjoyed each other's company in their own way, and Callie again experienced a surge of regret that she hadn't shared Aunt Caroline's last years. Walking to the kitchen, she imagined that she could actually smell the fresh banana bread her aunt had been so fond of baking. She smiled as she looked at the bright room and the sunlight streaming in through the glass panes of the two doors.

The old-fashioned black stove took up much of the room, and the broad wooden counters curved away on each side of it. The small round table, covered by the same yellow and white oilcloth Callie remembered, and the same two straight-back chairs were in the middle of the floor. Off to one side was a low sink and a cylindrical mahogany pot cupboard. For a moment, the smile faded on Callie's lips; the kitchen had been her and her aunt's favorite spot to sit and talk on Sunday mornings. How could her aunt have begun to hate her so intensely? She smoothed her hair back; perhaps the woman had cared after all: she *had* left Callie the house.

"Look at this," Logan exclaimed, breaking into her musings and pointing to the counter. "Fresh banana bread, a basket of fruit, and a pot full of hot coffee. It looks like you have a friend in the community."

Walking up beside him, Callie lifted the clear plastic wrap from the plate of still warm bread. "What a kind thing to do. Now, I wonder who was so thoughtful."

"I don't know, but I'm going to have a slice," Logan commented.

Callie indicated a heavy round table visible through the entryway of the dining room. "Sit in there. I'll get the coffee." While Logan carried the bread to the table, she took two cups from the cupboard and filled them.

After they had eaten, they both felt better. "I'll show you the upstairs," Callie said, standing up. A little more energetic after the snack, she hurried up the stairs, stopping at the top to wait for Logan. To her surprise, the upstairs was as clean and orderly as the downstairs. Pressed, fresh white linen had been put on the beds, and again she wondered who had been so thoughtful. Of course, she reasoned, Ned must have had someone come in. She turned into the room that had been Aunt Caroline's and looked back at Logan.

"Why don't you take a nap while I go to the store?" she suggested, scanning his wan face. "You take this room. I think you'll be comfortable here."

Looking around the feminine room with a wry face, Logan nodded. "Yes, it will be fine."

Callie grinned at him. "Make yourself at home. This *is* our new home for a while, you know. I'll take the room down from this one. It's the room I used when I lived here."

"I hate to admit it, but a nap does sound good," Logan said, looking at the narrow brass bed. "I'm drained. I'll just go down and get the suitcases, then take a quick shower."

"There is no shower, I'm sorry to say, but you go ahead and get in the tub while I get the luggage."

"I'll do it," he insisted.

Callie dismissed his offer with a wave of her hand and turned on her heel. She ran back down the stairs and out the door and when she reached the car, she stood for a moment and inhaled deeply. She hadn't remembered quite how beautiful the valley was, with its few buildings and lush vineyards. There was something splendid about the rows and rows of leafy vines, just now developing clusters of small, green grapes. The fruit wouldn't mature until the fall, some of it not until November or December. Monterey county's cool climate resulted in a long growing season and the development of intense flavors, color, sugar, and fruit acids when the grapes were picked at complete ripeness. The harvest was a fascinating time, but it was also a hectic, busy time that destroyed the tranquillity of the valley. Consequently, Callie liked the lazy summer days of the growing season best.

She looked back down the road at Chandler's ranch, and though he had purchased it for cattle raising, she now saw no cattle. In fact, Chandler must have sold some of his acreage to Roy Dumontt; much of it was covered with vines. Turning away from the sight, Callie unlocked the trunk and took out the suitcases. She would have to put Chandler out of her mind somehow, but it was very plain to her that she hadn't been able to put him out of her heart.

Callie deposited Logan's luggage at his door, then took hers to her room. She smiled fondly when she stepped inside. Instantly, she was transported back to the first time she had ever seen the room; Aunt Caroline had decorated it in anticipation of her coming, and she had done it like a young child's room instead of a teen-ager's. The old woman had been so proud of it that Callie had never had the heart to change it, and today it was still decorated with pink and white gingham curtains, a canopied bed with a pink chenille spread, two white nightstands with doll lamps, and a highboy with a teddy bear perched on top. She remembered how Chandler had chuckled the first time he had seen the room, and she had turned scarlet with embarrassment. He had told her he hadn't realized that he was marrying such a girl, and she had fiercely and foolishly insisted that she knew as much about life as he did. Reminding herself that she had been dreadfully wrong, she shook her head to clear it of the bittersweet memories.

She set the suitcase in front of the highboy, then walked around the room, wondering if her aunt's letter were somewhere in it, tucked away so that only she could find it. When her search proved futile, she went to the other rooms in the house, looking in nooks and crannies just in case there really was a letter waiting for her. No letter was to be found, and she returned to her room and began to put her personal items away. After she had finished, she hung her clothes in the cramped little closet, then looked longingly at the bed, deciding that she needed a rest, too. Following Logan's initiative, she went to the only other bath in the big old house, piled her hair on her head, and ran herself a tub of warm water. She started when the noisy pipes gushed and grumbled; she had forgotten how cantankerous the plumbing was.

She didn't dally long in the bath, leaving it to return to her room only minutes later. Letting her striking blond hair fall down around her shoulders, she picked up the beautiful antique brush Chandler had given her and gazed for a long moment at the delicate painting on the back before vigorously stroking her hair a hundred times. She knew it wasn't necessary to perform such a ritual, but Aunt Caroline had insisted that it was good for the hair, and Callie had long ago fallen into the habit. Besides, over the years it had become a method of relaxing before going to bed. She smiled ruefully as she recalled the three days she had been sick in bed with the flu; Chandler had brushed her hair each night before she had fallen asleep. She finished her hair, laid the brush down on the bureau, and slipped into her gown, wanting to suppress the memories of Chandler that lurked in her mind and rose suddenly with devastating swiftness. How could she begin to forget the past when her mind insisted upon recalling every minute detail? Lying down on the bed, she dozed easily, completely forgetting that she needed to shop if she and Logan were to have anything for dinner.

When Callie awakened, the sun was slipping down behind the mountains and she was filled with remorse at the sight. She shouldn't have slept; now it was too late to shop for groceries unless she drove all the way into Salinas. She and Logan would have to eat more of the banana bread and fruit. Lightly massaging her temples, she rose and trailed to the closet for a robe, barely able to see in the falling darkness.

As she stepped into the hall, she imagined that she smelled the delicious aroma of steak cooking downstairs, and she was surprised to find Logan mixing a green salad when she entered the kitchen a minute later.

"Where on earth did you get the food?" she asked.

He looked up, startled by her entrance, then grinned broadly as he walked over to the pantry and opened the door so that she could view the full larder. "Someone stocked this and the refrigerator."

"What a blessing," she murmured, thinking of the paltry amount of money she had in her purse. She had been afraid that she would have to ask for an advance on her salary, and she hated to start working under those circumstances. This food was a lifesaver. "It must have been Ned. He's been so kind."

"He'll bill you, don't worry," Logan said with a laugh. "Let's eat before I starve to death." He placed baked potatoes and steaks on plates and carried them to the dining room table. "There's even a bottle of white wine."

He and Callie seated themselves and Logan poured the wine. "Welcome home, Callie. I hope you won't be sorry you've come back here," he said, holding up his glass.

Callie raised hers. "Of course I won't be," she murmured, but a painful premonition told her the words were a lie.

Monday dawned bright and beautiful, and Callie awakened, unsure for a moment where she was. Stretching languidly, she pushed her golden locks away from her face and looked around the delicately decorated room. So many years had passed, and it seemed that nothing had changed. It was like waking up there again that first morning, only now she was a woman who had known the anguish of love lost. And that made all the difference in the world.

She sighed, then stretched again before going to peer out the window. Her room was at the front of the house and she could see Chandler's house down the way. Her eyes were drawn to it and the thousand remembrances it held for her.

Did Sung, the Chinese servant, still wake the mistress of the house with a cup of coffee and a wildflower? She felt a fierce fluttering of her heart. Who was the mistress of the house now? Did Nadine live with Chandler? She looked away, not wanting to consider the possibility any further.

Her gaze fell on the huge old oak tree, and for a moment her thoughts were diverted by the sparrows playing among the leafy branches.

Turning her back on their gay chatter, she walked to the closet and removed a severely styled but attractive daffodil-colored dress. She knew it outlined her shapely hips and slim waist without being provocative, and because she was going to the winery today, she wanted to look professional. She hoped Roy would put her to work right away, for neither she nor Logan had earned a single penny for the past three months. He had been much too ill to work and she had spent most of her time caring for him. Somehow he had pulled through, but Callie hadn't been able to lose her fear that his condition might worsen again, and she was afraid for his life.

After she had bathed and dressed, she swept her hair up in a tight bun, then applied a touch of lip color and just a hint of powder. Shunning nylons, which she found confining and unnecessary, she slipped her feet into high-heeled white sandals with crisscrossed straps. She stood before the mirror critically examining her legs; she had long ago determined that her long, shapely legs were one of her major assets—along with her hair and eyes. Her cheekbones were too prominent to please her, although she had been told that they were attractive and exquisitely defined. Her bust was too small, she thought, as she studied her reflection.

A sudden treacherous memory filled her mind and she shivered as she recalled Chandler's hands and mouth on her body. He had often told her how beautiful he thought her high, firm breasts were. Her heartbeats increased as she remembered the way he had touched and teased her nipples, arousing her to desire.

Although she fought to suppress the question, she found herself wondering if Chandler still found her appealing. She quickly discounted the idea. What did it matter now? Besides, she had learned the hard way that it was what a man saw with his heart, not his eyes, that counted.

She went down to the kitchen for a quick breakfast of coffee and a piece of toast with butter and strawberry preserves. Leaving a note for the still sleeping Logan, telling him that she was going to the winery and then to Ned's office, she walked out to her car and climbed in.

She tried not to look at Chandler's house as she drove past, concentrating instead on the grapevines, sparkling and velvety dark after their morning bath from the sprinklers. She gazed up at the tall, stately rows of eucalyptus trees that formed a shield against the sometimes destructive summer winds. Minutes later, she turned into the hedged driveway of the tall, neat, Spanish-styled winery. Looking up at the red sign proclaiming Dumontt Winery, she smiled to herself. It would be good to see Roy again. She considered him a friend, and she had missed her friends while she was away.

She had entered the wine room on her way to the office when Chandler appeared out of nowhere. Callie gasped slightly as she collided with the muscular wall of his chest. Her heart pounding wildly, she stepped backward as if she had been burned. Her glance involuntarily swept over the maroon shirt and white slacks, which emphasized his powerful body.

"Good morning," he said coolly, his eyes traveling over her shapely figure, outlined in the daffodil dress. His gaze lingered on her high, well-defined breasts, then roved down to her long legs, accentuated by her tall heels. When his eyes met hers again, Callie felt a fiery tension in the air.

Her eyelashes fluttered as she attempted to hold his hard gaze, and again she fought the ridiculous temptation to fling herself into his arms and beg him to tell her why he had hurt her so deeply that night four years ago. It would be so easy to press her body against his and feel his strong arms hold her close. So easy to— She shoved the traitorous thoughts into the recesses of her mind.

"Good morning, Chandler." She was surprised that her calm, cool voice gave no indication of the rebellion and desire churning inside her. She lowered her eyes momentarily, alarmed by the pained expression she saw in Chandler's. His attitude confused her, and she experienced an absurd feeling of guilt.

Suddenly, Chandler took a single step closer to her and Callie felt terribly vulnerable and threatened by the movement. "Who is Logan?" he demanded sharply. "Are you two lovers?"

Callie felt circles of scarlet stain her cheeks, and she tried to maintain her composure. "Chandler, Logan is—"

She jumped as Roy Dumontt came down the hall, his voice booming loudly. "Callie! Callie, girl! How are you? It's been too damn long since we've seen your pretty face in these parts. You look wonderful. More beautiful than ever, doesn't she, Chandler?"

Callie's glance skimmed over Roy's short, barrel-chested frame, taking in the salt-and-pepper hair and warm brown eyes. He grabbed her in his beefy arms and hugged her. "Damn, it's good to see you!"

"It's good to see you, too, Roy," she said, smiling at him. "I've missed you and this winery. I've come about the job." She glanced awkwardly at Chandler; in spite of the tension brought about by his presence, she felt his intoxicating appeal as strongly as ever.

The smile died on Roy's lips as he looked at Chandler, then back at Callie. For a moment the three of them stood there in awkward silence. Callie's heart sank; she needed the job so desperately. She was counting on it, and Roy appeared to have changed his mind.

"You want it, then?" he said at last, his big voice compensating for his short stature. Callie breathed a sigh of relief, even though Roy looked at Chandler again, his expression peculiar, his smile tentative. "Well, Chandler?" he asked, a flush darkening his already ruddy complexion.

Callie was momentarily confused, wondering if Roy were deferring the matter to Chandler, or inquiring what he wanted at the winery today. Surely he was simply being polite because they both had arrived at the same time. There was certainly no reason for Roy to consult Chandler about Callie working here.

"Take care of your business with her," Chandler said. "I can wait."

Callie glanced at him uncomfortably, then followed Roy into the office. She was aware of Chandler standing behind her, watching her. When she reached the office, she told Roy, "He was here first. I can come back later."

"No, no," he murmured, glancing back over his shoulder. "He'll wait. I'll talk to you first."

Roy indicated a chair and Callie sat down opposite him, listening as he quickly explained what would be expected of her before discussing a more than generous salary.

Callie stared at him for a moment, surprised by the figure. Surely wages hadn't gone up that much here in the last few years. It suddenly occurred to her that Roy felt sorry for her, and she was appalled. Proud and independent now, she would be no one's charity case. She wanted no obligation to anyone, regardless of how dire her situation was. She sat a little straighter in the chair. "I can't take such a large salary," she stated unequivocally. "I didn't expect half that to start, and I don't want any special consideration."

Roy looked nervous for a moment, then he waved a heavy hand. "Now, come on, Callie. Don't talk foolish. You'll be worth it. You were the best tour guide we ever had, and everybody knows a pretty face is a selling point in itself. When can you begin?"

"It's really too much money for the work, Roy," she stated.

His brows met in a frown. "That's what the job pays if you want it. Now when can you start?"

She hesitated, uncertain about the money, then she told herself to count her blessings. She would work hard for Roy, and she did need every penny she could get now. "Tomorrow," she replied. "Perhaps you can refresh me today while no one's here for the tour."

"Fine," he boomed heartily, his happy demeanor regained. "I'll take you to the processing plant as soon as I talk to Chandler. People are showing up for the tours now."

"Yes, summer always brings them out," she said knowingly.

Roy left the room only briefly. "Chandler is in no hurry," he said, his face a bit grim. "I'll refamiliarize you with the tour before I talk to him."

Callie stood up and walked with him from the room, past Chandler, who was leaning languidly against the wall, his hand carelessly inserted in his pocket in what appeared to be a casual posture; but Callie sensed a tenseness in him. She rushed uneasily past him, and she told herself that she would have to talk to him, too, when Roy finished his business with him. The sooner the air was cleared between them, the quicker she could set about forgetting Chandler and rebuilding her life.

When she and Roy entered the plant, she walked along beside him, occasionally gazing up at the huge oak wine casks and storage bins, and listening intently as he briefed her. She was eternally fascinated by the way grapes were turned into wine. She had always been in love with the business of winemaking, and she was pleased that she would be working here again.

"Briefly note the difference between white wine and red wine, explaining that the grape skins determine the color, and that white wine ferments in closed tanks while red wine ferments in open tanks. Describe as simply as possible how the grapes are processed, starting with the crusher-stemmer, then the press, fermentor, storage tank, filter, holding tank, and then into bottles," he said, pointing as he went. He looked at her and grinned. "You remember all this, don't you?"

"Yes, most of it," Callie said. She laughed lightly, the gentle sound echoing merrily in the cavernous room. "It all sounds so easy when you explain it."

He chuckled. "But you and I know that people will have a thousand and one questions, and you have to adequately answer every one. Well, if you have this down, we'll get back to the wine room, and I'll give you the price list and tell you about stocking the shelves and putting out the cheese tray." He was already leading the way out. "I have a couple of good current wine books you can borrow if you want to update your knowledge."

"Of course, I'd like them." She walked rapidly beside Roy as he went back into the other building. "I know a lot about wine," she commented, "but there's always someone who knows more."

"You bet. It's a booming business now. Many small operators and hobbyists are getting into it. Cottage industry wineries, they're being called. It's quite competitive these days, not like when I first started," he mused speculatively. He added a little bitterly, "It takes a lot more money these days. The wealthy and big business are getting into winemaking now, too."

Callie thought she detected a desire in Roy to continue the discussion at length, but knowing that Chandler was still waiting for him caused her to hurry along. Fleetingly, she wondered what business Chandler had with Roy. She knew the two men were acquainted, and that the remains from the grape pressings used to be sold to Chandler to mix with fodder for his cattle. She shook her thoughts aside.

What business Chandler had with Roy was none of her business. She had problems of her own, and for now she was determined to submerge her thoughts of Chandler and concentrate on her job. She needed it too much to let anything jeopardize it, and she wanted to make sure that she was worth the generous salary Roy intended to pay her. She would lose herself in her work and drive the past from her mind. This was her home now, and she vowed not to let Chandler chase her away again. As soon as she had money, she would get the divorce and cut the final tie.

Roy held the door to the wine-tasting room open and Callie walked inside. The phone was ringing in the office and he indicated a list on the counter. "Look that over and I'll be right back."

Before she could finish reading the list, Roy had returned. "Chandler's meeting me in the plant. Can you mind the store for a few minutes?"

"Sure." Callie stored her purse in the back room where she had always kept it and then settled down on a high stool at the counter to peruse the wine list.

Roy was gone only a few minutes, and when he returned, he brusquely indicated a large false clock on the wall. "The tours are still given at ten-fifteen and two-thirty. When you've completed one tour, turn the hands of the clock, showing that the next one won't begin until two-thirty." His hand swept along the shelves behind her and the counter beneath the cash register. "Wine is kept here, and, of course, there's a supply in the storeroom. The tasting glasses are here under the counter. Any questions?"

Callie was stunned by his suddenly curt manner, and she wondered what had brought it on. She carefully noted the way everything was arranged, then smiled nervously. "No, I don't have any questions right now."

Roy nodded, then looked away. He glanced back at her, seeming to have something to say, then shook his head.

"Is something wrong, Roy?" she asked, her brows meeting in a frown. At just that moment a group of Japanese men straggled into the room.

"Do me a favor, will you, Callie?" Roy asked. "Take them on a tour before you leave." He ran his hand over his chin. "I have something I really need to take care of right now."

"Fine," she agreed, but she didn't understand Roy's attitude at all. She discounted her uneasy feelings; perhaps Roy really did have problems in the plant and was preoccupied by them. Forcing her best smile, she greeted the visitors. "Good morning, gentlemen. What may I help you with?" She was a little uncomfortable about the first tour in light of Roy's brusqueness. And it had been a long time since she had explained the winemaking process.

The spokesman for the group smiled politely. "We have come to see how the wine is made," he said in perfect English. "And to buy some wine, of course," he added with a sedate smile.

Callie stepped out from behind the counter and indicated the door. "Right this way, please." She did love the wine business, and she felt a sudden surge of confidence as she led the way to the plant and began to talk to the men. Her guests were very quiet, but attentive, and it appeared that they had few questions until the tour was almost over. One reserved gentleman standing in the back raised his hand, and Callie nodded to him. "Yes? May I answer a question for you?"

"Why are the bottles green?"

"Dark glass is used to prevent light from damaging the wine," she explained. Her eyes searched the group. "Any other questions?"

"How many acres of land are cultivated for this winery?" the same gentleman asked.

Callie's mind raced furiously, but she wasn't sure about the acreage now. Just when it seemed that her poise had deserted her, Chandler appeared behind them.

"Two hundred acres," he answered smoothly.

Although Callie was grateful for the information, Chandler's sudden appearance and overpowering presence unsettled her. She wished he would leave. "Thank you," she said coolly, then turned back to the group.

"Callie."

She glanced at Chandler, her patience stretched to the breaking point. They did have to talk, but here and now wasn't the time.

"Come here a moment, please."

Feeling vulnerable and defensive, Callie excused herself to the group and marched over to him, her head held high. Her voice was low and crisp. "I can't talk to you right now, Chandler. Roy asked me to take these men on tour." She was annoyed that he felt that she was at his beck and call and that he could make demands upon her.

He looked deeply into her blazing brown eyes, then his gaze shifted to the small group studying the bottling machine. "I wanted to see how efficient you were," he drawled when his eyes again met hers.

Callie felt herself bristle, but she tried to remain outwardly calm. "It's really none of your business," she replied in a firm voice.

"Oh, but it is," he retorted with equal firmness. "You might have noticed that I'm in the business of raising vines now myself, and I have an interest in this winery."

"You may have an interest in this winery, but you do not have an interest in me," she said with conviction. "Now if you'll excuse me, I'll finish the tour. I don't want Roy to think I can't handle this."

"I'm not worried about what Roy thinks." His voice was insolent and he crossed his arms and stared down into her eyes in that way Callie despised.

"And I'm not worried about what you think," she snapped, turning on her heel. Before she could walk away, Chandler grasped her arm and spun her around to face him.

"You should be."

"Why?" she demanded, her anger overtaking her intention to remain composed.

"Because *I* own the winery."

It took Callie a moment to digest his reply, then she could only stand there, white-lipped, while she gawked at him. "You *what*?" she managed to rasp.

"I own the winery. Roy sold out to me two years ago. He's my manager now, and you're working for me."

Callie felt faint for a moment. She should have been used to Chandler's duplicity by now, but why had he gone to such lengths? "Whose idea was it to hire me?" she hissed, her fingers curling into tight fists at her sides.

Chandler's eyes searched her face, his expression unfathomable; then his gaze moved back to the men, who now stood looking at them both curiously. "Your group is waiting," he said abruptly. Turning away from her, he coolly sauntered from the room.

Weak-kneed, Callie walked back over to the men to make a few concluding statements. She tried her best not to reveal her agitation, but she was terribly shaken by Chandler's cruel revelation. She needed the job; she was depending on it, but of course she never would have taken it if she had known Chandler owned the winery. She had confidently come all this way, only to be misled. She felt she had been tricked and betrayed. She couldn't possibly stay on. She would have to find another position somewhere—somehow. She sighed wearily, then remembered to smile as she escorted the little group back into the wine-tasting room.

"Shall we sample some wine now?" she asked too brightly, hoping she could contain her distress until they left. The men nodded in unison and she handed them each a wine list. "I'll be happy to give you a sample of any of them," she said, forcing a lightness into her voice.

They discussed it among themselves, speaking rapidly in Japanese, and it was all Callie could do to keep her mind on the business at hand. Finally, the leader indicated a particular wine. When Callie had poured a small amount in each of their glasses, the man asked very politely, "How do we judge it?"

Callie poured a little into another glass and held it up by the stem, swirling it gently. "Check for clarity. Legs, the wine that streams down the glass, are also an indication of good wine." She watched as the men followed her instructions, murmuring among themselves while they imitated her gesture of spinning the wine, and she wished they would quickly make up their minds so that she could deal with her pressing problems. Why had Chandler hired her? What on earth did he hope to accomplish with such a move? Did he want her under his power again? When the men looked at her, she raised her glass with a hand that wasn't quite steady. "Wine should have a bouquet. The white wine which we sell here should have a fruity aroma."

"Ah," the leader murmured, obediently holding the glass to his nose. The others emulated him, then they chatted among themselves. Soon several wines had been sampled, and the small group had purchased a number of bottles.

Callie inhaled deeply when they had gone. Letting her ragged breath slip through her lips in a sigh, she leaned against the counter. She had done quite well with her first tour, except for the question about acreage. She smiled at the irony; it didn't matter how well she had done. She would give Chandler notice, sell the house, and leave the area. She couldn't work for him—*wouldn't* work for him —and her resolve to stay here had disintegrated at the first encounter with him. It was only too evident that she had been foolish to come back.

She looked up sharply when she heard the ominous tapping of stiletto heels, and she felt physically ill when her eyes met the malicious ones of Nadine Harris. The very last person she wanted to deal with at this moment was Nadine.

"Well, well," the sultry beauty drawled mockingly, "if it isn't little Callie Hart come home to roost. What on earth are you doing here in the valley?" Before Callie could reply, Nadine pursed her plum-colored lips in annoyance and tapped her foot. "Oh, yes, how could I forget? You're here to claim that dreadful old barn your aunt called home. That is *all* you've come to claim, isn't it, Callie?" she purred. "You don't have anything else in this valley, you know."

Callie managed a smile, despite the instant fury racing in her veins. "There's nothing else *worth* claiming in this valley, Nadine," she replied with an amazing calm she was far from feeling.

Nadine's lips formed a startled "O," and her green eyes danced with fire. "Now, I wouldn't go so far as to say that, dear," she retorted at last, obviously surprised by Callie's comment. "But, at any rate, you seem to have learned a few things in your absence."

"What do you want?" Callie asked a bit coldly. She was in no mood to play games with this woman, and she realized suddenly that responding had been her downfall in the past; she never should have allowed herself to be baited by Nadine.

Nadine cocked her head, looking at Callie with new interest. Again she regained her poise, her arms folding across the front of her green pleated silk dress. "What I want, you don't have—and never did."

Dismissing the redhead without comment, Callie turned away with the intention of getting her purse and leaving. She looked back over her shoulder when Nadine spoke again.

"I'm looking for Chandler, but I'm sure you don't know where he is." She patted a bright curl and laughed falsely. "You never did, poor dear."

Callie turned around fully to face the other woman. "Feeling insecure today?" she asked seriously. At the woman's flustered expression, Callie laughed briefly. "I know the feeling well," she commented.

Clenching her fists, her lips pursed, Nadine spun angrily on her heel and strode away. For the first time since her meeting with Chandler, Callie honestly smiled. She was no longer intimidated by Nadine, and it was a good feeling—an uplifting feeling. Her triumph was brief; she had a serious problem on her hands without this job. She and Logan had to have a steady income, and she had been so confident about this.

She retraced her steps, leaving the counter to hunt for Roy. Nothing—nothing would make her work for Chandler. She would get some other job if it meant scrubbing floors and washing dishes. Roy wasn't in his office, and she turned back to the wine room, frustrated and upset. Roy had been part of Chandler's deception, and Callie resented it deeply. She reached up to the top shelf to grab her purse, then whirled around when she heard footsteps behind her. Chandler was standing there, his arms crossed, his feet spread in an arrogant stance. She despised the way he glared down at her so condescendingly, and she fought a desire to slap his face.

"We'll talk now, Callie."

"Oh, we most definitely will," she agreed quickly, her mouth twisting angrily. "Why did you perpetrate this deception, Chandler? You knew I wouldn't work for you, so why did you hire me?"

"I'll ask the questions," he growled coldly, causing Callie to suck in her breath painfully. "Tell me who Logan is now!" he commanded in a positively threatening tone.

Callie felt a little surge of satisfaction that he was so bothered by Logan; she hadn't meant to keep him in suspense or toy with him over the matter, and things had worked out that way only because he had jumped to rash conclusions. She smiled and the smile was full of bitterness. "Don't judge me by your standards, Chandler," she retorted coolly.

Chandler looked angry enough to explode, and before Callie could explain, he demanded, "Do you fancy yourself in love with him?" His brows merged into a heavy, ominous line and his stormy blue eyes glittered hatefully. He stepped closer to her, his eyes narrowing menacingly, and abruptly his steel fingers bit into her upper arms and he dragged her to him. "Damn you, answer me!"

Callie gritted her teeth and attempted to pry his fingers from her arms. "Logan is my stepfather!" she hissed between her teeth. "Let me go!"

Chandler gazed at her uncomprehendingly for several seconds. "Your *stepfather!*" he repeated harshly. "What kind of fool do you take me for?"

"Logan Bartholomew really *is* my stepfather. He married my mother and they went to Montana after leaving me with Aunt Caroline." She tried again to free herself from his painful grasp, but it was like fighting a beartrap.

"And you think you're in love with the man?" Chandler questioned in an insulting and incredulous tone.

"No!" she cried. "I'm not *in love* with him, but I do love him as a relative. He's been very good to me, and I feel extremely loyal to him. But then, you don't know much about loyalty, do you? Now, let me go, dammit!"

Chandler's eyes held a question and before Callie could protest further, he had pulled her against his hard length, his hands molding her body to his as his mouth ravished hers in a possessive, demanding kiss.

Trembling violently, Callie fought down the desire to wrap her arms around his broad back as she used to do. He had always possessed the power to fire her blood and she discovered that he still had that power. His very touch sent her senses reeling, and her anger was devoured by her treacherous need for him. It had been so long—so very long since she had been here in his arms. Her struggle was more mental than physical as her hips molded to his of their own will. Callie had very little strength to resist him, and she was breathless when he pulled away from her.

He studied her with a perplexed expression. "Why did you leave, Callie?" His fingers stroked her arms where his hands still rested. "You haven't forgotten me in these past years," he drawled perceptively.

Callie would have slapped his face if he hadn't been justified in his remark; she hadn't forgotten him. She couldn't hide her response to his touch. It was written all over her face, evident in every line of her body, in her rapid breathing and her quivering lips. She averted her eyes, unwilling to have him read the desire there and know the truth of his statement. After all this time, she was still in love with Chandler Matthews, and she had wanted so desperately to hate him. She had lied to herself; she had tried to deceive her heart. She should have known that she never could forget her husband of one year. The man she had known so intimately and so volatilely so briefly. He was branded on her heart—her love for him seared right through to her very soul and the knowledge was the ultimate humiliation.

Chandler's voice was strangely gentle when he spoke again. "Was there someone else? Why, Callie? Why did you go away?"

She refused to look at him. He was playing her for a fool again: he knew she knew about Nadine. She wouldn't give him the satisfaction of seeing the misery that had surfaced in her eyes.

He cupped her chin firmly, forcing her eyes to meet his. "Callie?"

A vision of Nadine flashed painfully into her mind, and the woman's words, spoken a few short minutes ago, burned into her brain. "You bored me, Chandler," she murmured impulsively. "I grew tired of you."

She looked away from him quickly, feeling the savage pounding of her heart at the bold lie. She had wanted to hurt him as he had her, to punish him for thinking that she was the same young fool he had married, but she hadn't intended to make such a rash and foolish statement. She wouldn't admit it to him, however. She had been sure she had grown out of her weakness and desire to bend to his will at his merest touch, but she was finding out that Chandler's presence had the power to distort the painful past. She had never been able to be cool and rational when he was near: that hadn't changed at all, but she was determined not to succumb to him again.

A hush fell over the little room, and Callie felt like rubbing her arms briskly to ward off the descending icy chill. She didn't need to look at Chandler's face to know how angry he was. His voice was flat and bitter when he spoke again.

"I realized when I married you, Callie, that we were taking a chance. You were young and inexperienced—we hardly knew each other—but I wanted you too much. When you left, I hoped that you would use the time to mature, to find yourself, and to realize that you loved me." His hand gripped her chin punishingly, biting into the tender flesh as he again forced her eyes to meet the fiery anger in his. "I was wrong. You didn't love me, but you made a vow to me, and, God as my witness, I will see that you keep it. I meant it when I said 'till death do us part.'"

Callie gasped at his audacity. How could he stand there and say such a thing to her when she had caught him in Nadine's arms? Indeed, in the very act of preparing to run off with his mistress! What about *his* vow to her? But then, he wasn't talking about himself. He had never said he loved her, only that he *wanted* her. "I'll never, never be your wife again," she declared tremulously, her brown eyes flashing angrily. "Incidentally," she rasped, recalling the woman who had caused her so much misery, "Nadine was here looking for you. Shouldn't you run along and see what she wants?"

Chandler silently glowered at her for what seemed like an eternity, and Callie could see his body tense with rage. Her eyes met his defiantly; she would never again back down to this man. After a long electric moment, Chandler gave her chin a rough jerk, then released her and stalked from the room.

When the door had been closed, Callie sank down on an empty wine crate. Of course he had gone when she mentioned Nadine. Hadn't Nadine always commanded top priority? She shut her eyes and drew a deep, shuddering breath. Damn Chandler and his winery and his lies and his mistress! She hated them all! She caught her lower lip between her teeth and bit down on it. She could hate her husband all she wanted, she could despise him for what he had done to her, and she could condemn him to hell, but the sad truth was that she was married to him until death—just as he had said. She knew deep down inside that she could never marry another man.

Like the strong, flourishing vines of the grape, the vines of love had twined around her heart and made it Chandler's captive. She knew that she would belong to him as long as she lived—she was tied to him by those bitter, hurting vines of love. The knowledge was painful and degrading, and she made herself a solemn promise that Chandler Matthews would never know how she felt about him. It would be her cruel secret, and somehow she would live with it locked in the dark part of her heart.

CHAPTER THREE

For a long time, Callie sat on the wine crate, lost in her misery. Finally, she made her way to the bathroom, freshened her makeup, and walked purposely to the office. She clenched her fists when Roy answered her knock, and she couldn't keep back a sharp remark. "You could have told me," she accused. "I had no idea that you had sold the winery to Chandler!"

Roy rubbed a big hand across his face and looked properly repentant. "I'm sorry, Callie, but I was in a bind when Chandler bought it from me and I needed a job myself. I was too grateful that he kept me on as manager not to go along with his wishes concerning you. I wanted to tell you this morning, but he told me to stick strictly to business." He hung his head, diverting his eyes from her face. "I'm ashamed of my part in it, but I didn't see how it could hurt you. After all"—he looked back at her sheepishly—"you left him. I thought things were over between you two."

Callie swallowed hard and nodded grimly; Roy wasn't to blame because Chandler had involved him in this. "Things *are* over between us," she said tightly, "but I certainly don't want to work for him. I won't be coming back tomorrow, of course. With such a generous salary" —she looked at him meaningfully—"I won't be difficult to replace."

A frown drew Roy's brows together and he looked at her pensively. "I'm real sorry, Callie."

Noting his long, sad face, she closed her eyes briefly and shook her head wearily. "It wasn't your fault, Roy."

He gave her a hesitant smile before turning back toward his office chair. Callie quietly left and closed the door behind her. It wasn't until she was in her car, driving past Chandler's house, that she had doubts about what she had done. What was she going to do for a job? Should she have swallowed her pride and stayed on at the winery until she found something else? She brushed at her hair. No, the injustice of such a thing would have been too great. She didn't want to be around Chandler, much less feel indebted to him for her salary. She had been falsely lured into the job, and she would simply have to find something else.

Afraid of upsetting Logan, she didn't tell him that she had taken the job and already quit. He would have to know soon enough, but in the meantime, she would only tell him that she wouldn't start to work until later.

She and he shared a simple lunch of cheese sandwiches and a green salad before Callie left to see the lawyer. Her mind was in turmoil as she drove down the long road to his small office. Within five minutes of entering the room, she had learned a most distressing fact about Aunt Caroline's house: it had a second and third trust deed that accounted for most of the value of the house, and it seemed that the lender had been very generous. He had even deferred the monthly payment until Callie could be located.

Her heart sank at the unwelcome news. She didn't have money for monthly payments, of course, and that was just one more reason to sell the house. "I had no idea my aunt was so in need of money," Callie murmured unhappily, knowing that she would realize very little profit when it was sold. She had been counting on a goodly sum as a nest egg against emergencies.

"Your aunt experienced hard times in the last few years," Ned explained, looking at her sympathetically.

Callie nodded and thought absently that Aunt Caroline had never mentioned them while she and Chandler were married. The information about the house was the second blow of the day. "Who is the lender?" she asked.

Ned smiled wanly. "You send the payments to me, and I forward them to the lender. He's a businessman and his investments are made under the corporation name of West Enterprises."

"I see." It really didn't matter who the lender was. What mattered was that the house wasn't free and clear. Having no job was dreadful enough; now Callie would realize very little profit from the sale of the house. Inheritance taxes, a broker's fee, Ned's bill, and mortgage payments would have to come out of that amount as well. Crestfallen, Callie concluded her business and stood up. "About that letter Aunt Caroline is supposed to have left for me—do you think it really exists?"

Ned shook her head uncertainly. "The last time she talked with me, she said that there were things she had to say to you if she were to die with a clear conscience. However, she was much too proud to dictate such a personal message to my secretary, and she insisted that she would write the letter in her own hand, even though she was quite feeble there at the end. She was very definite about the matter, but she never gave the letter to me. She said you would know where to find it when you came home."

Callie sighed in disappointment; how like Aunt Caroline to remain proud and stubborn to the very end. She didn't know where to find the letter, of course, and she had already searched the house. "I've looked everywhere I can think of," she told Ned. "It may sound silly to everyone else, but it's important to me for my peace of mind. My heart would be lightened considerably to know that she still loved me."

"Of course she loved you," Ned insisted gruffly, peering

at Callie over his bifocals. "She was a hateful old woman to most people, Callie, but I've known her all my life and you and I know she had a good heart."

Callie clutched her purse tighter, thinking that disappointment seemed to dog her path every way she turned. She looked down at Ned as he sat hunched over his desk. "You don't know anyone who needs a secretary in the community, do you, Ned?"

He shook his head again. "No. Who's looking? You? Aren't you going to work at the winery?"

"I think not," she said, her voice suddenly cool. Ned surely knew that Chandler owned the winery, and that she wouldn't work for him. She barely remembered her manners as she turned to walk out of the room. "Oh, yes, thank you for keeping the house up. It was so pleasant to come and find it clean and well cared for. And we might have starved without the food," she said lightly, trying to force a smile. "I forgot to go to the store when we arrived."

Staring at her unblinkingly, Ned cleared his throat. "I didn't do it, Callie. Chandler did. I didn't think you would mind."

Callie felt the skin on her face blanch, and she lifted her chin the slightest bit. "No. No, of course not," she murmured. "It was very kind of him." Then she rushed from the room, not even speaking to the secretary as she fled out into the warm sunshine. Chandler! Why had he done it? What was he trying to prove?

She could hardly keep her mind on her driving as she made her way to the small neighborhood real estate office to put the house up for sale. She and Logan would have to move into the city anyway, so that she could find work, and there was no point in procrastinating. Suddenly she felt that the most important thing in her life right now was getting away from Chandler again.

The agent she spoke with, James North, was friendly,

but not very encouraging. He explained that he was familiar with the house, and that there might be very little demand for it. After all, it was a very old house, not in good repair, and it was set in the midst of the vineyards. Also, Aunt Caroline's property was small; over the years, she had gradually sold most of it off for money to live on.

"Well, please do your best," Callie requested. "I do want to move as soon as possible."

The agent gave her his most professional smile. "Of course I'll do my best, but I think it will take a very select client. I'll work on it." He scratched his head thoughtfully, then pressed his fingertips together. "I just might have someone who is interested," he mused.

Callie thanked him and returned to the car. Her situation certainly wasn't looking very promising, but, fortunately, she would have her hands full looking for a new job, a new place to live, and keeping the house immaculate so that she could sell it as rapidly as possible. She wouldn't have time to brood over Chandler, or to think about the way she had trembled in his arms, thrilling to his touch when he had kissed her.

She forced a smile to her lips when she parked the car in front of the house and stepped out. There was no reason to involve Logan in her misery. Opening the front door, she marched confidently into the living room. "I did it!" she exclaimed brightly. "I put the house up for sale."

"Oh?" Logan's look was quizzical, and he raised his eyebrows and watched her as she settled on the sofa beside him. He laid down the magazine he was reading and his gray eyes met her brown ones. "I thought you were going to wait a little while."

She shrugged carelessly. "I decided it would serve no purpose to settle in since we're going to move anyway. There's no reason to wait, really."

Logan spread his hands in a helpless gesture. "Whatever you say. It's your house. How do the prospects look for a sale?"

"I'm not sure. Mr. North, the agent, admitted that it might take a select client." Callie fidgeted with her purse, then stood up, not wanting Logan to press her on the issue. "I think I'll work out in the backyard for a while. I'd like to enjoy the sun before I have to start working every day." Without waiting for his response, she slipped up the steps to her room to pull out a pair of blue and white cotton shorts and a brief blue halter. When she was dressed, she freed her hair from the bun and let it swing down about her shoulders like a cloak of spun gold.

For a while she aimlessly inspected the bushes and flowers, trying to think out her unhappy situation. She picked up a worn green garden hose and absently sprayed the grass and the brilliantly colored flowers thriving in the rich soil. Unaware of the frown creasing her brow, she showered the thick-trunked grapevines climbing wildly over the rickety old red lattice-work arbor. She had faced problems before, of course, problems more serious than this, and she had survived. The loss of the job was a setback, and it was true that she didn't want to sell the house right now, but in the end matters would work themselves out; after all, life was a series of compromises. A faded orange hammock of coarse nylon hung under the vine-covered arbor, and Callie looked longingly at the shadowed coolness where it rocked gently in the afternoon breeze. She had lain there in that same old hammock and dreamed a hundred daydreams on such a hot summer afternoon. She pursed her lips pensively: she rarely had time for daydreams now and she had little belief in them. Many of the daydreams she had reveled in there in the swaying old hammock had been about Chandler and her future with him. She turned away from the hanging bed and its memories, forcing herself to concentrate on her work in the yard that she loved so.

When Logan came into the backyard, she was digging in the moist, rich earth with a two-fingered trowel she had found in the old lean-to Aunt Caroline had used for storage. "Your Mr. North called," he informed her. "He wants to bring a client out this evening, and I told him that it would be fine. He certainly doesn't waste any time, does he?"

Callie's face lit up; this was indeed good news. "No, he apparently doesn't waste time, thank God," she said, shading her eyes with her hands as she gazed up at him. "I told him I wanted to move as soon as possible, but I didn't really expect any action so quickly."

Logan looked around the backyard and breathed deeply. "It's so peaceful here," he said pensively.

"Yes, it is." Callie had a suspicion that Logan hated the thought of selling as much as she did, but it simply couldn't be helped.

"Are you ready for dinner?" he asked.

She rolled her head in a circle, easing her cramped neck muscles, then stood up and stretched. "Yes. We didn't eat much lunch, and I am hungry." Brushing her hands together, she cleaned off some of the clinging dirt. She put the trowel back in the plastic wastebasket where she had found it and took it back to the shed.

"I've made up for lunch with dinner," Logan told her, grinning proudly. "Come on in and clean up while I get the food on the table."

"You're a treasure." She winked at him. "I never thought I'd have my own cook." He laughed openly as she followed him into the house.

Upon returning from washing up, she saw that Logan had prepared a tempting meal consisting of baked chicken, boiled ears of golden corn, and a large avocado salad. She settled down in a straight-back chair eagerly. Her fork was poised for the first bite of salad when the doorbell rang.

"I'll get it. It must be the realtor." Barefoot, she hurried to the front door and pulled it open. Chandler was standing on the porch with James North, and Callie felt her breath catch in her throat. "Yes?" she demanded breathlessly, her heart beating furiously at Chandler's unexpected appearance. Each time she saw him, she had that absurd urge to throw her arms around his neck, and she struggled to suppress the ridiculous desire.

"I think Mr. Bartholomew was to give you my message," Mr. North said, looking a little dismayed at Callie's less than enthusiastic greeting. "I told him I wanted to bring out a prospective buyer."

When Callie stared at him blankly for a moment, he asked, "Did he tell you?"

Her hand flew to her throat in a revealing nervous gesture. Chandler! Chandler was the client? She gazed at him, her anger rising at the turn of events. "You?"

Before Chandler could speak, Mr. North made the introductions. "Miss Matthews, this is Mr. Chandler Matthews."

"We know each other," Callie told him, "and it's Mrs. —Mrs. Matthews."

Mr. North looked more confused then ever. "You mean you two—"

"Yes," Callie said grimly, her eyes meeting Chandler's. Why did the interested party have to be Chandler? She didn't want him to have the house, and she couldn't imagine why he would possibly want it. Was he playing some cruel little game with her? "Why?" she asked, glaring at her husband. "Why do you want this house?"

Chandler's eyes swept coldly over her tall, shapely form, taking in her long legs, temptingly exposed in the brief shorts, her small high breasts straining provocatively against the skimpy halter top, and finally they rested on the shimmering gold cascading down her shoulders before they settled on her angry, upturned face. "I don't want it," he drawled at last, his perusual seeming to make him tense and angry. "I want the land to expand my vineyards, and I don't need to tell you what premium land this is for grapes. I hardly think I can purchase the land without the house, but it's really too old to save."

Callie felt betrayed and she knew she had no reason to. She didn't want to sell to Chandler, but common sense told her he might very well be right about the house, and that he might be the only interested buyer. But still it seemed a cruel injustice that he was the one who was interested. Hadn't he hurt her enough? Did he have to commit this final humiliation—taking the only thing she had in the world? She couldn't make herself tell him he could have it. She simply couldn't. "I've decided not to sell," she declared rashly.

"But Miss—Mrs. Matthews," Mr. North sputtered, "I thought you were eager to sell. I assured my client that you wanted out of the house as soon as possible."

Callie felt a blush creep up her neck, and she licked her lips. "I'm sorry to have inconvenienced your—your client," she managed to reply, "but I've changed my mind."

Mr. North looked at Chandler helplessly, his eyes wide. "I don't know what to say," he muttered unhappily. "She told me just this afternoon that she wanted to sell."

Chandler glanced briefly at Mr. North, then glared at Callie. His jaw muscle was twitching ominously and his eyes sparked with anger. "Mrs. Matthews has always had a fickle nature," he said tartly; then he turned on his heel and stalked off the porch toward the car.

Callie quickly shut the door and leaned heavily against it, her eyes bright with anger and threatening tears. Why Chandler, of all people? The why was obvious, she told herself; he had said he wanted the land. She looked up forlornly as Logan walked in from the dining room.

"What happened?"

Stiffening her spine, Callie met his gaze. "The interested

party is Chandler. He seems to be trying to move in on every area of my life, and I don't want him to have this house," she exclaimed. Her eyes shifted from Logan's to stare at her hands as they twisted together nervously, and she sighed in resignation. "Actually, he doesn't want it. He says it's too old to save and he wants the land for expansion of his vineyards."

Logan studied Callie's flushed face, his pale gray eyes sympathetic. "I know how you feel about the house, Callie, but perhaps Chandler is right. It is old and in disrepair. You can keep the furniture, and I think that's what really makes this place."

Callie massaged her temples wearily, experiencing the first dull pains of a tension headache. "It's not what will become of the house so much, Logan," she said. "It's selling to Chandler. I'd almost rather walk off and leave it than sell it to him."

Logan arched his brows and looked at her pensively. "It's yours to do with as you wish, Callie, but he may be the only interested buyer."

He couldn't be, Callie told herself unhappily. Fate couldn't be so cruel. "Do you think I should sell to him?" she asked bleakly. "After all, you are involved in this, too."

"Only through your generosity, honey," he said with all humility. "I have a few dollars, and I'm too sick to work. I don't know what would have become of me if you hadn't been there in Montana when you were, and I don't know what I'd do without you now. If you don't want to sell to Chandler, then don't. Someone else will be interested sooner or later."

Callie balled her hands into fists. "Oh, Logan, I really don't want to sell to him, but we may be in real trouble if I don't. He owns the Dumontt Winery now—not Roy Dumontt. *He* hired me to work there, and when I found out, I quit." She spread her hands before her in a helpless gesture. "I don't have a job now," she finished miserably, "and when our money runs out—that's it."

A frown creased Logan's pale face. "Oh, I see why you wouldn't want to sell to him. What's he trying to do to you?"

"I don't know, but what if no one else is interested? What if the house is too old to save, as he said?"

Logan's face appeared a little whiter than usual—or was it merely her imagination? "Different people see things differently. Come on and let's eat before the chicken gets cold. We'll worry about the house later."

Callie couldn't worry about it later; it was on her mind now, but she didn't want to hurt Logan's feelings after he had worked so hard on the meal. She walked to the window and lifted the edge of the drapery. Peering out, she was just in time to see Chandler and Mr. North pull out of the driveway, and she quickly dropped the drapery, as though it had singed her fingers. Damn Chandler Matthews. He had lured her here with the offer of a job, and now he wanted her house. Was he determined to strip her physically as well as mentally? Was he bent on breaking her for leaving him?

Callie followed Logan back to the dining room, but she could only pretend to pick at her food, and as soon as she had eaten enough of it to be appreciative of Logan's effort, she excused herself from the table. Without saying anything else, she went back out to the yard. Taking all her uncertainty and anger out on the ground around the plants, she dug at the soil furiously. She kept at it until the sun started to dip low in the painted pinkish-orange evening sky and the coolness settled comfortably on her shoulders.

As night slowly covered the yard with a soft, velvet darkness, Callie sat down heavily on the thick, green grass, listening to the croaking of bullfrogs and the chirping of crickets as the evening creatures came out of hiding to socialize with each other. She pulled her knees up to her chin and rested her head on them until the solitude of her surroundings dissipated her misery. A frog hopping too close for comfort roused her from her meditations. Finally, realizing how late it was, she rose and trailed back into the house, stopping at the kitchen table, where Logan sat reading an old magazine and sipping a cup of coffee.

"May I join you?" she asked, suddenly feeling guilty that she had shut him out while she pondered her situation. He couldn't have helped her, but she should have included him, she told herself.

He agreed immediately, his gray eyes brightening a little. "Yes, of course. Sit down and I'll get you a cup."

"No, stay where you are," she insisted, waving him back to his chair.

He ignored her gestures. "I'll do it. You look beat, and I know you're tired after working out there with the grapevines."

She smiled shyly. They both knew she hadn't done any real work; the only result of her activity had been to dispel her hostility. She sat down in a chair and watched Logan as he walked from the room. He looked old and tired, and again her concern for him filled her mind. His shoulders seemed more slumped than usual, and she nervously fidgeted with a strand of hair as he left the room. It was only seconds later that she heard a gasp, then a muffled crash from the kitchen.

Knocking her chair backward in her haste, Callie raced to the room, to find Logan leaning against the counter, clutching his chest. Before she could reach him, he fell to the floor. A broken cup lay at his feet and for a moment Callie was mesmerized by it.

Although she had rehearsed this particular scene in her mind many times, she was immobilized temporarily by her shock. Managing to gather her senses sufficiently for action, she rushed into the living room. Her heart pounding madly, she phoned for an ambulance, then went back to make Logan as comfortable as possible.

Callie had paced the hospital corridor a hundred times when a doctor finally came out to speak with her. She was stunned to hear him tell her that Logan would live, but that he would need bypass surgery on his heart if he were ever to function normally again. Without it, he would be little more than an invalid and in danger of dying.

"Thank God, he's alive and can be helped," she breathed gratefully. She felt the blood pound in her temples, and she couldn't keep the critical question from her lips. "How much will it cost?"

"It's quite expensive, unfortunately, but Mr. Bartholomew's insurance will probably cover most of it."

"How expensive?" Callie persisted, knowing that Logan's insurance was little better than useless. She was staggered by the sum when the doctor told her, and her hand flew to her mouth. She didn't know where she would get the money; a bitterness rose inside her and she swallowed hard. One disaster followed another here, and she regretted her decision to come back home. Her worst fears had been realized: Logan was desperately ill and they were without funds. Even if she sold the house, she knew she would never clear enough to pay for the operation. There had to be *some* way to get the money.

Callie pushed her pride way back into the dark corners of her mind; the situation was grave, and she had to accept her forming thoughts. She would be forced to sell the house to Chandler now, no matter how abhorrent the idea was to her. There was no time left to consider her own feelings about the matter. She would do all she could to help Logan, and that meant that she would have to be grateful for Chandler's interest in the house—and it meant that she would need the job at the winery. The salary was too good to pass up—Chandler's generosity, she thought unhappily. She fought down the gall rising in her throat: she wished she were still in Montana, for she had found nothing in the Salinas Valley but old pain, sharp disappointment, and new, bleeding wounds.

The doctor patted her hand clumsily. "Try not to take it too hard. Really, things could be a lot worse. He'll do just fine once he's had the bypass."

Callie's smile quivered on her lips. "Thank you, Doctor. I'm grateful to you." Logan *would* have the bypass, because Callie would get the money somewhere. She just wasn't quite sure how right now. "May I see him?"

"Not at this time," the man said. "He's in intensive care. Why don't you phone in the morning? I think he'll sleep through the night, and you'll be notified if there's any change."

Numb with unhappiness, Callie whispered her agreement. Then she stumbled down the hall, suddenly realizing that she didn't have any way to get home. She took change from her purse, found a pay telephone, and called for a taxi, resenting the money it would cost.

When she had gone out in the dark, cool night air to wait for the cab, she became aware of how scanty her attire was. She had slipped her feet into shoes, but she hadn't changed from her shorts and halter, and the thin blouse she had hastily pulled on did little to drive away the coolness. Callie pressed her lips into a thin line and quickly lost herself in her thoughts. What if Chandler refused to let her stay on at the winery? She wouldn't put it past him. And how humiliating that she must turn to him at all, and especially now after she had refused the job. What if he wouldn't buy the house either? Even Chandler couldn't be so cruel, she told herself, but a memory of him standing there on her porch, so tense and angry, filled her mind. Chandler wouldn't be above making her crawl for help, she thought miserably. She was relieved that she had told him Logan was her stepfather, for surely he would refuse her requests otherwise.

The cab eventually came, and Callie ignored the driver as his eyes skimmed interestedly over her. In a cool tone, she gave him her address and climbed inside the car.

It was a tired and drained Callie who paid for the ride and stepped out at her front door. The house had never felt so empty and barren as it did when she went inside, and needing some distraction, she roamed through it, again searching for her aunt's letter. But it was all to no avail, and again doubting the existence of the letter, she trailed upstairs to the bathroom. She bathed quickly, brushed her tousled hair, pulled on a flimsy nightgown, and slid beneath the white sheet on her bed. The heart of the night, the loneliest time in the world, dearily draped her room with its gloom before she finally secured the elusive, healing solace of sleep.

The next morning Callie phoned the hospital as soon as she awakened, and she was tremendously relieved to learn that Logan was resting and doing as well as could be expected. She left word that she would see him later in the day, then went to dress. Today of all days, she wanted to look her best. And today she hoped Chandler would be at the winery. Slipping into her most appealing pants outfit, she noticed the way the cinnamon color set off the golden highlights of her blond hair and complimented her skin. She camouflaged the dark circles beneath her eyes with more than her usual light makeup, then slid her feet into functional sandals. Today she didn't feel like being an aloof businesswoman: today she was Callie Hart Matthews, and she was going to have to humble herself before the man whose name she bore.

With single-minded determination, she drove to the winery and got out of the car. She held her head proudly, hating what she had to do, and knowing there was no alternative. Her entire body rebelled at the thought of the humiliation she must face, and her mind encouraged rebellion. She felt a weakness in her knees, but she refused to give into her quivering limbs and she pressed onward. When she knocked at the office door, she found only Roy there, and she faced the heavy man.

"Has anyone else been hired for the job of tour guide?" she asked.

Roy shook his head. "Not yet. We haven't had time to look for anyone."

Callie licked her lips nervously. "Did Chandler speak to you about it yet? Was he terribly angry because I refused the job?"

Roy smiled half-heartedly. "He was angry, all right, but he didn't say anything to me about it. Why?" he asked a bit impatiently. "Have you changed your mind?"

"Logan, my stepfather, has been hospitalized in serious condition, and I really need this job." She was ashamed to find herself in this position, but there was no help for it now. Her gaze lowered to the wooden floorboards, then she looked back up quickly, her eyes imploring Roy to make this a little easier for her. "I—I can't afford to lose the job, and I hope Chandler will let me stay on."

Roy looked at her with compassion in his shrewd eyes. "What's wrong with your stepfather? Is he going to be all right?"

Callie sighed tiredly. "He has a heart condition and needs surgery if he is ever to live a normal life. Oh, Roy, I can't give up this job now, and—and I hate to face Chandler."

Roy nodded. "I'm sorry to hear about your stepfather, Callie, but you'd better talk to Chandler as soon as you can. He really is mad—apparently about a lot of things. I know you refused to sell him the house, too, and he's not a man who takes an insult lightly. I don't know what he'll say about the job, but he's got temporary help for emergencies."

Callie's heart sank at the news that Chandler was terribly angry; even though she expected no less from the man, she knew it made her plight more uncertain. "I've changed my mind about selling the house, too," she told Roy, sweeping her pride aside. "I need the money, and I don't think even the profit from the house will be enough for Logan's operation. He has very little insurance." Her eyes searched Roy's face. "God, Roy," she murmured, "I'm so desperate, and I wish so fervently that you still owned the winery."

He smiled sadly. "I wish I did, too, honey, but wishing doesn't make any difference."

She nodded, knowing only too well the truth of his words. "I've no right to ask you, but will you try to soften up Chandler for me?"

"I'll see what I can do," he promised, "but you'd better go on over to the house and talk to him, Callie. He's not coming in today."

"Oh," she murmured. Wasn't that just the way her luck was running? She shuddered at the thought of going to the house she had shared with him all those months. Still, she had no choice but to confront him, and there was no use putting off the inevitable. Ruefully, she decided to get it over with. "Thanks, Roy."

Turning away from him, she walked stiffly from the room. She got back into the car and drove directly back to Chandler's house without giving herself time to mull over her situation any longer. She almost couldn't make herself turn into his drive, and several times she started to go past, but she suddenly made a sharp turn. All the way to the front walkway, she struggled with a grim desire to keep driving rather than stop, but finally she halted the car in front of the house and sat for a moment summoning her strength. It was all a matter of mind control; the man could do nothing but say yes or no, and when he said one or the other, she could flee back to her own house. Regardless, it was difficult to make herself leave the car. Abruptly, she jerked the door open and marched up to the front door, lest she lose all heart and throw the car into reverse.

The door was open and she could hear soft music playing inside. With a shaking finger, she pressed the bell and told her wildly beating heart to be silenced. It was hard enough to stand there and wait for a response; she felt weak all over and her mouth tasted of cotton. It appeared that Chandler wasn't going to answer the door at all, and Callie wondered where the household help was. She looked hopefully at the refuge of her car, then whirled around sharply as she heard the purr of a female voice.

"Well, little Callie. How good to see you again!"

Callie stared up into Nadine's glittering green eyes, and her heart plummeted. She hadn't anticipated the redhead being there, not now of all times, and her shame was even more unbearable as she asked, "Is Chandler at home?"

She had no sooner asked the question when the man appeared behind Nadine. Once again Callie was struck by what a handsome couple they made, and the thought caused her heart to beat more rapidly. Did Nadine live with Chandler? Must she talk to him in this woman's presence?

"Yes?" he demanded coldly, his eyes raking over her disdainfully.

Callie had to force the words to her lips. Stiffening her spine, she stood rigidly before them, hating her position, yet powerless to tell them both off and leave. "I need to speak with you, Chandler," she said through tight lips, glancing from Chandler to Nadine, then back again.

"Speak," he said curtly, his eyes taunting her.

She seethed with instant anger. He was making this as hard on her as he possibly could, and she despised him with every bone in her body. "I prefer to speak with you alone," she bit out, "but I will speak with or without Nadine here."

Chandler's lips quirked in an ironic smile and he tilted his head to one side. He was laughing at her! It was only by the sheerest shreds of willpower that Callie was able to stand there under his torment. She wanted nothing more than to slap that smile off his lips and rake her nails down Nadine's flawless cheek, but she stood silently before them, her chin held high, her posture tense.

"Come in," Chandler invited after a long, humiliating moment.

Nadine and Chandler both stepped aside for her to enter, and just when Callie was sure Chandler intended to make her degradation complete by forcing her to plead for her job in front of Nadine, he turned to the tall woman. "I'll see you at eight."

Nadine's eyes swept ruthlessly over Callie before she flounced out the door. She looked back over her shoulder and smiled broadly at Chandler. "Don't be late." Then her eyes returned to Callie, and the smile lingered on her lips. "So good to see you again, dear."

Callie shook her head, half-amused by the charade. "You saw me yesterday, Nadine, remember?"

The redhead's green eyes flashed hatefully for only a second. "Of course I remember. And I remember what we talked about. I hope you do, too."

"But of course," Callie returned, remembering only too well.

Nadine smiled broadly. "Good girl. See you later, Chandler." Then she strolled confidently down the walkway to her car, her hips swaying provocatively.

Callie couldn't stop the sigh of relief that escaped her lips at the woman's departure; she could think of nothing more horrible than having to humble herself before Chandler in the presence of his mistress.

"Will you sit down?" he asked, and Callie heard a forced politeness in the words.

"Yes, thank you." She was grateful that he had offered, for her legs were unwilling to support her much longer. She seated herself in the nearest chair, and she was surprised to see that it was the rocker Chandler had purchased for her when she had admired it in an antique store. She sat very still, not wanting the chair to rock; she didn't need more memories of her life with Chandler to seep into her consciousness. Even hating him didn't dull the fascination he held for her.

Chandler perched on a nearby couch arm, idly swinging one long leg. "What can I do for you, Callie? Surely you aren't here on a social call. Have you come to tell me you'll sell me the house after all?"

Callie's head jerked up and she gazed into Chandler's mocking eyes. Mustering every ounce of dignity she could summon, she held his glittering gaze. "Yes, as a matter of fact, I have."

"Oh?" He looked terribly amused. "Why the change of heart?"

"Logan's very ill," she explained hurriedly, afraid her tongue would fail her, "and I need every penny I can get now. He needs a bypass operation and it's so expensive. He has almost no insurance."

Chandler gazed at her flushed face without speaking, but the gleam in his eyes faded and was replaced by hardness. Callie rushed on. "I'd also like to keep working at the winery if I may," she stated with more confidence than she felt. Damn the man for letting her hang like this. Her eyes lowered, and she looked down at her tightly clenched fists and saw that her fingers were turning white from the unnatural pressure.

"Are you asking for my charity?" Chandler drawled at last with no hint of humor in his voice.

"I am not!" she denied, raising angry brown eyes to his

face. It would be a cold day in hell before she would ask *him* for charity.

His eyes stared evenly into hers. "If you had the money for the operation, you wouldn't want to sell the house or to continue working for me, would you?"

"No, I wouldn't," she told him frankly, despising his condescension. "I wouldn't be here at all, but I'm asking nothing from you without reciprocation. I don't want anything for nothing!"

"How expensive is the surgery?"

When she told him, he whistled between his teeth. Then he scrutinized her face before looking away from her to stare out the open door. Callie waited tensely until his eyes again met hers, and then she experienced the most dreadful foreboding. Chandler was playing with her. There was something cruel about his frosty gaze.

"I know the house has a second and third mortgage on it, Callie. Even if I were very generous, which your attitude certainly doesn't warrant, I couldn't give you a lot for it. It's in a sorry state, no matter how much you'd like to think that it isn't. Besides, I want only the land. You might sell it to someone else, but you aren't going to find buyers very eager for it with my land surrounding it."

Callie had a sinking feeling in the pit of her stomach; the profit would be very small, and from that she would have to pay so many debts. But she would die before she would ask Chandler for more money. She had already told him how desperate she was, and it was obvious that he didn't care.

"However," he said, looking levelly at her, "if you want to wait for another offer, that's certainly your prerogative."

Callie raised a hesitant hand to finger the pins of her tight bun. Slowly, she shook her head. She didn't know what she would do for more money, but she couldn't wait for a nonexistent buyer. She knew the hospital wouldn't any interest in her at all now, it was purely sexual—so why pretend that the marriage meant anything? What was he trying to prove? That she would do as he demanded? What? Why bother to have her return as his wife?

Suddenly she knew that she would be more than willing if only there were some chance for them again, but she had long ago admitted that it could never be. Trying to resurrect what had been between them that summer would be as futile as trying to bring life back to a beautiful plant that had bloomed magnificently and briefly in the spring, then had been violated and abused by summer heat and autumn winds.

Her eyes defiantly met his and she glowered at him. "No! Never!" she cried vehemently, rising to her feet. He wouldn't get the chance to break her heart and shame her in this community a second time. Turning away from him, she quickly walked toward the door.

Before she could escape him, Chandler grabbed her and pulled her roughly back to crush her against his chest. "Was our marriage so unbearable?" he asked hatefully. Tilting her chin so that his stormy eyes could probe her distressed ones, he vowed, "You'll come back, Callie, and on my terms."

Then his lips lowered ever so slowly to hers. In contrast to his painful kiss of yesterday, this one was tantalizing and seductive. Callie felt the provocative pressure of his muscled body as he gently pulled her against him, and his hands played lightly in caressing circles on her back as the kiss gradually increased in intensity, progressing from sweet temptation to passionate hunger.

She tensed in his arms, trying to pretend cold indifference, insulted that he resorted to such tactics, but she found herself reliving a thousand other such kisses that Chandler had given her, and even in her rage, she felt her body give in to him. She knew that she had to get away from him while she was still in control of her senses. She wait for payment from Logan. She looked up at Chandler, hating him for his callousness about her predicament. She knew she would have to sell to him, and still she heard herself murmur, "I don't know."

She was startled when he walked over and stood by her chair, seeming taller than ever. "How badly do you want Logan to get well?" he growled.

Her eyes brilliant with anger, she glared at him. "That's a ridiculous question! I want desperately for him to get well. He must get well."

"And to get well, he has to have this operation?"

Why was he toying with her like a cat with a cornered mouse? Did he enjoy dragging out her agony? Would he help her or not? For herself, she would never have come here, but for Logan, she had had to. "Yes," she cried. "Why do you think I'm here?"

Chandler fiddled with the band of his expensive gold watch. "There is one way he can have the money," he said reflectively, his voice low and ominous.

Callie waited breathlessly, wondering if he were really going to help her, but he made her ask the question. "How?"

"Come back and live with me as my wife."

Callie was aghast. Stunned, she stared at him, her mouth open in surprise. "Why?" she whispered. "Why?"

His expression was indifferent, but his voice was hard. "I told you when I married you that I only intended to marry once. I also told you yesterday that I meant it when I said 'till death do us part.'"

Callie grimaced as a wave of shame washed over her: Chandler didn't love her, of course. He wanted to punish her for running out on him, to show her that she was his to do with as he wished while he was free to engage in his illicit affair with Nadine. A woman didn't leave Chandler Matthews until he told her he was through with her—and he hadn't gotten the chance to tell Callie that. If he had attempted to pull away, but steel arms pressed her more tightly to his masculine length, and her nipples tautened as her breasts molded to his chest. She could feel every virile line of Chandler's lean, muscled form, and she felt a burning warmth all along her body. Remembrances of other times in his arms filled her mind and she experienced strong stirrings of desire for him. Because she was so hungry for him, he was easily able to stoke the fires of her passion. The warmth turned to a hot heat as his hips moved slightly and teasingly against hers, causing ripples of desire to radiate throughout her loins. She didn't want to want Chandler, but they had always enjoyed the most ecstatic of sexual unions; and she realized she was responding against her will.

She reminded herself of the numerous reasons why she must turn from his touch. He had cheated on her, humiliated her, tricked her into coming back for a job, and he had tried to get her house, but now he was using his most powerful weapon to make her bend to his will. She refused to be a slave to her desire for him. Her pride and honor forbade such an outrage.

His kiss became increasingly passionate, and his fierce grip lessened again as his long fingers played sensuously on her back. Callie knew only too well that she hated him as much as she loved him. His desire for her was a cruel mockery of the love she felt for him, but she also found that she was fast losing the battle to her own rising desire. Once again she knew his power over her as he broke down the last fence of her resistance. What was the use in trying to control her responses when every area of her body had already told Chandler of his effect on her? Her nipples pressed against him like hard buttons, her hips molded to his as if that were the only purpose for which they had been created, her lips were supple and willing under the coaxing pressure of his mouth, and even her tongue touched his when it explored the soft recesses of her mouth.

Finally the turmoil in her mind revolved only on what Chandler was doing to her physically. With a ragged sigh, Callie found herself returning his provocative kiss, lost to all but the response that raged inside her. It had been so very long, and she had dreamed of being in her husband's arms a thousand times. She was helpless to stop her hands from finding their way to the curly black locks she loved so well. She felt a betraying weakness in her legs as they pressed against Chandler's muscular ones. It was useless to deny that she wanted him, that she was his at this moment to do with as he so desired.

She couldn't fight him and her body no longer wanted to. Chandler took advantage of her weakness; leading her to the couch, he eased her down onto it, lowering his long body gently beside hers. She closed her eyes, trying in vain to keep him from seeing the love that she felt so deeply for him. Her pride had been consumed in the flames of desire, her hurt and pain had been overrun by passion. Placing his hands on each side of her face, Chandler raised her head up so that he could better ravish her softly parted lips, and Callie felt a rising urgency to give herself to him completely. She shivered with desire when his large hand cupped her breast, and she longed to have him ease the blouse over her head so that his lips could close down on the rosy tip. His hand stole down to her thigh and caressed it through the material of her pants. Callie trembled when his teeth teased her earlobe, then took love bites along the length of her throat.

Then she heard his hoarse words. "I've wanted you so, Callie. I've longed so many times to hold you in my arms, to have you again. No woman has ever been able to drive me crazy with her body as you did."

Not even Nadine Harris, she wanted to shout bitterly, his words bringing her out of her trance of love. "Oh, I don't doubt that, Chandler," she murmured hoarsely. She had always been enticing as a sexual plaything for him, but not enticing enough to keep him out of Nadine's arms. Abruptly, she pushed at him, her hands hurting against the hardness of his chest. It was plain that he wanted her only physically, and she was glad her self-respect had surfaced in time. Chandler hadn't said a single word about love, and she wasn't so desperate for him that she would settle for sex. Had he thought to seduce her back into his home with his irresistible lovemaking so she could be a convenience for him? Did he think so little of her—or did he think she thought so little of herself?

He looked at her oddly for a moment, and she saw the desire gradually fade from his eyes. It was replaced by a hard, cynical glare, and at last he slid his body off hers.

Callie sat up quickly, straightening her clothes and grabbing at the pins falling from her hair.

Chandler sat a little distance from her, silently glowering at her. After several moments, he spoke in a cold tone. "Well?" he demanded.

"Well, what?" she asked, refusing to look at him.

"Do you agree to my terms?"

Of course she didn't want to, but what else could she do? Logan had to have the bypass, and she had already made a fool of herself in Chandler's arms. "Have I another choice?" she retorted. It would be humiliating indeed to return to him, knowing full well that he was still carrying on his affair with Nadine. Did he see this as a way of having both of them?

Her shame rose at the thought. She told herself that she was sacrificing her happiness for Logan, but an insidious thought crept into her mind: she had wanted nothing more than to have Chandler make love to her less than two minutes ago. Was she sacrificing herself for Logan, or was she so desperate to be back in Chandler's arms at any cost that she would use any excuse to salvage her pride while she crawled back to him? No, she told herself sternly: it was for Logan's sake. She would return to Chandler for Logan's sake, but she would hide the love she harbored for him deep in her heart, lest he discover it, and see for himself how much of a fool he was really making of her.

"For how long?" she asked sharply, trying to cover her confusion and her shame.

"What do you mean?"

"How long do you expect me to live with you as your wife?" If only he knew how hard it was for her to go back to him at all, loving him as she did, and knowing that he loved another woman. It was humiliating and pride-stripping and too much to ask of any woman, especially one in love. When he was tired of her again, she would go through the agony of losing him a second time. "You can't think that Logan's surgery is payment sufficient for me to sell myself to you for the rest of my life."

Callie watched his beautiful lips tighten into a thin, cruel line, and his hands clenched convulsively at his sides as his posture became ramrod straight. For a solitary moment, she was sure that she had provoked him to strike her. She had never known him to be violent, although she had been exposed to his temper on several occasions. Frigid blue eyes glowered down at her. Suddenly he gripped her chin in a punishing vise, jerking her face toward his. Callie's breath was sucked away by the sudden move, and she blinked back instant tears as his hard fingers bit into the sensitive skin of her face and neck.

"For one year, the same as before," he growled savagely. "An expensive year, but surely you'll be bored again by then!"

Callie felt his hot breath on her face, and seeing his pulse throb at his temples, she flinched before his fury. She struggled to be free of his hurting hand, but he held her immobile until he was ready to release her. Then he shoved her from him with an expletive. Only by supporting herself with her hands was she able to remain upright, and she was more frightened of his anger than she wanted him to know.

Chandler stood up with swift, angry motions and glowered down at her. Summoning her courage not to lower her gaze, Callie stared at him.

"I'll have the check for you tomorrow. We'll invite some people over for a ceremony Saturday night, so wear something special. I'll have Pastor Nathan come for a renewal of our wedding vows."

Unable to believe what she was hearing, Callie protested. "Surely that isn't necessary. Do we need to put on a show?" she asked in a hard, nervous voice.

His handsome features were fierce. "Yes, we do. Besides," he added cruelly, "you're at your best with a crowd, aren't you? How many people were there at the barbecue? Eighty? A hundred?"

"I only remember Nadine Harris," she stated pointedly, her ire rising at the mention of that fatal night.

"Yes, I remember her, too," Chandler replied coldly. "She helped me hunt for my wife that night." His eyes were stony as they glared into Callie's. "She consoled me when I found your note."

Chandler's little game was becoming increasingly cruel, and Callie rose to her feet before she lost all control. "I'm sure she did, Chandler." Brushing past him, she walked stiffly to the door.

"Have you something special to wear for the ceremony, or would you like some money?" he asked, grabbing her arm and whirling her around to face him. He reached for his wallet with his free hand, but Callie shook her head emphatically.

"The only thing I want from you, Chandler, is money for Logan's surgery."

He laughed harshly, then pulled her closer. "Is that really all?" he murmured low, his voice suggestive.

Pulling free of his hands, she stepped back to put some distance between them. "Yes, believe it or not, that's all!"

He laughed again, and Callie reached for the doorknob. "Don't go to work at the winery," he called after her. "Your job is not part of the agreement, and I don't want my *wife* working." His tone was mocking. "I'll see you tomorrow morning at your house."

Callie nodded without turning back. Then she forced one foot in front of the other until she was out of Chandler's house. As she walked to her car, she whispered bitterly, "And you'll see Nadine tonight."

CHAPTER FOUR

The next day Callie spent half an hour with Logan, who was still weak and not allowed to see anyone for longer periods of time. She didn't tell him about the deal she had made with Chandler, though she knew he had to know before long. For now he didn't need the shock, and she thought that later she could convince him that she had grown lonely and decided to return to Chandler on her own. She did tell him that she had a buyer for the house, and that he need have no money worries.

It was a pale and anxious Callie who peered out the window to watch Chandler stride up the steps to her front door later that morning. She recalled the many times she had waited impatiently for him to knock on her door when their love was new and exciting, and it only made the mockery seem more unjust now. She had been wrong to come here; she remembered the adage that one can never go home again. She had never understood how true it was until now.

She made Chandler ring twice before she had the courage to answer. She wanted to hate him for what he was doing, but she found a traitorous excitement growing inside her at the sight of him standing there on the porch, so tall and commanding. He was dressed in jeans again and a pale blue shirt that accented his startling blue eyes.

"Are you going to let me in?" he asked, his tone taunting.

She spoke sharply to hide her emotional upheaval at the sight of him. "Is there any way to avoid it?"

"Not if you want my money," he snapped.

Callie gasped at his retort, and she couldn't keep the tartness from her voice. "I *do* want your money," she said, motioning for him to come inside, "but that's all I want."

Briskly stepping inside, Chandler walked down the wide hall to the living room, and without Callie's invitation, he seated himself on the sofa and pulled two checks from his shirt pocket.

"The money for Logan's surgery," he said, slapping the piece of paper down on the round table. "And payment for the house. I took the liberty of making out this check since I want the land and you don't need it. You'll live with me, of course. I won't demolish the house for some time, so when Logan gets out of the hospital, he can stay here until your year of—indenture—is up." The last words were cold and cynical, and Callie winced at his belittling tone.

She almost protested that she hadn't made up her mind to sell him the house, but that was absurd, of course, and she swallowed her foolish pride. It was much too late for game-playing. He was right, naturally. In all probability, no one else would want to buy the house in its present condition, especially with Chandler's land all around it.

Besides, she would feel so much better with money of her own, and the money left after Logan's surgery could be earning bank interest. It would be a nest egg for the future —a hedge against the time when Chandler no longer wanted her. When her year with him was up, she would move far, far away from the valley, maybe even start that little plant shop she occasionally dreamed of. She could never forget Chandler; that had been brought home to her quite painfully, but she would not subject herself to the torture of his presence. She would leave him once more and she would never, never be foolish enough to come back. She would get a divorce and throw herself into a career.

"Callie."

She glanced up quickly. What on earth was she doing examining her future while Chandler sat there staring at her? She had almost forgotten that he was there. "Yes?"

"You do want to sell the house and the land?"

She nodded dumbly.

Chandler carelessly tossed the other check on the table. "Good. Then that's settled. What things would you like for me to take back to the house?"

She frowned at him. "Things?"

"Yes—belongings." He laughed hatefully. "Or do you intend to outfit yourself from head to toe with my money while you have the chance?"

Callie marched over and glared down into his face, amber sparks blazing in her brown eyes. "I don't want you to buy me anything, Chandler. I wouldn't take these"— she bent down and slapped her hand on the checks—"if there were any other way to see Logan get well. I *do not* want anything from you, believe me!"

She started to straighten up, but Chandler reached up and grabbed her shoulders to pull her down onto his lap, twisting her around so that his warm lips found hers and ...ed them thoroughly. She held herself rigid, refusing to give in to his caresses, no matter how much he stimulated her body. She would not fall for his seduction today as she had yesterday. She had seen how eager her body was for him, and she wouldn't let it happen again.

But Chandler was a master at the art. Although she wanted desperately to turn away from his touch, Callie soon found herself lying on the sofa with Chandler's long, muscled body pressing provocatively against hers. His lips sought the exposed column of her throat, and she felt the thunder of her heartbeats as he continued his seduction with skilled hands and teasing lips. When he sought the rigid peak of her breast with searching fingers, Callie knew she was losing all will to remain impassive, and she struggled to get up. It proved impossible; all her movements only served to increase her passion as well as Chandler's. She looked into his face as his gaze lowered to her taut nipples straining against the thin brown material of her dress, asking to be loved. His eyes met hers, and Callie sank into the misty blue depths before his lips returned to her mouth and his massaging fingers found the hard nipple of her breast.

"Are you sure I don't have *something* you want, Callie?" he asked in a husky voice when his lips had left hers to nibble at the slender column of her neck once more.

"I hate you, Chandler," Callie whispered raggedly. "I truly do hate you." But it was herself that she hated at the moment, and as if to mock her, her body denied the words her lips had spoken. Her arms wound around Chandler's neck, pulling his head back down so that his lips met hers in a fiery, demanding kiss. Her back arched so that her breasts were molded firmly to the hardness of his chest, and she raised her hips to meet the pressure of his.

Chandler moved against Callie, his body like a magnet, drawing her thoughts away from anything but the shivers of pleasure slipping up and down her spine. There had been no other man in her life; she had missed Chandler's loving, and her body had been too neglected not to respond now. It refused to forget those tantalizing nights in Chandler's arms in their marital bed. Her pride was shoved aside, along with her other convictions concerning Chandler, and she thrilled to his exciting touch. No matter how firmly her mind said no, her body and heart cried yes!

Chandler undid the buttons of her dress, letting it slip into folds along her sides, and a small moan escaped her parted lips as his mouth found its way down to her breast. His tongue slowly circled the rosy tip, and Callie found her own tongue tracing her parted lips as Chandler set fire to her soul. She ran trembling fingers through the thickness of his dark, curly hair, and he gazed up at her, his eyes full of desire. She made one last token protest, but she knew she didn't want him to stop what he was doing. His hand moved down over her belly to the tender skin of her thigh and he caressed it sensually, causing Callie to ache somewhere deep down inside for him. She closed her eyes and was lost to the desire racing in her blood as Chandler worked his magic on her body. Opening her eyes, she looked up when she felt him move away from her, and she expected him to undress and make love to her fully and satisfyingly. But she was wrong.

Standing up and smoothing his shirt down where it had slipped over the belt of his jeans, Chandler turned away from her. "I'll call for you Saturday evening at six, Callie," he said over his shoulder, his voice thick and broken. "I'll send Sung for whatever you may wish to have brought to the house."

Callie gazed after him, even when he had left the room and shut the door. So, he was tormenting her! He was just trying to see what he could expect for his money in that year she had consented to be his wife again, and like the fool that she was, she had tumbled eagerly into his arms. Where was her pride? Didn't she have any left? *Did* she want Chandler badly enough to accept him on his degrading terms? Of course not! Shame caused her face to turn a flaming red as she recalled the way she had pressed her body to his, mad for his love, his burning touch. And he had just walked away at the peak of her passion and left her smoldering with desire! She lay back down on the sofa and bit at her lower lip in frustration. She wouldn't be such a fool next time. Chandler would find that she wasn't still the young woman he had married, lapping up all the attention she could get from him, making love to him long into the darkness of night.

Her aroused breasts tingled as she gathered her dress together to close the gap Chandler had left open, and a new rush of humiliation colored her cheeks. Chandler had bested her at every turn since her return, and she couldn't let it happen again. She had agreed to be his wife for the year, but only she could make herself his fool. She buttoned the buttons and smoothed back her hair as she sat up. She would curl up and die before she would let her body betray her like that again. And she was only too aware of how willing it was to lend itself to anything Chandler wanted it to do.

Her body throbbing, her mind aching with shame and humiliation, she went to the bathroom and ran a tub of warm water. After quickly taking off her clothes, she stepped in and sank down up to her neck, trying to forget about the way Chandler had driven her to the edge of ecstasy, then walked out on her, leaving her aroused and hungry for him. But then, she reminded herself painfully and deliberately, he didn't need her to satisfy the blazing fires of his passion: he had Nadine for that.

When she had dried off, Callie slipped into sea-foam green shorts and a green-silver top. Taking her long-handled brush from the vanity, she stood pensively brushing her blond hair free of the tangles created by Chandler's long fingers as she studied her figure in the mirror. Her hand poised above her head, she told herself that Chandler did at least still desire her. Not that he would ever put her in such a position again, she vowed, the color rushing to her face at the memory of him walking out on her—not even when she was officially his wife again. She had agreed to no conditions, and in view of the situation, she saw no need to share his bed. He had inflicted all the humiliation upon her she would tolerate. If he thought making love was included in their bargain, she would be happy to enlighten him.

She smiled unhappily. If their encounter an hour ago were any indication, she would be the one who needed enlightening; she had been the one shaking from their passionate loving. Chandler had gotten up and walked away as if they had been discussing the weather. Leaving her mortified and ashamed and angry—and terrified to return to his arms lest he commit such an injustice a second time. Abruptly, she tossed the hairbrush down on the vanity in frustration. What a situation she was in! She knew instinctively that she would earn every penny of the money Chandler gave her for Logan's surgery—and she would pay for it with her heart.

She went downstairs to the kitchen and took a loaf of bread and a jar of mayonnaise from the refrigerator. Choosing a golden ripe banana from the fruit bowl, she carefully sliced it lengthwise on one piece of bread and spread the dressing thickly on the other slice, then sprinkled lots of coarse pepper on the fruit. It was her favorite sandwich, and it had always driven Chandler to distraction to see her eat it. To him, bananas were strictly fruit to be eaten as such with no enhancement. As she bit into the sandwich, she remembered that Chandler had provided the fruit, and she was a little surprised that he had filled the basket with so many bananas. She shook her head as she poured a glass of milk and took her lunch to the big round table in the dining room. She had gotten herself into a terrible mess by coming back here, and yet she knew in her heart that only her pride kept her from being thrilled that Chandler wanted her again. She would give anything if circumstances were different and she and Chandler were reuniting because of love instead of hate. But wishing wouldn't make it so. She had just sat down when she heard someone at the front door. Drawing a deep breath, hoping it wasn't Chandler again, she went to answer.

She cried out in delight when she saw Sung standing on the front porch; she adored the old Oriental man with his short stature; thin, long goatee; and beaming face. "Sung!" she exclaimed. "How wonderful to see you! Come in. Come in."

"It is wonderful to see you, missy," he said in his soft, reverent voice. "You have been away too long. Old Sung has missed your smiling face." He bowed politely before he entered the house, and Callie curtsied. It was a ritual she had enjoyed with the man from the first moment she had met him. When he had bowed to her then, she hadn't been sure what to do, and though Chandler had told her a thousand times after that that she didn't need to curtsy to Sung, she continued to do it because she respected the old man and his customs.

Callie led him to the living room. "I was just having lunch—a banana sandwich," she added mischievously, for Sung, like Chandler, deplored the fruit on bread. "Will you join me?"

Sung made a sour face. "No, missy. Why not let me prepare something good for your lunch?"

She laughed. "A banana sandwich is wonderfully nourishing, Sung, and well you know it. May I get you some tea?"

He shook his head again, and he waited until Callie indicated a chair before he sat down. "No, thank you. I've come about your personal belongings. Mr. Matthews instructed me to fetch whatever you want to be taken to the house."

"So soon?" she asked. "I won't be moving there until Saturday." Suddenly she sat down on the couch by Sung and touched the sleeve of his pale green Oriental smock. A question had been nagging at her, and though it wouldn't make any difference to her situation now, she really wanted to know the answer. "Sung, has Nadine been staying at the house?" she asked in a low voice, ashamed of her need to know.

Sung made a clucking noise with his tongue. "Missy, you know I can't talk about Mr. Matthews' private affairs, even with you."

Callie felt her cheeks turn pink, and, properly chastised, she lifted her head proudly. She shouldn't have asked him, of course. She had been out of line. "I'm sorry," she murmured. Chandler had told her a hundred times that one did not discuss personal affairs with the household help, but Callie considered Sung her friend, and she had always felt very close to him. He was very loyal to his first master, apparently, no matter what he thought of Callie, but she was sure that since he had evaded the question, the answer was yes. And somehow, it made her despise Chandler more for asking her to be his wife again.

"Is Molly well?" she inquired, wanting to change the subject.

Sung made another sour face. "Molly is always well."

Callie's light laughter filled the room. She had always been amused by the pretended hostility between the housekeeper and Sung. A sturdy middle-aged woman with an overbearing manner, Molly had no sense whatsoever of her place in the scheme of things. She towered over Sung and she ruled him, and anyone else she came up against, with an iron hand. Sung kept out of her way as much as possible, but when Molly went into the kitchen, which Sung was sure was his domain, tempers flared and the battle could be heard all over the house.

Suddenly Sung's little black eyes became solemn. "I

hope you will be happier this time, missy. The house hasn't been the same since you went away." He waited politely for Callie to speak, and when she didn't, he stood up and bowed to her. "The wine man is coming, so I must get your possessions and go back to the house. Mr. Matthews said for you to join them for lunch."

Callie arched her brows quizzically, annoyed that Chandler had sent Sung with such an order. She was still recovering from their encounter and she had no wish to meet anyone. "The wine man? Who?"

"Mr. Joseph. He comes and talks with Mr. Matthews about the soil and the weather and the pests so that Mr. Matthews can keep the vines healthy and productive."

"What happened to the cattle ranch?" Callie asked, standing up beside Sung. "Why did Chandler give it up?"

Sung shrugged. "Mr. Matthews is a businessman. He has become very rich from the vines." His face lit up as he smiled. "Now we serve our very own wines with dinner, and they are quite delicious."

"I'm sure," Callie conceded, but she didn't comment about Chandler's wealth. He had been rich before he began the vineyards. "Come with me upstairs," she said. "I suppose I might as well have you take my clothes and odds and ends with you now, since you're here."

She and Sung spent the next half hour putting her clothing and personal items in the back of his small compact car. Callie kept only a few articles to wear during the three days that remained until Saturday, and a lovely gold organdy dress for the party. It was definitely her prettiest dress, and she did want to look her best. She was resolute about looking cool, confident, and contained. Chandler's friends might point, whisper, and speculate, but Callie had made up her mind to hold her head high and endure until the end. She had no other choice.

When the car was packed, she declined the lunch invitation. "Tell Mr. Matthews I've eaten," she said. She could see that Sung wasn't happy about her decision, but he climbed into the car without a word. Callie watched as he drove away before she returned to her sandwich and milk.

The bread was beginning to get hard and the milk was warm; she found that she wasn't hungry after all. Her appetite had diminished considerably in the past few days. Leaving the table, she called the hospital to see how Logan was doing, then she wandered out back to the peaceful coolness of the yard. Automatically, she was drawn to the hammock hanging under the vine-covered arbor. She climbed into it and settled down with a gentle sigh. The world would be so much nicer if her life consisted of only the backyard and the gently swaying hammock. She swung in it for some time, letting her thoughts take her where they might, unless they wandered into the unhappy areas of Logan or Chandler. The day began to seem less unpleasant, and Callie's eyelids began to grow heavy. She hadn't slept well last night, and as she listened to a solitary sparrow singing a sweet song in the old walnut tree, she closed her eyes and drifted into the soothing blackness of sleep.

Callie thought she was dreaming when she felt the butterfly lightness of a kiss on her lips. She smiled contentedly and sighed. It was a warm, gentle, undemanding kiss such as dreams are made of. Then she felt it again and it seemed very real. Opening her eyes sleepily, she stared up at the lush green vines hanging overhead. To her surprise, Chandler was standing before her. She almost spilled to the ground in her haste to stand and, to her dismay, Chandler had to hold the hammock steady so that she could get out of it.

"Afternoon, Callie," he said coolly.

She raised dark eyes to his face and, seeing his proud demeanor, she wondered how she had ever imagined that she was actually being kissed as she slept. Certainly not by this man. "Chandler," she responded with a nod. She wished she at least had shoes on, for though she was reasonably tall, she always felt very vulnerable with Chandler towering over her, so bold and masculine.

"Why didn't you return to the house with Sung?" he asked, his tone revealing annoyance.

"I didn't want to," she replied. "It won't be Saturday for three more days." Saturday would be soon enough to begin her painful year with him, and to again become a subject of gossip in the community. She needed time to adjust to the idea.

Irritation etched deep lines into Chandler's handsome, dark face. "Don't try my patience, Callie," he growled. "Get whatever you have remaining in the house and let's go."

Her calm voice belied the tension twisting her stomach into knots. "I'll come Saturday, Chandler. I will not be bullied into going any sooner."

Storm clouds gathered in his intense blue eyes. "What difference can it make to you if you come today or Saturday? You'll be safer at the house than here in this rambling old barn that's stood empty for so long. Everybody in the vicinity knows no one has lived here for many weeks. We had to clean out debris left by some itinerant farm workers who had been staying here furtively."

"If you're trying to frighten me, it won't work," she replied. "I've been alone before, and I stayed here last night and nothing happened. What difference can a few more days make to you?"

"I simply don't see any point in the delay," he stated.

"Who cleaned the house?" Callie asked, dismissing the subject of going to Chandler's house. She didn't want to argue with him and she didn't want to relent.

"Molly and Sung. Why?"

"Did either of them mention finding a letter? Aunt

Caroline was supposed to have left a letter for me, but I can't find it, and Ned doesn't know where it is."

"What kind of letter?" His eyes lit up with interest.

Callie shrugged. "A personal letter. It wouldn't be of any interest to anyone but me."

"Sung and Molly didn't find it, or they would have told me. They did store some things in the attic, but there were no letters or papers among them."

"I didn't think so." She was unreasonably disappointed, even though she had suspected that the letter hadn't been found.

"Well, come on. Let's go," Chandler prompted impatiently.

Her eyes met his evenly. On principal, she would not bend to his will. "I'm not afraid to stay here and I'd prefer to come on Saturday."

Chandler watched her for a moment, his expression unreadable, then suddenly he whisked her up in his arms. "I can't wait until Saturday."

Callie gasped, and when she overcame her surprise, she instinctively drew back her hand and slapped Chandler soundly across his face. Her eyes widened with alarm as she heard a sound deep in his throat. She had only a moment to stare into his cold blue eyes before he turned around and dumped her unceremoniously into the hammock, which swayed and rocked precariously under her uneven weight.

For a few seconds she was so busy righting herself that she didn't think about the consequences of her action. A rush of red ran up her neck, and when she looked into Chandler's unsmiling eyes, she muttered, "How I wish I'd never married you!"

He watched her briefly from beneath heavy lids, half-lowered. "I gathered as much," he responded harshly. Without a backward glance, he turned on his heel and walked away.

Callie gripped the sides of the hammock and gazed unseeingly at the grapevines that covered the arbor. Chandler was determined to extract his pound of flesh to punish her for leaving him. It was almost intolerable to think of spending another year with him, feeling as she did about him. If only she hated him, it wouldn't matter so much—but she didn't hate him. She was very much afraid that she would never be able to hate him. She felt hot tears build in her eyes, and she was powerless to stop them as they streamed down her flushed cheeks. She cried harder and harder, letting her anguish and her bitter resentment of the situation and Chandler's attitude toward her spill from her eyes until she had released her pent-up anger and unhappiness. Finally her sobs became a shuddering sigh and ceased altogether.

She was returning to Chandler for Logan's sake, she reminded herself quietly. She was indenturing herself for one humiliating year so that Logan could live; she would take the days one at a time, and one day the year would be over. Other people endured unpleasant situations and were able to put them behind and go on, and she would, too. She would not listen to the whispers of her heart, telling her that she wanted this year with Chandler—that she was actually foolish enough to hope that some miracle would occur in that year that would make theirs a real and loving marriage. Callie knew no miracle was in the offing as long as Nadine was still around, and Nadine would always be around.

Carefully getting out of the hammock, she stood on trembling legs while she wiped traces of her tears from her cheeks with her fists. She would survive the year somehow. She had to.

In the evening, Callie visited with Logan, and she was pleased to discover that he was doing reasonably well. She stayed with him as long as she was permitted, then ate a hamburger in the hospital coffee shop before going home.

After she had bathed, she put on her nightgown and picked up her hairbrush. Sighing wearily, she mechanically brushed her hair a hundred strokes. Having completed the ritual, she prowled restlessly about the empty house, feeling vaguely ill at ease because Chandler had told her about the farm workers.

She wasn't the kind to be frightened of shadows, since she had spent four years in an isolated mining camp, but the last few days had played on her nerves. Tense, edgy, she roamed from room to room trying to find something to take her mind off her whirling thoughts. Finally, she settled in an overstuffed chair to watch a program on Aunt Caroline's little black-and-white portable set. The only channel she could get clearly featured a murder mystery movie, and she quickly flipped the station off, hating such movies. She was surprised to find herself growing increasingly uneasy in the old house she had spent so many years in. She had never felt afraid before, but then she had never been alone here before.

Damn Chandler! This was his fault, too. Around ten o'clock, she finally went upstairs to her bedroom. Lying down, she closed her eyes and tried to induce sleep, but she remained wide awake. In desperation, she resorted to counting backward from a hundred and gradually she fell into a light, restless sleep.

Sometime later, she was awakened by a noise. Opening her eyes wide in alarm, she sat up in the middle of the bed and tried to decide what had awakened her. She jumped when she heard two tomcats engaging in an age-old battle for supremacy down below in the yard. She listened for a few minutes, then turned over on her side and tried to get back to sleep. It had been difficult the first time; now it was impossible. She sat up and turned on the bedside lamp to glance at the clock. Damn! she thought unhappily, it was only midnight. After turning the light back off, she tried taking deep relaxing breaths, but it was futile. Sleep was out of the question.

She turned the light on again. Finding an old Civil War romance book, she opened it and started to read. She had read it, she thought frustratedly. She dropped the book down on the bed table and flipped the light switch. Even if she couldn't sleep, she would rest. She lay there as long as she could bear it, then tiredly turned the light back on. There was no point in punishing herself further. She might as well go downstairs and make a cup of hot chocolate, and perhaps the warm milk would soothe her jangled nerves and help her fall asleep.

Quickly, Callie heated the milk in a small aluminum pan, then poured it into a large brown mug. She stirred in a heaping spoonful of chocolate mix and sampled the rich beverage. It was just the way she liked it, lukewarm and sweet. Switching off the kitchen light and turning the hall one on, she rounded the corner and started up the steps to her room. Suddenly she heard the distinct and chilling rattle of the front doorknob. Someone was trying to get in! She spun around in fright, the abrupt motion spilling much of the contents of her mug down the front of her flimsy amber-colored nightgown. "Ouch!" she cried as the warm chocolate touched her skin and raced down the front of her gown. Dropping the cup to the floor, watching as the liquid spilled over the rug, she covered her mouth with both hands. Of course she hadn't wanted anyone to know that she was there.

A fierce pounding shook the door. "Callie! Callie!"

She drew a deep breath and slowly let it slip through her lips. It was Chandler, she realized, as a tremendous wave of relief washed over her. She rushed to the door, opened it, and then stood gaping at him, the relief she had felt turning to anger. Was he trying to scare her to death now?

"What are you doing here at this time of the night? You frightened me," she cried, more as a tension release than anything else. Feeling a trickle of milk run down her leg, she looked at her gown, then brushed furiously with both hands. Droplets of chocolate milk dripped off the bottom of the gown, making a puddle on the floor and wetting her bare feet.

Chandler shoved his way inside, his gaze falling on the dark wet stain molding the material to her breasts and clinging to her stomach. Shutting the door, he demanded, "What's going on here?"

Embarrassment caused her to speak coldly. "That's what I want to know. Why are you here, beating on my door?"

"I saw your light go on and off three times, and I thought something was wrong. Now, what's going on?"

Callie stared at him in disbelief for a moment. The concern on his face was quickly giving way to ire. "What's going on," she replied, "is that I couldn't sleep, so I turned my light on to see what time it was, then to read. Then I came down to make some hot chocolate." She pointed to her gown and to the mess on the floor. "This is where the chocolate went when you pounded on the door."

Chandler looked in the direction of her finger, then back at her nightgown. A broad smile spread over his sculptured lips and he chuckled. "You are a sight," he murmured.

An angry flush crept up Callie's neck. She knew she was a mess, and she didn't need for him to remind her. Her pride had been stripped away as it was since her return, and she wouldn't be standing here like this before him for all the world. "I'm not the one who ran over here pounding on the door like a madman, just because a light was turned on at midnight."

The smile left Chandler's mouth. "The light wasn't just turned on; it was turned on and off several times."

"Did you think I was signaling for you?" she asked sharply, wanting him to look like as big a fool as she.

"Were you watching the house, looking for any excuse to charge over here?"

Chandler gazed at her for several minutes, and she didn't know why he had the power to make her feel guilty. "I couldn't sleep either, Callie, and I had gone outside to investigate a noise that I thought was cats when I glanced in the direction of your house and saw the light." His eyes met hers evenly. "I shouldn't have to find reasons to come here, Callie," he said softly. Turning around, he opened the door and stepped out into the night.

Callie didn't know whether to laugh or cry. He had come because he was concerned about her, and she hadn't even been gracious. She gazed forlornly at the door for a long time, then, shaking her head disconsolately, she went to the kitchen for a mop and paper towels to clean up the floor. When she had finished the chore, she walked to the bathroom, stripped off the soggy gown and took a quick bath. After she had dried off and slipped into a clean gown, she turned off the light and climbed back into bed. An image of Chandler appeared before her with amazing clarity.

"Oh, Chandler," she whispered into the lonely darkness, "where did we go wrong?"

CHAPTER FIVE

Callie spent the days until Saturday visiting with Logan and deliberating over the upcoming year with Chandler.

Each day she expected him to come to the house, but he didn't. She began to regret her hasty refusal to go to his; it would have made the transition less painful and embarrassing, she soon realized, if she had spent time there before the party with all the guests in attendance. It was too late to do anything about it now. She couldn't admit her error to Chandler: she could never tell him that he had been right after all.

Logan was feeling stronger, and he and Callie talked about the possibility of his surgery. The doctor had told him that it was necessary, but neither the doctor, at Callie's request, nor she had given Logan an idea that the cost would be so exorbitant. He would need to regain his strength before it was attempted, so Callie felt no need to talk about particulars just yet. He would be in the hospital for several more days before the surgery would be scheduled, and she was grateful that he wouldn't be home when she was reunited with Chandler.

Saturday afternoon arrived much too rapidly. Callie hadn't slept well the night before, and she was high-strung all day. How could she face all those people again? Those same people who had last seen her the night of the barbecue more than four years ago? Would Chandler really be so cruel as to invite them all? She toyed with a strand of blond hair. Of course he would. She knew he would. She would simply have to stick to her resolution about being proud and self-contained and not let any of them see how a repeat of that disastrous night humiliated her, or how she trembled inside.

And the questions. She prayed that only the boldest or the rudest of the guests would be insensitive enough to ask where she had been and why. But, of course, she had probably been talked about for the last four years. Not much exciting went on in the little community, and she was sure to have been a frequent topic of conversation. She tossed her head back and lifted her chin proudly, imagining what might have been said then and now. She suspected that many people thought, as Chandler had, that she had returned to the valley with her lover. And on top of this scandalous fact, she was going to reaffirm her wedding vows to Chandler after being here a week. She was overwhelmed by it all.

Lowering herself onto the bed, she permitted her mind to run down the list of possible guests, many of whom she had once considered her friends. They had watched her grow from a thin, long-legged, shy teen-ager into a young woman. They had taught her in the local school, or, as her peers, had shared silly, girlish secrets and dreams with her. But there were others, of course. Nadine would be there with her family, she could bet on that. God, she thought bitterly, what would one of Chandler's parties be without Nadine Harris?

Callie had never been able to get along with Mr. and Mrs. Harris—not because she didn't try, but they had so obviously wanted Chandler as their daughter's husband and they considered Callie an interloper, regardless of circumstances. And there was old Mr. Harris, the grandfather, who watched her with stern eyes and an indifferent smile; however, he was kinder than the younger Harrises. Nadine had a great-aunt who lived in San Francisco and sounded especially formidable; since she hadn't even come to the wedding, though, it was doubtful that she would come to the party. Surprisingly, she had sent a beautiful mantel clock that Callie had loved, and even though Chandler had known the aunt well himself, Callie often thought when she heard the loud bonging of the chimes that the clock was meant to remind her that Chandler had first belonged to Nadine and the Harrises. She smiled faintly to herself; such a notion seemed terribly silly now, but then she had been suspicious of everyone's motives when it came to Chandler.

There were other people coming, perhaps, who looked

on her more sympathetically, or indifferently, but she didn't know or mind them so much. A picture of Mr. and Mrs. Matthews, Chandler's mother and father, surfaced, and Callie frowned thoughtfully. She didn't know how they would react to her; they had always been warm and loving when she had lived with Chandler, but now—well, it was too late to worry about it, wasn't it?

She made herself breathe slowly several times. She would not be intimidated by the guests. She had been cowardly in her method of leaving Chandler, it was true, but it had been expedient and less painful at the time, and she had been right to leave nevertheless. Having married him in the belief that he would love her and be faithful to her, she had certainly been justified in expecting those two traits in him. She ran her hands through her hair. It didn't matter how anyone behaved toward her; she would survive the night, and maybe it was best to confront them all at once.

Chandler certainly hadn't tried to ease her reentry into his life by throwing this party, but then what else had she expected under the circumstances? A man bent on revenge didn't dwell on the niceties of life. Still, he could have phoned or dropped by today. Apparently he was still punishing her because she hadn't gone home with him when he came for her that day, and she had admitted to herself that she hadn't behaved very appreciatively when he had come to check on her that night. Surely he could see that she was both embarrassed and frightened. Yesterday he had sent a note by Sung, telling her to be ready by six o'clock and to look her best. She smiled wryly to herself. Look her best, he had ordered. It wouldn't do for Chandler Matthews to remarry a wife who was less than up to standards. But she *would* look her best, of course, for she would need every shred of confidence she could summon.

Standing up tiredly, she went to the closet to pull out her gold dress. She walked over to the mirror and held the garment up in front of her, appraising it critically. She scrutinized the delicate sheer material, the deep V of the bodice, the waltz length, the belted waist, and the gently flaring skirt. Yes, it would do nicely. She need have no fear about the dress being flattering, and if she matched its beauty, she would get through the evening's experience. She spread the dress out on the bed and found the tall, gold shoes with thin, wraparound ankle straps, which completed the outfit. Setting the shoes on the floor by the bed, she went to enjoy a long and, she hoped, relaxing bath.

When she had stepped out of the tub and dried on a thick terry towel, she returned to her room and began the painstaking ritual of hair and makeup. Parting her long hair down the middle, she intricately braided each side, starting high up on the crown so that the plait framed her face. She looped the two braids into a very attractive figure eight at the nape of her neck and secured them with an exquisite gold clasp. Then she outlined her eyes with a light brown pencil, making them look deep and velvety brown. She chose two lip creams and blended them on her lips until she had the rich plum she wanted before carefully outlining her mouth.

As a finishing touch, she dusted her clear skin with a light powder. When she had slipped into her dress and shoes, she studied her reflection in the mirror: she was well-pleased with the image of the pretty, sophisticated woman with dark, interesting brown eyes in a coolly beautiful face with delicately plum lips.

Callie scrutinized the vision very carefully, turning this way and that, and she decided that she looked fine. No one would ever know that the girl inside still bore traces of young Callie Hart Matthews, Chandler's naive bride, or that she was so nervous about the upcoming event that she was almost physically sick. Drawing a deep breath, she held it for a count of twelve, then let it slip slowly from her lips, hoping the tight feeling in her stomach would ease; but it didn't.

The time she spent waiting for Chandler was the longest in her life. The party was scheduled for six, and when it was almost time, Callie went down to the living room to wait. She had to consciously resist the urge to run to the window to see who was arriving at Chandler's house early, or if Chandler were on his way to her house. Six o'clock on the dot had come when the doorbell finally rang. That meant that other people would be at the house before she was, for sure, and Callie hadn't wanted that to happen. Her heels clicked rapidly as she walked down the hall and pulled open the door, ready to tell Chandler just how cruel he was being to keep her waiting. To her chagrin, Sung stood on the porch. Chandler hadn't bothered to come for her at all! He was going to make her walk into a room full of their acquaintances after a four-year absence—all alone.

"Where's Chandler?" she demanded, her fingers curling into fists at her sides. "Damn him, why didn't he come himself?"

Sung looked anxious. "The guests are already arriving, and the Harrises came early. Mr. Matthews stayed to entertain them."

Callie blinked her eyes as hot tears of humiliation gathered in them. So, it was Nadine again! Even tonight! She didn't know who was the bigger fool, she or Nadine. What kind of woman came to a wedding reunion party for her lover's wife? A very confident mistress, she told herself bitterly.

Sung looked away from Callie's face. "Are you ready?" he murmured.

Callie stood a little straighter. Chandler wouldn't get the best of her—and neither would Nadine. Not ever again. "I'll be just a moment," she said evenly. Rushing back to the bathroom, she dabbed at her eyes with a cold cloth, and when she returned to Sung, she was somewhat composed. "I'm ready," she said in a cool, remote voice.

But despite her determination, when they approached the house and Callie heard the music and party noise, she developed a terrible case of nerves. Her legs were unsteady by the time Sung opened the car door for her, and she felt uneasy on the high heels as she walked purposely toward the house. She noted a number of cars, and some part of her seemed to die deep down inside at the mere thought of subjecting herself to this outrage. Looking at Sung, who walked by her side, she asked, "Are there many people already here?"

He gazed into her eyes and his were carefully devoid of any emotion. "There are quite a few."

Callie struggled to keep down a rising panic. She would not let any of these people—especially Chandler—know how upset she was by this affair. She closed her eyes for a moment and escaped to a small spot in her mind where she had learned to draw strength. Attempting to still her quivering insides, she lifted her head haughtily, opened the front door, and entered the house.

Immediately, the room became hushed, as all of the guests, about thirty in number—some, Callie noted, all the way from San Francisco—turned their eyes in her direction. The throb of the soft music was oddly loud in the sudden silence. Callie's eyes swept around the room boldly and defiantly, and she caught sight of Nadine in a stunning pistachio gown that caused her brilliant red hair to look like a flame on top of her head. The Matthews were there, too, as well as the older Harrises. For a single moment, Callie was suddenly frozen to the spot where she stood; then, forcing a broad smile to her beautiful lips, she walked purposely toward Chandler, who was approaching her from the middle of the room. Her gaze traveled over him and she conceded that he looked magnificent and commanding in a rich sand-colored suit, a raisin-brown shirt, and a broad beige tie.

"Good evening, all," she murmured, inclining her head slightly for a brief time while her glance raked over the party-goers, then went back to Chandler. "Darling," she said huskily. Wrapping her arms around her astonished husband's neck, she kissed him warmly on the lips while the crowd looked on.

Callie felt Chandler's cold, sensuous lips twitch to life under the pressure of hers, but she pulled away from him before he could overcome his surprise at her dramatic entrance. His arm slid possessively around her waist and she noted her lip color on his lips as he hugged her to his hard, muscled length and turned to face the others.

"A toast to my wife's homecoming," he said smoothly, holding up his wine glass. Although Callie almost lost her hold on her hard-earned composure at the remark, the silence was broken by it, and the crowd, too, simultaneously seemed to recover from her entrance. Only Callie had nothing to drink as the guests began to sip and murmur quietly in response to Chandler's toast.

Someone changed the music to a fanciful love song and the party chatter picked up, either because of the sheer tension created by the occasion or the blatant curiosity of those assembled, and those still coming. Clearly there were more than a few people who had hoped for some tantalizing confession from the reunited couple, but Chandler set his glass down on a nearby table and drew Callie into the circle of his arms to lead her slowly to the music.

"Touché!" he said in a low voice, staring down into her eyes.

Callie experienced no elation even though she had carried off a grand entrance. Obviously Chandler had anticipated her entering the room meekly and greatly embarrassed, and it was the first time she had seen him caught unprepared for even a single moment.

His lips turned back in an amused grin. "You've changed, Callie. In subtle ways—and some not so subtle ones."

Looking up into his eyes, she smiled bitterly. "You haven't, Chandler. You still have your way at the expense of other people. It's not an attractive trait."

An unfathomable expression darkened his eyes, and a smirk gradually twisted his mouth. Eventually it gave way to gentle laughter. "There was a time," he murmured at last, "when you said much kinder things about me, but then that was a time when I thought you loved me. Perhaps we both were wrong."

Her smile quivered before she could control it. "There was a time when I couldn't have imagined you setting up such an affair"—her eyes left his to scan the room—"in a deliberate attempt to humiliate me."

A frown furrowed his forehead for a few seconds, then he abruptly maneuvered her through the sliding glass doorway that led out onto the patio. "When did you begin to hate me so intensely?" he demanded of her when they were out of the hearing of the others. "Is that why you think I arranged this party—so I could humiliate you?"

Callie gazed at the blue water shimmering in the pool, which was lit by several underwater lamps. The moon was just beginning to rise as dusk fell. "Why else?" she whispered.

His grip tightened on her waist. "Ah, Callie." He sighed deeply. "I thought this was the easiest way to stop the gossip and speculation. I want no one to doubt that you are again my wife."

As she looked into his hard blue eyes, Callie wondered if he were telling the truth. After all, she had told herself that it would be easier to see all these people at once and be done with it. Still, she didn't want to start making excuses for Chandler's behavior; he shouldn't have put her in this position at all by insisting that she live with him again as his wife.

His eyes held hers, and suddenly she felt very vulnerable. He watched her speculatively for a few seconds, then his head lowered. His lips touched hers in a gentle caress, and Callie was almost persuaded to believe that he really was concerned about her feelings.

"Oh, there you are," Nadine sang out, and Callie twisted out of Chandler's arms to stare at her as the woman approached.

"We'll be right in," Chandler announced in clipped tones.

Nadine looked a bit ruffled, but she flounced off. Callie laughed nervously. "I suspect that she thought I had disappeared again already."

She hadn't even considered it, of course, and she was taken aback when Chandler's fingers bit cruelly into the flesh of her upper arms. "Do it," he muttered in a savage tone, "and you'd better run to the ends of the earth to hide this time, because I'll track you down and break your pretty little neck."

Although Callie was alarmed by his vehement retort, she had no intention of letting Chandler know it. "Why, Chandler," she said, looking at him coyly from beneath lowered lashes, "I wouldn't dream of disappointing you after you've gone to such trouble. I'll do my year. You did give me the money, after all, and that's what this is all about."

His hand firmly encircling her shoulder, Chandler looked at her through narrowed eyes. Callie was sure he was going to respond to her remark, but abruptly he led her back into the living room, where he guided her to a number of guests, many of whom were still arriving. He cleverly and smoothly began making polite comments and initiating small talk, involving Callie in conversation as if four years hadn't elapsed since the last time she spoke with these people. There were awkward moments, especially when he led her to the couch where the Harrises sat, one protectively on each side of a smoldering Nadine; but, on the whole, the evening progressed much better than Callie had dared hope. Chandler's mother and father were friendly and charming and seemed genuinely pleased that Callie was back with their son. Nadine's grandfather hadn't come, so Callie was spared that ordeal.

Finally dinner was announced and Chandler escorted Callie to the long table in the dining room. Although it seated a number of people comfortably, it was impossible to serve everyone there; consequently, several tables had been set up out on the patio. The sliding glass door was left open, and Callie could see the other guests as two temporary waiters helped seat everyone. To her consternation, the Harrises were seated at the main table—Nadine on the other side of Mr. Matthews, who sat next to Callie.

Forcing her lips into a faint smile, she pretended that it didn't matter, but it bothered her terribly. Chandler, sitting on Callie's right, had gotten Nadine as close as he dared under the circumstances. In fact, Callie was surprised that he hadn't seated his mistress right beside him. Why hide what everyone knew?

Wine was served, and to Callie's astonishment, Chandler stood up. "This is going to be the season's finest wine," he said, lifting his glass. "You are the first to sample it before we market it. I've named it Callét, in honor of my wife."

A big fuss was made over the wine, and Callie feigned delight, but she was appalled that Chandler would go to such lengths with his charade. Why was he doing this? She smiled and pretended to be flattered, but she ached inside that he would taunt her return and her love for him. They both knew that their reunion was one of bitter necessity on her part and cold revenge on his.

Callie heard Nadine's voice behind her, and suddenly wine spilled down the shoulder of her gold dress, rapidly racing across the thin material. "Oh; I'm so dreadfully sorry. How clumsy of me," Nadine purred, bending down and putting her arm around Callie's shoulders. "I was just going over to compliment Chandler on this delectable wine, and I tripped on the chair leg."

"That's all right," Callie replied evenly, making herself sound polite, but she despised Nadine and they both knew the redhead had intentionally spilled the wine.

"Let me wipe it off before it stains your lovely dress," the woman offered in a sugary voice. "A little cold water should take care of it."

The entire table seemed to be waiting for Callie's response, and she had no choice but to slide her chair back. "Thank you," she managed to say. "You're too kind."

Her face flushed, she walked beside Nadine to the bathroom. When she had stepped inside and closed the door, she declared, "I can manage alone, thank you. Go back to the table." Picking up a washcloth, she dipped it into cold water and began to dab at the dark stain. The tension in the small room was electrifying, and Callie felt a burning sensation in her stomach.

Standing behind her, Nadine crossed her arms and watched. "Callie," she snapped suddenly, "you know Chandler has never been yours, and your coming back here won't change a thing. He's always been mine, even when he was married to you."

Callie whirled around to face the redhead, her breathing rapid. "Then why didn't he marry *you*?"

"Oh, my dear, believe me, he wanted to," Nadine replied mockingly, "but I wasn't naive enough to think a woman could put a ring in the nose of a man like Chandler. He's the kind who will occasionally take some young thing to his bed, but those affairs don't mean a thing. You and I both know the only way you succeeded in getting him to marry you was because I had married another man. He did it to get even with me." Her gaze lowered briefly to her long nails and she pretended to study them. "We both realized we'd made a dreadful mistake."

Callie had no doubt that the woman was telling the truth, but she wouldn't give her the satisfaction of admitting such a fact. "Excuse me," she said coolly, tossing the washcloth into the sink and brushing past Nadine. "Dinner will be served by now, and I mustn't keep the guests waiting." Her cool manner was in sharp contrast to the quivering way she felt inside, and she wanted to escape before her emotions were exposed.

Nadine grasped her arm before she could open the door. "Don't make a bigger fool of yourself by going through with this little farce of a ceremony," she said hatefully. "Don't you know that Chandler is making you the laughingstock of the community? He's doing this to embarrass you as you did him when you left."

Callie fought the painful sensation in her chest. "And what does it make you look like, Nadine?" she asked, her voice only a little higher than usual. "At least he's marrying me twice. He's never made any pretense of lending any respectability to your relationship with him." Opening the door, she walked outside the room.

"Bitch!" she heard Nadine hiss, and it brought a bitter smile to her lips.

Chandler stood up when Callie returned, but she didn't even look at him as he slid her chair back so that she could be seated. Nadine had reminded her of things she didn't want to think about and she hated Chandler afresh. Somehow she managed to make light conversation and to endure dinner, despite that fact that her stomach was tied in knots. As the meal progressed, she even dared to hope that Chandler wouldn't actually have a renewal of the wedding vows, since Pastor Nathan hadn't yet arrived. Surely there was no need to mock the holy state of matrimony by doing this. Her hope was short-lived, for the pastor showed up when dessert was being served.

Everyone gathered in the living room again and, not for the first time that evening, Callie's face turned scarlet. She made it through the ceremony, and managed to repeat her vows, but she couldn't even manage a semblance of a smile. She had long ago discarded her wedding band; she had, in fact, thrown it out the window of a taxi on her way to the airport when she left Chandler, but, to her amazement, he produced an exact likeness of the first orange blossom band. Callie wanted to refuse to let him slip it on her finger, but she didn't dare make a scene now. Later she would simply remove it and conveniently misplace it.

When the rite had been performed, the crowd's curiosity seemed to be satiated as much as they expected it to be, and they began to filter out of the house. Many said their good-nights pointedly to Chandler, and Callie was aware that a certain amount of hostility was felt about her for her "desertion," but she was too numb to care what the others thought. Nadine had stayed for the entire party, even the repetition of the vows, and Callie wasn't surprised to find her still lingering, though her parents had been among the first guests to leave.

Callie was grateful that none of the out-of-town guests were staying the night, as they often had in the past. At last Nadine stood up and walked toward her and Chandler as they bade the only other guest good night.

"Well, Callie," she said with stretched sweetness, "I hope your new attempt at marriage is more successful than your old one was." Turning to Chandler, she touched him gently on the arm. "Good night, Chandler."

Callie froze in rigid anger as Nadine raised her head and gently brushed Chandler's cheek with her lips. Callie gave him a stormy look as Nadine pivoted on a shapely leg and sauntered out into the night.

"I'm surprised at Nadine's . . . good wishes," Callie

remarked tartly. "Didn't you tell her that there is no way this 'new attempt at marriage' can be successful? Of course, there was really no need to tell her, was there?"

Chandler watched her from beneath lowered lids. "Did you want me to tell her?" he asked in a quiet voice.

"Honestly," she replied with pretended indifference, "I don't care what you tell Nadine. What you say or do is of no interest to me." She started to walk away, but Chandler caught her arm and dragged her back to him.

"Really?" he asked. "Of no interest? Well, we'll see about that, won't we?" Before she could step away again, his lips swooped down possessively onto hers. She gasped a little at the swiftness of the maneuver. Pressing her hands against his chest, she tried to push him away. Only when he was ready did he raise his head.

"What's wrong, Callie? You're my wife again—in every sense of the word. Are you refusing me my husbandly rights?"

Callie smiled weakly to hide her frustration. "What's your rush? We've spent four years apart. I didn't eat much dinner, and I think I'll have a snack before bed."

"I'm hungry, too," he said in a low, seductive voice, trailing a finger over her lips. "But not for food."

She was suddenly nervous and shy under his penetrating gaze. In her heart, she wanted nothing more than to have him carry her off to their bedroom and make mad, passionate, unrestrained love to her as though nothing had ever parted them, but she knew he was only toying with her now. And she knew, too, after their last embrace, that her pride demanded that she not allow herself to fall into his arms, no matter how enticing they were. He had turned away from her on Wednesday, and she wouldn't be his fool again. It was apparent that he was only trying to torment her, and she wouldn't succumb this ti would find out soon enough that if he expected at his beck and call in the bedroom, he was in for a surprise.

His finger tipped her chin up so that she was forced to look into his eyes. "Callie, come with me," he murmured. "I have a gift for you."

For an instant Callie was flattered that he had been so thoughtful, but then she wondered about his sincerity. Forgetting about the sandwich, she followed him to the bedroom they had shared for a year, and she opened her eyes wide in surprise. Everything had changed. Nothing was familiar to her. Even the mantel clock Nadine's aunt had given them was gone. Well, she thought angrily, perhaps Nadine hadn't liked her choice of decor. She had redone the bedroom completely when she and Chandler had married, and at the time he had complimented her on her decorating skills. She smiled bleakly. Obviously he hadn't been honest with her then either. She let her gaze sweep over the dark wicker furniture and the huge round bed, bare of a headboard. It looked like a man's room, she mused. Chandler had needed something exotic and masculine for his trysts with Nadine. But it was attractive in a warm, expansive way, and it looked very comfortable in every respect.

"Here," he said, handing her a brightly wrapped package.

She took it reluctantly, her thoughts on the bedroom.

"Well, open it," he prompted. When she fumbled with the pink paper and red ribbons, Chandler ripped the paper apart and handed her the box. Hesitantly, Callie lifted the lid and removed a long, white satin gown. It was breathtakingly lovely and involuntarily she murmured, "Thank you, Chandler."

"I want you to be beautiful when I make love to you tonight," he said. "It's been a long, long time, Callie."

"I see," she said, her tone devoid of any warmth. It

wouldn't come to that anyway; she was determined that it wouldn't.

"I'll disappear while you change," he told her, moving swiftly from the room and closing the door behind him.

Feeling terribly disheartened that they were playing such cruel games with each other, Callie went to the huge Roman tub and ran water for her bath, liberally sprinkling rose-scented perfume into it. For a while she gazed at the tub forlornly, then she slipped out of her clothes and sank down into the warm water. The bath was relaxing and soothing, but it did little to make Callie forget her situation.

Those hauntingly familiar memories ran freely in her mind, making her remember other times best forgotten. Times when she had been so sure of Chandler's love. Times when Nadine was gone from the valley. She used to spend hours soaking in the tub that first glorious summer, waiting for Chandler to come home from the pastures or his other pursuits, and she had waited so expectantly for him to come and find her soaking. She would usually pretend to be reading a romance novel, which she did frequently, and Chandler would take it from her hand. Then he would help her from the water and dry her with a fluffy towel, sprinkling kisses over her naked skin as he did so. Laughter had filled the house during those times. After Chandler had dried her off, he would carry her to the bed, and they would tumble down on it and make love for a sweet eternity. She closed her eyes on the memory: tonight that wasn't what she anticipated. She opened her eyes and looked around the lushly decorated bathroom.

This had been her home, a home she and Chandler had once filled with love—or at least she had thought it was love then—and everything was so different now. Tonight he would try to make love to her because he was angry with her and wanted to punish her. Chandler might find physical—as well as mental—satisfaction if Callie let him claim her, and her body might respond to his ministrations, but what had made their lovemaking precious and special was dead between them. The muscles in Callie's throat tightened. Even if there had never been any real love between them, she hadn't known it at the time, and she had reveled in Chandler's desire for her. The thought of making love now in that same bed he had shared with Nadine filled her heart with pain. She stepped out of the tub and briskly toweled her body dry. She wouldn't let him take her—she couldn't. Dabbing Chandler's favorite perfume at the base of her throat, behind her ears, and trailing a tiny amount between her breasts, she fought to suppress the memory of the untold times she had thrilled to Chandler's touch. She smoothed creamy, scented lotion on her feet, legs, and hands, then slipped into the lovely gown, wondering what could come of this need they felt to punish each other.

The gown was stunning, but Callie took no pleasure in Chandler's gift. If only she and Chandler weren't just pretending to renew their wedding vows—if only they were putting all the past behind them and honestly giving themselves this one precious year to try to rebuild their lives together. She sighed disappointedly; they *were* pretending, and that was that. As long as Nadine remained in Chandler's life, there was no hope for him and Callie.

Walking to the bathroom vanity, where all her personal belongings had been attractively arranged, Callie discovered a beautiful ivory-handled hairbrush with a painting of a man and a woman holding hands on the back. *Chandler,* she thought, feeling unreasonably angry that he was buying her presents under the circumstances. Freeing her hair from the braids, Callie brushed it quickly, refusing to take pleasure in the beautiful brush. When she had put a hint of lipstick on her lips, she settled down on the bed to await her husband.

As she gazed about the room, she noticed for the first time that the draperies of the sliding glass door were partly open. She walked to the door and peered out for a few minutes, seeing the patio that ran the length of the long house and the oblong swimming pool only a few feet away. For a few seconds, she stood staring trancelike as she recalled the times she and Chandler had slipped out of the bedroom and swum in the pool late at night. A blush of shame touched her face as she thought of their lovemaking there in the water when the servants were away from the house. Abruptly, she jerked the cord, closing the drapery and her mind on the pool.

A short time later, Chandler opened the bedroom door. Callie gasped ever so slightly as he entered the room dressed in long royal-blue silk pajama bottoms. The dark hair on his chest was a curly, glistening mat spread over well-defined muscles, and she tried not to stare as he approached the bed in the scant light of a single bedside lamp. The faint scent of her favorite aftershave drifted toward her, and she smiled sadly, thinking of the waste they were both making of sweet scents, old memories, and a once blazing desire.

Chandler's eyes roved over her slowly, and she almost felt like hiding under their appraisal. Instead, she raised up on her elbows in a provocative pose, allowing her blond hair to flow down her back like a golden stream, the ripples created by her braids glistening in the glow of the bedside lamp. For the briefest of moments, she saw a look of hunger mingled with regret in Chandler's eyes and she was distressed by it. She saw that he was struggling to control his emotions, and a cold look entered his eyes. "You look absolutely ravishing, my darling," he said in a deep, but strangely remote voice.

Callie could have replied that he did too, but she took herself sharply in hand. She would not yield to him as she had done before. She would control her body with her head instead of her heart for once. If he thought to humiliate her, embarrass her, throw his mistress in her face and make her pay for a broken marriage that was his fault, he could think again. He was only angry because she had gone away. Their marriage had been over anyway, except for the formalities, since he had obviously been planning to tell her that he was going away with Nadine. Was he so bitter now because he hadn't gotten the chance to carry out his plans four years ago?

The snap of the bedroom light being turned off echoed loudly in the room, and Callie heard herself breathing raggedly as Chandler settled on the bed beside her. Her heart began an erratic beating. There was an animal warmth about him, and she felt her flesh burn when he pulled her close to his long, muscled body. His well-shaped lips descended to hers, and it took all her willpower to respond with only her body. Her emotions were in turmoil as his hungry, fiery touch sent thrills of desire cascading over her.

She wanted so desperately to abandon herself heart, soul, and mind to his loving, and forget that their reunion was one of revenge, anger, disappointment, and financial need. She wanted to tell him that she needed him. She wanted to beg him to tell her that his affair with Nadine had been a mistake and that he hadn't really shared his bed with another woman. She wanted him to tell her that the past was behind them and that they would begin afresh to rebuild their relationship. She wanted to tell him that she could forgive and forget the past if there were any hope for a future for them. She wanted to, but she smothered the words in her throat and tried to keep her head while her body was clearly lost to Chandler's teasing touch.

Chandler's hands began to make caressing circles over h   h and she fought the longing to surrender herself
       tally. She tried to picture Nadine as she had

looked kissing Chandler when she left the party, and for a few moments she managed to hold the image in her mind, but when Chandler eased off the bed to slip out of his pajamas, Callie felt a wild excitement burning in the pit of her stomach. He gathered her against his chest, and before she could make the effective protest, he had eased her gown over her head and was holding her naked body to the nude expanse of his broad chest.

She felt as if her breath had been sucked away when he eased her back down on the bed and began to scatter kisses over her quivering, yielding flesh. A growing need was building inside her, and she was quickly losing her determination to turn from his touch. His hands moved over her skin with a tantalizing caress, and one hand stole down to her thigh to stroke it with provocative movements. As his thumb played high up on her leg, she felt a flood of warmth fill her loins. Callie knew she was lost as desire surged higher and higher inside her, and she moaned softly.

It had been so long since Chandler had held her like this and had done such exciting things to her hungry body. This was the man she loved, and when his lips closed down over a rosebud nipple and suckled it gently, it became very plain to her that she could refuse Chandler nothing. Her plan would go begging with her pride, for she couldn't turn from him while her body was his slave. The seduction continued and she found herself gripping his hair tightly, wanting him to claim her totally and end the agony and ecstasy she had involuntarily been thrown into.

But Chandler was in no hurry. Savoring every delicious moment, he continued to stroke, fondle, and caress her flaming body until she thought she could stand no more of his provocative touch. A fire was burning hotter and hotter inside her as Chandler's mouth moved down lower and lower on her body, causing her stomach to quiver as though it had been filled with a thousand butterflies.

Chandler's tongue snaked out to trail a moist path down to her thigh, and Callie gripped his hair more fiercely when he gently nibbled at the tender skin with his teeth. His mouth retraced the same fiery path, moving ever so slowly over her belly, her breasts, and neck, his body pressing down tantalizingly on hers as he worked his way upward. Just when Callie was sure he was ready to join her totally, his lips found hers again and closed over them in a scorching kiss. Callie could feel the maleness of him as his body touched hers intimately, rocking against her gently, but he still did not become one with her.

"Chandler," she murmured as his lips found her throat and he tickled the sensitive cord with his tongue. "Oh, Chandler."

All motion stopped as he arched his body over hers and gazed down into her eyes. Even in the darkness of the passion-filled room, Callie could tell that he was staring down into her face. "Do I bore you now, Callie?" he asked in a husky, ragged voice, as if it were a terribly important question.

She felt herself grow chilled in his arms, even as he paused above her, waiting for her reply. He was treating her cruelly, and she wanted nothing more than to tell him yes, but the lie was too great. She was too much in love with him to insult him with such a statement again, and she needed him too much. Yet her pride was such that she struggled for a minute before she could phrase a denial. And in that single minute, Chandler mistook her hesitation for an affirmative reply.

"I see," he said coldly, all the warmth draining from him instantly as he slid across her body and moved off the bed. The suddenness of his departure rendered her momentarily unable to respond at all. She watched in bitter disappointment as he stalked from the room, not even bothering to pick up his pajama bottoms. He didn't close the door, and for a long time Callie lay still where he had left her, staring out into the hall where he had disappeared. The feverish desire she had known minutes ago had vanished as irrevocably as a flaming sunset, and she was left feeling cold, abused, sick at heart, and very, very alone.

CHAPTER SIX

Callie awakened the next morning to streams of sunlight filtering through the shell-colored draperies. She opened her eyes cautiously, unwilling to face the day after last night's fiasco in Chandler's arms. She had no doubts about where she was, for the memory of his naked body pressed so provocatively against her flooded her with a sense of loss because they really weren't man and wife again. She glanced down and saw that though she was still naked, she was under a dark blue sheet now. Her gaze darted quickly to the door, and she saw that someone had closed it. She wondered if it had been Chandler, but he had been so furious when he strode away that she couldn't conceive of him returning for any purpose. She ran her fingers through her hair. Today would be almost as painful as last night, but she might as well face it. Besides, she had to see Logan and discuss his surgery with the doctor, and she knew his doctor made rounds at eleven.

She had shoved the covers aside when she heard a gentle rap on her door. "Yes?" she queried hesitantly, her heart suddenly picking up its pace.

"Missy?" came the familiar question, and Callie relaxed. She pulled the covers back up.

"Come in, Sung." She could use a cup of hot coffee before going to join Chandler for breakfast; that is, if she were, indeed, supposed to join him.

Sung opened the door and when he smiled at Callie, she felt a little better. Sung, at least, was glad of her homecoming. She saw the pleased look in his eyes as he came forward with a tray containing a steaming cup of coffee, a single slice of buttered whole wheat toast, and a tiny, delicate Oriental vase with a few lovely lavender violets.

Sitting up in bed, she gathered the bedclothes to her body. "Thank you, Sung. I really do appreciate this."

He bowed, and automatically Callie lowered her head in response. "It is my pleasure, missy." He turned to go and Callie asked nervously, "Is Chandler up?"

"I'm going to wake him," Sung said, discreetly not meeting her eyes. "He is asleep in the adjoining bedroom." Then he backed out of the room and closed the door.

Callie stared at the door absently. She had taken Chandler's bedroom and she felt a ridiculous pang of guilt because he had been inconvenienced. Today she would remove all her belongings and put them in the third bedroom down the hall. She glanced at the bathroom, then at the adjoining bedroom. One had only to enter the bathroom from it, then come into this bedroom. She drew a weary breath. What did it matter? Chandler hadn't done so in the night, and now he wouldn't get the chance. Walking swiftly to the door, she closed it, and not a minute too soon; immediately after, she heard the shower water being turned on. He had gotten up and was bathing.

Returning to the bed, she climbed back in and quickly drank her coffee and ate her toast, then went to the closet that ran the length of one wall. Hunting among her clothes, she decided on a brown and white striped dress with short sleeves and a gathered skirt. When she heard no more sounds from the bath, she tentatively opened the door. It was empty, and Callie could see into the bedroom where Chandler had slept. It, too, was empty, and she saw the bedclothes scattered wildly about the bed, and a pillow bunched up into a ball. Several magazines and a book lay on the floor. Callie closed the door to the bedroom, then climbed into the shower.

After she had finished her bath, she brushed her hair and carefully secured it on top of her head with a brown comb and concealed rubberbands. As she was working with it, she caught sight of her wedding band, and for a moment she stood and stared at it. It meant nothing, of course, and that was part of the tragedy. Picking up her dress, she slipped into it and a pair of soft brown sandals. She checked her appearance, then left the room to make her way past the familiar rooms of the house.

Chandler had given her unlimited funds when they married and he had let her indulge her fantasies and whims in the house, even though it had been beautifully appointed when she had moved in. Now it seemed strange to see so much of her personality and handiwork in a house she had long ago ceased to occupy. Even the wall hangings, one a whimsical needlepoint she had done when she was sixteen, were exactly as she had left them. The macrame hangers she had made herself still held plants, although, Callie observed with a frown, under Molly's black thumb most of the former plants had apparently perished, and the ones she remembered were in a sad way. She stared unhappily at her croton, which had once been tall and full of dark green leaves with bright yellow spots. It was still tall, but now it was leggy and pathetic, with a few sparse leaves. Molly hadn't pinched off the new top growth to keep it looking pretty, and it had obviously been overwatered. Her eyes moved to the weeping fig, looking pitiful and paltry in the huge white container that housed it. Callie was sure it was the same plant she had purchased, but it had been mistreated, not intentionally, she was sure, but mistreated all the same. The leaves looked dull and dwarfed, and the plant should have grown tall and beautiful in the past four years. She shook her head. Why was she worrying about those poor plants when she had so many more serious things on her mind?

When Callie entered the dining room, she glanced up in surprise as Molly collided with her. She had been so lost in thought that she hadn't looked where she was going.

"Why, Miss Callie!" Molly exclaimed, bracing Callie with a large hand. The woman's eyes took on a stern look. "So you are home—and it's high time, too. You scared us half to death running off like that, and then nobody heard a darn thing from you."

"Yes, I'm home," Callie said simply, unable to think of anything else to say.

Molly's snapping black eyes swept measuringly over her figure. "Well, it's good to see you, and you've changed, child. You're pretty as a picture, I declare, but you're thin. Mighty thin. I'll have to take you in hand."

Callie laughed lightly as she let the housekeeper scrutinize her. She had no doubt that this domineering woman, with iron gray hair, a body that spoke of power and stubbornness, and a will that would not bend, would try to take her under her wing again. When Callie had been mistress of the house, Molly had treated her as the novice homemaker she was, and had firmly and confidently instructed her on furniture, fabrics, budgets, and the other responsibilities of running a house. Molly had been amazed that Chandler had let Callie replace all the items in the house to suit her fancy; she had spoken up about it, even to Chandler, but he had only laughed. He alone refused to be run by Molly, despite the fact that she had been his parents' housekeeper in San Francisco, and had known him since he was ten.

"You go on in and eat breakfast. Mr. Matthews is waiting—and you be sure to drink your orange juice. Vitamin C, you know. And you need it, from the looks of you."

"Yes, Molly," Callie said with mock obedience, and she was a little amused that the housekeeper picked right up where she had left off four years ago. "I'll drink every last drop," she said in a teasing voice.

"See that you do now," Molly retorted, determined to have the last word.

Callie nodded again, and smiling broadly, walked into the dining room. Her smile vanished when Chandler glanced up from the paper he was reading.

"Callie," he acknowledged with a nod. His eyes traveled over her indifferently, then returned to his paper. Callie sat down some distance from him at the long oak table and gazed around the room, attempting to keep from looking at Chandler. Glancing up, she noted the heavily beamed ceiling, and then her eyes lowered to stare at the quarry tile floor. She had always loved this room with its warmth and graceful country French furnishings. Molly had told her that the pieces she had added didn't mix with the long oak table, but Chandler had seen the room and proclaimed it charming. Callie smiled a little: she had loved him for saying that, but now, as she viewed the room more objectively, she saw that Molly had been technically right. She surreptiously studied her husband as he read the paper. He had been so caring and supportive during that first summer, and she had been sure at one time that he had loved her.

"What will you have to eat, missy?"

She glanced up quickly when Sung came up beside her. Looking at Chandler's plate, she saw the remains of pancakes and blueberry syrup. "I'll have pancakes and another cup of coffee, please."

After Sung had smiled and vanished into the kitchen, Chandler lowered his paper to look at Callie.

Now that she had his attention, she spoke rapidly. "I'll

move my things out of your bedroom so that you can have it back. I had no intention of inconveniencing you."

With deliberate motions, Chandler laid the paper down on the table, then pressed his fingertips together, watching her intently. A dark brow arched up. "Will you?" he asked at last. "I think not. When I took you back as my wife for a year, I meant in *all* ways." His voice lowered to a deep growl. "And believe me, Callie, I *mean* all ways. That includes sharing a bed and a bedroom."

"I never agreed to that!" she retorted sharply.

Chandler's eyes met hers levelly. "How much of a fool do you really think I am?"

Callie couldn't hold his hard gaze and finally her gaze wavered to fall on her hands, which twisted in her lap. Not nearly as big a fool as he thought she was, she wanted to tell him, but the words were trapped in her mouth.

She glanced up when Chandler stood up. "Sunday is business as usual at the winery, and I have some matters to take care of. I'll return by ten-thirty and we can go to the hospital and make the arrangements for your stepfather's surgery."

"That won't be necessary," she announced. "I'll handle the arrangements. You've given me the check, and I don't need any further help from you."

When she saw Chandler's jaw muscle twitch, she knew she was pushing him past all patience, but she couldn't seem to help herself. He put his hands down on the table and leaned dangerously near her. "I'm paying for the operation, and I'll make the arrangements. Besides," he added less harshly, "I know a heart specialist in San Francisco, and I think it's best that Logan go to a hospital there."

"Oh?" she murmured. She hadn't considered that, but of course she realized that it might be in Logan's best interest.

"Yes, so you be ready when I get back." Without waiting for additional comment from her, Chandler left the room.

Callie leaned back in her chair and sighed. This truly was going to be impossible. If anything, their reunion would make them hate each other more intensely. However, Chandler did appear to be trying to do what was best for Logan, and she would have to go along with him in this matter. She wanted Logan to have the best possible care, but she was at a loss as to how to explain Chandler's appearance. Sung soon returned with her breakfast, and picking up her fork, she ate the golden cakes absently as she pondered her situation. Bowing to Chandler in the matter of Logan was one thing; remaining in his bedroom entirely another.

She found that she wasn't terribly hungry, and she left most of her breakfast and returned to the bedroom. She was going to be in Chandler's home a year, and she wanted to make it as bearable as was physically possible. Sharing a room with Chandler under the circumstances would never work. Walking to the closet, she flung her clothes across her arm. When Chandler came back, she would be settled in the third bedroom, and there would be little he could do about it. Her arms full, she hurried down the hall to the other room and laid her clothes down on the bed. Then she slid open the closet door.

Her mouth gaped open in surprise when she saw that the closet contained a number of women's dresses, gowns, and slacks. She realized with consternation that this must be the room Nadine occupied when she stayed over. No, she told herself sharply—that was ridiculous. This was the room in which Nadine kept her clothes. Obviously, she spent her time in Chandler's room. And to think that he hadn't bothered to have these articles sent to Nadine when he bribed Callie into becoming his wife again! She pulled out a flimsy pink nightgown, and her mind flashed back to the night four years ago when she had seen the clothes in Nadine's suitcase.

The nightgown looked like one of those she had seen, and she was surprised that Nadine had kept her clothes so long. But then, she reasoned angrily, her clothes didn't get much use when she spent her time with Chandler! She pulled out another item, this time a long blue evening gown. Her anger became more intense because Chandler hadn't made any pretense of moving his mistress out of the house. Did he mean to carry on the affair right beneath her nose? And he had asked how much of a fool she thought *he* was!

She marched out into the hall. "Molly!" she called.

The housekeeper took her own good time, but she finally strolled down the hall in response to the summons. "Yes, Miss Callie?"

Callie pointed a shaking finger at the clothes in the closet. "Box those things and donate them to charity."

"That's a good idea—" Molly said, and Callie interrupted her. This was one time when she had no intention of discussing a matter with the household help.

"Just do it, Molly—and quickly."

Molly raised heavy eyebrows, but she didn't reply as she ambled back down the hall. When she returned, she had two large boxes and she quickly and efficiently emptied the closet and carted the boxes away. By the time Chandler returned to the house, Callie had hung all of her clothes in the closet and was sitting in the living room, glancing through a magazine.

"Ready to go?" he asked.

Callie nodded, and without further ado, they drove to the hospital. They reached Logan's room in time to speak with the doctor as he was leaving. To Callie's surprise, Chandler introduced himself, explaining that he was Logan's stepdaugher's husband, and that he intended to pay for whatever Logan needed.

The doctor looked at Callie, and she smiled faintly. Chandler slipped his arm around her waist and began to talk with the doctor about the surgery, explaining that he knew a heart specialist in San Francisco and that he thought perhaps that would be the best choice for such an operation. He looked at Callie only briefly as she slid from his grasp and stepped around the two of them to go into Logan's room. She was still trying to think of some way to tell him why she had gone back to Chandler without arousing his suspicions.

He was lying with his eyes closed, and for a moment she thought he was asleep, but when she approached the bed, his pale gray eyes flickered open.

"Callie," he said. "How good to see you." A smile spread over his lips and he tried to sit up against the bed pillows.

"Lie still," she insisted with a forced smile. "How do you feel?"

"Much better. Much better," he told her, and he did sound better. "How are you? Have you found a job?"

"Sort of," she responded vaguely. Taking his hand in hers, she patted it gently. "I have something to discuss with you." She held up her hand, displaying the gold band. "I've gone back to Chandler."

"Gone back to him?" Logan asked incredulously, a frown marring his forehead. "Why?"

Her smile was sheepish and she fought in vain to keep the flush from staining her cheeks. "You know I love him, Logan." At least that much wasn't a lie, she told herself. "And when he found out about your illness—he wanted to help. We started talking, and—" She shrugged. "And I guess I just couldn't resist him." She pretended to laugh and looked away from Logan's frowning face. "He is handsome and charming, isn't he?"

His hand tightened around hers. "Honey, it's not because of me, is it? I don't want you to—"

Her eyes met his again, and she murmured teasingly, "Listen to you. You don't really think I'd go back to Chandler just to make your life easier, do you?"

He grinned in embarrassment. "Well, I thought perhaps—"

"Even for you, I couldn't live with him if I didn't love him," she insisted. "You must know that. Now, don't give it another thought."

"But what about Nadine?"

Making a careless dismissing motion with her hand, Callie said, "I overreacted when I saw them together." She averted her eyes again, staring blankly at the window, hoping the lie she was about to tell didn't choke her. "There was never anything really serious between them." *Oh, if only that were true,* she thought despairingly; she would give almost anything.

Logan ran a hand through his hair, and when Callie looked at him again, she knew he wasn't satisfied with her explanation. "Logan," she said evenly, "I'm a fool for that man. I can't help myself, but he's the only man I've ever wanted."

"I only want your happiness," he said, his eyes searching hers. "Can you be happy with Chandler Matthews?"

"I can't be happy without him." She knew that was true. "This is what I want," she forced herself to say with conviction. "And besides, he wants to make me happy, and we would be unfair to ourselves if we didn't at least try again."

"Callie, honey—" Logan looked at the door as Chandler and the doctor entered the room, and he stopped midsentence. Callie stood beside his bed, lightly holding his hand, as Chandler and the doctor discussed the operation with them. Logan objected at first to going to San Francisco, but when he realized that it would simplify the situation and Callie urged him to go, he became reconciled. It was decided that he could have surgery right away, since he was well enough and there was no reason to postpone it. Chandler would make the arrangements for transportation and the new doctor. Callie and he would drive up to see that Logan was settled in comfortably and to discuss the operation with the surgeon. Fortunately, the trip would only take about three hours. Logan wouldn't be far away from them if there were an emergency and Callie was needed.

When the medical talk had ended and the doctor had gone, Logan turned to Chandler. "About this little girl here," he said, shaking Callie's hand. "I want you to promise me that you will do everything in your power to make her happy. She's very special to me." His face was friendly, but Callie could tell that he was upset, and she knew it was important that he not become emotionally distraught. Freeing her hand, she wound an arm around Chandler's waist.

"Logan, there's absolutely nothing to worry about. We couldn't be happier. Chandler loves me. He doesn't want to see me hurt ever again." She raised her eyes to Chandler's face, daring him to deny her words, and for a moment she was startled by the vulnerability she saw in his blue eyes.

Hugging her to his side, he lightly touched his lips to her forehead. Callie was sure she felt the tension in his body, but he spoke calmly. "I *do* love this woman, Logan, and I intend to see that we're never parted again."

Logan looked from one to the other. He obviously wasn't convinced about the wisdom of their reunion, or by their display of affection, but he saw something in the two of them that resulted in a visible relaxing of his tense face muscles. Callie wondered what he thought he had seen, but then, Chandler had sounded so convincing that she might have believed his words herself if she didn't know the situation.

A smiling older woman arrived with Logan's lunch, and

Callie and Chandler decided to leave so that he could enjoy his meal. When she kissed him good-bye, she felt suddenly depressed. Even with Chandler ensuring that he get the very best care, she would still worry about him. He might think that she had Chandler now and would be taken care of, but she knew that Logan was all she had—all she would ever have, for she could never love another man as she loved Chandler, and she would never marry again and raise a family of her own. The experience had been much too painful to consider again anyway. Holding her head high, she walked out of the room with her husband, and she was surprised when he took her hand in his after they were out in the hall.

"He'll come through this just fine, Callie," he said reassuringly as if he had read her mind. "I'll see that he gets the very best that money can buy."

Unthinkingly, Callie replied in a strained voice, "Your money can't buy everything, Chandler."

His gaze probed hers for only a moment. "How well I know it," he stated harshly, dropping her hand as if he found her touch unpleasant. Callie felt an inexplicable rush of tears fill her eyes and she pressed her lips frimly together to hold the tears at bay. A new wave of bitterness engulfed her, and she regretted again that their lives were so entangled.

Neither of them had anything to say as they drove back to the house. Sung was busy in the kitchen when they went inside; Chandler settled down in the living room while Sung finished lunch. Callie wandered out on the porch and stood looking out over Chandler's property. Her gaze fell on Aunt Caroline's monstrous old house, and she felt a twinge of sadness because it belonged to her husband now.

"Callie." She was stirred from her musings when Chandler appeared by her side. "Are you ready for lunch? Sung is serving it on the patio."

Callie nodded, avoiding his eyes as she walked back

inside with him. She had always found eating on the patio very romantic, but now there was no romance between them.

"Why don't you put on your swimsuit?" he asked unexpectedly. "We'll take a quick swim before lunch."

Her eyes met his and her first impulse was to refuse. Chandler was trying to pretend that four years and a thousand heartaches hadn't come between them. Perhaps he could do it with ease, but she couldn't.

"Come on," he coaxed with sudden softness. "It will be good for you to get a little exercise and loosen up. You look tight as a spring." He stepped up behind her and a slow smile spread over his beautifully sculptured lips as he reached out to lightly massage her tense neck muscles.

It was true that she was rigid with tenseness, and she found herself giving in, against her better judgment. "All right. I'll meet you out on the patio." She moved away from him quickly, afraid of his magical touch. She went down the hall to the bedroom where she had put her clothes; to her shock, when she opened the closet door the space was empty. Whirling around, she ran down the hall to Chandler's room. All her clothes had been neatly hung beside her husband's. Anger raced in her veins as she turned around to leave the room. Just as she reached for the doorknob, Chandler opened the door and walked inside.

"Is anything wrong?" he asked coolly, but Callie was unable to miss the arrogant thrust of his strong jaw.

"Who hung my clothes back in here?" she demanded.

"Molly," he replied with lazy indifference. "Upon my order."

"Have her return them to the other room," she insisted. "I'll live here as your wife, but for us to share a room is an injustice to both of us. We're miserable enough sharing the days; at least let us rest in peace at night."

"Fine, if that's the way you want it."

Callie was astonished at his easy acquiescence, and she watched him warily when he walked across the room to the phone resting upon the nightstand. When he picked it up and dialed a number, her curiosity got the best of her. "What are you doing?"

"Calling the hospital."

"Why?"

"Apparently we've struck no bargain after all," he responded calmly. He turned so that his eyes met hers. "I won't pay for Logan's surgery under the circumstances. I've already been your fool once. I won't repeat that mistake."

"*My* fool!" she cried. "*My* fool! You promised to pay for the operation if I agreed to be your wife again. This was your idea! You've made all the arrangements." She could hear the hysterical rise of her voice, but she was unable to speak naturally with her throat constricting so tightly. He wouldn't back out now. Logan had to have that surgery. "You gave me your word—and your check!"

"I thought we had made an agreement to live as man and wife. I was wrong. I didn't realize that you hadn't changed *that* much: your word is no better today than it was four years ago. I can still cancel the check."

"You wouldn't!"

"Don't you know me at all, Callie?" he asked softly. He turned his back on her. "Hello," he said into the phone receiver. "This is—"

Rushing up to him, Callie jammed her finger down on the button. "Please put the phone down," she said through clenched teeth. "If you want me so badly that you'll put a man's life in jeopardy, then take me." She thrust her face near his and glowered into his cold blue eyes. In contrast to her fevered face and harsh breathing, Chandler was cool and unruffled.

"You still flatter yourself," he commented. "I only insist that you keep up pretenses at this stage. I took you back as my wife in front of fifty people. And I've never said that I want you badly. Indeed, it will be you who will come to me eventually." His lips twitched almost imperceptibly and his cool gaze suddenly blazed with blue fire. "You can lie to yourself, Callie, but your body gives its own message."

Anger was surging inside her, but Callie truly did believe that Chandler would cancel Logan's surgery if she didn't go along with his demands. "Fine," she retorted hatefully. "You think anything you want to. I'll keep up the sham of our marriage—for whatever reason you want" —her eyes glittered as brightly as his—"but I will not go to you ever—for anything!"

To her consternation, he gave a short laugh, then replaced the receiver. "I know that beautiful body of yours better than you do." With that cruel remark, the smile faded from his lips. "Forget the swim," he said crossly. "Sung has lunch ready. Let's eat."

Callie gritted her teeth as she followed him out the door, but she didn't speak again as they went to the patio. The sight of the flagstone patio and the shimmering blue water in the oval swimming pool caused a new surge of memories to flood her mind, and she glanced away. Keeping her eyes on the intimate white wrought-iron table, brightly decorated with yellow lace, Callie walked purposely across the patio to the umbrella-shaded table and quickly seated herself.

Sung was working with skewers that held tender pieces of beef, bell peppers, and pineapple bits. As he slid the vegetables, fruit, and meat onto a snowy bed of white rice, Callie sighed wearily. She didn't realize the sound had been audible until Sung looked apprehensively into her eyes. Giving him a wan smile, Callie complimented him on the lunch. "It looks delicious, Sung."

He bowed. "Thank you, missy. I hope you enjoy it."

Automatically, Callie tilted her head forward in a partial curtsy and her eyes met Chandler's as he sat down across from her. Although his face was still set in angry lines, she couldn't miss the amused look in his blue eyes when she responded to Sung. Well, she told herself, it was too late to stop curtsying to Sung, just as it was too late to stop loving Chandler. Her admission surprised her.

After he had treated her so cruelly, why couldn't she hate him? Her gaze settled on the blue waters of the pool again, and she recalled the pleasurable times when they had swum there in the cool of evening. Her face burned with the remembrance of their sweet lovemaking, and she lowered her eyes. Finally, she looked up and saw Chandler still regarding her with a speculative look in his eyes. Could he read her thoughts? she suddenly wondered with dismay. Was she so obvious? Was that why he had boasted that he knew her body better than she did? *Did* he know how badly she wanted him yet? How desperately and destructively she loved him?

"Wine?" he asked her softly. Callie felt a dangerous beating of her heart. His anger seemed to have vanished now that he was once again in control and she had agreed to his wishes.

"Yes, please," she murmured quietly. What else could Chandler demand in order to keep the bargain? Did he mean to *force* her to share his bed and his love? She shook the thought from her mind. No; he intended to use more subtle means. She was sure of it. And she was equally sure that he would not succeed. She would not let him. Her principles and her convictions must be strong. He had blackmailed her into being his wife again, and she couldn't let him have his way with her and still live with herself.

Holding up her wineglass, she smiled enigmatically at him. "To love," she said mockingly. Then she tipped her glass and took a long drink of wine.

CHAPTER SEVEN

When they had finished lunch, Chandler offered to show Callie the vineyards. She almost refused. She didn't want him to involve her in his life any more than she already was, but she was curious about his property. Silently agreeing, she stood up.

Looking down at her feet, Chandler asked, "Are those shoes comfortable for walking?"

"Yes," she replied.

With Chandler leading the way, she walked a considerable distance through the vines flourishing on the gentle valley hills. They were lush and well cared for, but, of course, Callie expected no less from Chandler. He was a businessman through and through, and he took pride in whatever he did. He exposed a bunch of grapes and started to say something when a tall, lean man came up and interrupted them.

"Afternoon, Chandler," he said, taking off a brown cowboy hat. "Miss."

Chandler straightened up and smiled at him. "Good afternoon, Wesley." Turning to Callie, he said, "Callie, this is Wesley Joseph, our viticulturist. He's the man really responsible for keeping the vines growing and the wine delicious. Wesley, my wife, Callie."

Wesley didn't bother to hide his surprise. "This is your wife?" he asked, grinning broadly at her. Callie noticed the deep laugh lines on each side of his mouth and she knew instinctively that here was a man who enjoyed life and made the most of it. "How'd an ornery cuss like you get a pretty young thing like this to marry you, Chandler?" he asked, a teasing twinkle in his brilliant green eyes. His gaze roved blatantly over Callie, and he obviously liked what he saw.

Chandler wasn't amused by his remark. "I proposed to her," he said with a certain degree of sharpness.

"Dang it all," Wesley said, still smiling. "I sure am sorry you beat me to the punch with this one. Do you have any sisters?" he asked Callie.

She blushed at his flagrant flirting. Chandler was becoming angry, but Wesley paid him no mind.

"No, she doesn't," Chandler said coolly.

"Darn shame," Wesley commented playfully. Shoving his hat back on his head, he said, "It's sure nice to meet you, Callie. Maybe we'll see each other again some time."

"And maybe you won't," Chandler returned humorlessly.

"It's nice to meet you, Wesley," Callie murmured. She looked back at the vines when Wesley winked. He was a charmer all right, she told herself, but she knew she could never trust him. She much preferred a more serious man like Chandler. A bleak smile parted her lips; she couldn't trust Chandler either.

Obviously irritated with Wesley, Chandler watched him walk away, then held up the bunch of grapes again. He pointed out the color of the skins and commented on the texture, and although Callie was interested, she wouldn't let herself become too involved in the conversation. In a year, she wouldn't be here to see how Chandler's vines were doing, and it was foolish to pretend that his vineyard had any bearing on her life. She followed along behind him, giving him part of her attention as he talked about how well the winery was doing and his plans for expansion now that he owned Aunt Caroline's land. As she heard the enthusiasm in his voice, Callie decided she was glad that she had sold him the land, but still she regretted the loss of the old Victorian house.

After a time, her feet began to grow tired and she asked to return to the house. Chandler seemed most concerned for her welfare and he apologized for leading her so far into the vineyards. She smiled faintly at him; sometimes it was easy to think that he really did care for her, and those were the dangerous times. She *wanted* to believe that he cared for her, but she would not be such a fool a second time. *He* had destroyed their marriage by his unwillingness to give up Nadine, and no matter how much she longed to believe that he was sorry, she knew it wasn't true.

As though thinking of the woman had the power to conjure her up, Callie looked up to see the tall redhead sauntering toward them.

"There you are, Chandler," she called out. "I've been looking all over for you."

And no wonder you couldn't find him, Callie told herself; *you didn't expect him to be with his wife.* She brushed her thoughts aside when Nadine looked at her. "Callie," she said with a phony smile and a nod.

"Hello, Nadine."

Nadine walked up to them and turned her full attention to Chandler. "I've got something I must talk with you about, Chandler." She glanced back pointedly at Callie, then looked into Chandler's eyes.

"Why don't you go on inside and freshen up before we go to the hospital, Callie?" Chandler suggested. "I'll be right in."

"Of course." Callie briskly turned on her heel and walked away, but she was seething with resentment. The moment Nadine showed up, Callie was dismissed as if she were an unwanted guest. Well, it was a timely lesson for her. Hadn't she just been telling herself that she could almost believe that Chandler really cared for her? He might—if he didn't care for Nadine more.

Callie took a cool shower and changed her clothes, and she found that the action dispelled some of her hostility. She only hurt herself by getting so upset. She was well aware how things stood between her and Chandler, and wishing never had been a solution to anything. Seeking out Molly, Callie asked if there were any plant food and a spray container.

"You going to do something with those plants?" Molly asked.

Callie smiled. "If I can. Some of them look nearly hopeless."

Molly laughed. "I never claimed to be any hand at that, but Chandler wouldn't get rid of them, and he wanted the ones replaced that died off." She led Callie to an area in a walk-in pantry that contained supplies for the indoor plants. "Help yourself."

Chandler hadn't returned, and Callie busied herself in the living room with the croton, weeping fig, and an African violet that had somehow survived the years, although it didn't have a single blossom. She sprayed the croton and weeping fig and washed an accumulation of dust from the leaves. Then she set about repotting the African violet. When she had completed that, she hung it near a window where it could get good light, but not direct sunlight. She was on her way to the kitchen to doctor the snake plant, which had done reasonably well, no doubt because of its innate hardiness, when Chandler came into the room.

"I'll get a quick shower and we'll leave." Callie nodded coolly, but she didn't reply, and Chandler moved away from her without another word.

When they reached the hospital a short time later, they found Logan in good spirits. He was joking with a nurse, and Callie brightened upon seeing his smiling face and jocular nature. He hadn't been in a good humor in some time, and she was sure part of it was relief at knowing their plight wasn't as desperate since she had gone back to Chandler. This time he had no qualms about their reunion; in fact, she marveled at how well the two men got along.

Logan began to question Chandler about the vineyards and why he had sold all his cattle. The conversation turned to Logan's copper mine, and Callie was simply amazed at the questions Chandler asked. His interest appeared to be genuine, and he and Logan talked about the possibility of reviving the mine. One of the primary reasons it had gone under, of course, was Logan's lack of funds. He had poured every penny he could get his hands on into it, but he never had sufficient funds for wages or machinery. He had lost the house he and Callie's mother owned long before Callie went to Montana.

Callie smiled at the light that lit up his pale gray eyes when Chandler talked about looking into the setup and perhaps opening the mine up again. It was the tonic Logan needed, and she was very grateful for her husband's kindness, though she was sure he wasn't serious about it.

When Chandler went down to the cafeteria to get sandwiches for himself and Callie, Logan took her hand. "I like him, Callie," he commented. "I really do. I think you two can make the marriage work this time if you both try."

"Of course you like him, Logan," she teased lightly, squeezing his hand. "He might revive your copper mine."

Logan grinned, but he shook his head. "No, that's not why I like him, although you may be sure that he made points with me over that." He laughed softly. "Darn it all, I'm a fool for that mine, but I liked Chandler the first time I met him. There's something strong and reassuring about him. I'll tell you something—as little as I know him, I'd put my life in his hands."

You already have, Callie thought a little unhappily, but

she winked at Logan. "Or your copper mine, and that's more important."

They both laughed. They were making light conversation when Chandler came back into the room. He smiled warmly at both of them, and immediately joined in the conversation. After he and Callie had eaten, they visited with Logan for a while longer, then left.

Callie was grateful to Chandler for giving Logan a fresh interest in life, and she felt obligated to him. She took his arm when they were out in the hall. "I want to thank you, Chandler, for what you've done for Logan's spirits. I really appreciate it. I know you were just making conversation about the copper mine, but you've given him something to live for, and I'm grateful."

Chandler's blue eyes studied her face for a moment. "I'm glad you appreciate me," he said lightly, "but I wasn't just talking. I'm going to contact some people who know something about copper, and I may go into business with Logan. He still owns the mine and the land, he said."

"Are you serious?"

He smiled at her. "I'm a businessman, Callie. I love the winery, but I loved the cattle business, too. If I like the copper business and can see a profit in it, I'll get into it, too. Logan's a young man yet. I can rely on his expertise. He seems quite knowledgeable, and I believe he simply used bad business sense and went broke. I don't intend to make that mistake."

Nodding knowingly, Callie murmured, "No, I'm sure you don't. And you just may like the copper business at that. It takes a hard man to battle the earth and win."

Chandler laughed. "A man has to battle everything he does these days, and I like to think I'm a winner. Anything worth having is surely worth fighting for."

She smiled wanly as they continued down the hall. Yes, she told herself, Chandler was a winner all right. She had to hand him that. He was a success with business and with people—at everything except marriage, she thought wryly, and if he had married a woman willing to look the other way when he had affairs, he would have carried that off successfully, too. He had certainly won Logan over in a hurry.

She shook her head: Logan had been so sure that this man wasn't the man for her, and he had been furious when Chandler broke her heart. He had disliked the man intensely, sight unseen, and now—what did it matter? The relationship gave her stepfather new hope for the future, a hope he needed desperately at this time. But if the two men went into business together, it would be awkward and painful to see Chandler when she visited Logan. She brushed her hair away from her face with a trembling hand; she had enough things to worry about now without looking to the future. She would deal with the situation if and when it came to pass. For now she had all she could do trying to stay out of Chandler's arms and trying not to worry herself sick over Logan.

It was very late when they got home. Feeling a little depressed and weary, Callie went immediately to their bedroom, hoping Chandler wouldn't follow. Although she had few doubts that he would try to make love to her tonight, she was still unhappy about sharing his room. She would have been much more comfortable in one of the other bedrooms. This way was miserable for them both. She ran her hands through her hair and shook it out. It was what Chandler had insisted upon, and it would do her no good to make a scene. Perhaps if she bathed and went to bed, he would sleep in the second bedroom after all.

Closing the door to the bedroom, she went to the bath and ran a tub of warm water. When she had slipped out of her clothes, she slid down into the perfumed water and closed her eyes. It was heavenly. She almost felt that she could spend the night right here. She had been relaxing for about ten minutes when she heard the bedroom door open. She sat up, then immediately sank into the water again.

Chandler strolled to the bathroom door and grinned at her. "Comfortable?"

"I was," she said. "Close the door. I'm having my bath."

His smile broadened. "So I see, and a mighty pretty sight it is."

"Close the door!"

To her chagrin, he stepped into the bathroom and shut the door behind him. "I didn't mean come in and close it," she fumed. "Please leave until I've had my bath!"

The smile finally left his lips. "No," he replied calmly. "I'm going to take a shower, so if you'll just excuse me."

Callie's mouth gaped open as Chandler unbuttoned his shirt. "Can't you use the other bathroom or wait until I'm out of this one?" she protested.

He shrugged indifferently. "I suppose so." Reaching for the rose towel Callie had left out, he held it up. "If you're ready to get out, I'll dry you."

"You will not! I won't get out until you leave."

"Fine." He dropped the towel to the floor and slid his shirt down his arms. Callie watched for a moment in angry disbelief. When he undid his belt buckle and unzipped his pants, she averted her eyes. She heard him chuckle softly. A minute later the shower water had been turned on and she heard the door close.

Callie kept her eyes shut while Chandler showered. She couldn't believe that he was being so selfish, but surely he wouldn't take long. She wouldn't give him the satisfaction of driving her out, and besides, she didn't want to be in the process of drying off when he opened the shower door. Finally, she heard the water being turned off, and the door opened. She kept her eyes averted until she was sure he had had time to dry off. When she looked up, she found him before the mirror, clad only in a towel, wiping the mist away as he prepared to shave. He turned to smile at her and she threw a wet washcloth at him.

Chandler skillfully caught it in one hand. "Oh, you want me to wash your back?" he asked with feigned innocence.

"I do not!" she cried. "I want you to leave!"

"You don't and you know it," he retorted with a wicked grin. "Remember how you used to love for me to wash your back?"

"No," she said firmly, shaking her head for emphasis. But two telltale spots of red stained her cheeks: she remembered only too well.

The washcloth in hand, Chandler stepped toward her. "I don't want you to wash my back," she insisted again, but Chandler paid her no mind. Callie tried to decide if she should just grab the towel and hurriedly get out of the tub, or if she should stay and be subjected to his ministrations to avoid any further confrontation at this point. Resigning herself to what she considered the lesser of the two evils—surely he would content himself with washing her back and then go away—she braced herself for his touch. Automatically, she held out the bar of soap to him as he perched on the side of the tub.

Grinning at her, he dipped the cloth into the warm water, then soaped it with great care. Callie crossed her hands over her bosom and leaned forward so that he would have easy access to her back. When the cloth touched her skin, she felt as if it had been burned. Chandler didn't content himself with a simple washing. Handing the soap back to her, he began to slowly caress her back, making wider and wider circles with the soapy cloth until Callie thought he would drive her crazy with pure pleasure. He carefully bathed her neck and shoulders, moving the cloth with the same slow, teasing caress, and Callie felt the flames of passion begin to burn low in the most feminine parts of her body. Remembrances of other times when he had bathed her filled her mind, and she longed to return to those long ago times.

Bending near her ear, Chandler nibbled at it gently as he murmured, "You're very beautiful, Callie."

Callie knew she had to resist him at all costs, and forgetting that she held the soap in her hand, she tightened her hands into fists. Suddenly the soap slipped from her hand, arced in the air, and plunged into the water. Water splashed up into Chandler's face, and Callie covered her mouth with a soapy hand to stifle a giggle.

Abruptly, Chandler broke into deep laughter, and hearing him, Callie couldn't resist either. For a moment they looked into each other's eyes, their laughter filling the room. Dropping the washcloth, Chandler reached for a towel and took Callie's hand. She let him help her from the tub and she stood on a thick white rug, unable to turn from him as he slowly began to dry her body. With gentle motions, he started with her face, patting her skin softly and lightly brushing her lips with his when he moved the towel down to her throat and absorbed the moisture there. Her nipples stiffened into hard peaks when he dried them with a circular caress, and Callie moistened her lips with her tongue as she stood a captive to her burning desire and Chandler's ministrations. As he moved the towel lower and lower, Callie closed her eyes and she felt an excited fire race throughout her limbs as Chandler knelt down on the floor on his knees in front of her and dried her long legs with slow, soft movements.

When he stood up, he faced her, draping the towel around her back and patting it free of the water as his chest pressed against her breasts, his face inches from hers. Callie ached with wanting him, and she had been too long without him to enjoy much more of this sweet torment. Finally he wrapped her in the towel, then lifted her in his arms.

Only then did the smile die on her lips, for catching

sight of her reflection in the mirror, Callie was appalled at how quickly she had succumbed to Chandler's attentions. Her face was glowing with pleasure and anticipation, and from her eyes to the tips of her toes, she was a woman wanting her man. She was clinging to Chandler tightly—and just as he had predicted, she was ready to beg him to make love to her. The sight was a sobering one for her. "Put me down, Chandler," she demanded tautly.

He gazed into her eyes only briefly, then set her soundly on her feet. A hard look entered his eyes as he turned away from her and shut the door behind him.

For some time Callie stood before the mirror, trembling with the intensity of her emotions. She wanted her husband as much as he wanted her—possibly much more—but he was the one who had ended all the happy times and loving they had shared. She couldn't—she wouldn't—give herself to him when Nadine was still in his life. It violated everything she considered sacred about marriage and love. She was still too Victorian to have that kind of marriage. Today she had seen again that Nadine had only to call Chandler's name to have him bow to her wishes.

She sat down on the vanity stool before the mirror and deliberately brushed her hair a hundred strokes. Then she perfumed and lotioned her still flaming body. Whiling away more time, she filed her nails and cleansed her face, hoping Chandler would be asleep when she finally went into the bedroom so she wouldn't have to face him again. But her hope was short-lived.

He was lying on his back, his hands behind his head. She walked purposely to her side of the bed and switched off her lamp. "Good night," she murmured coolly as she slid under the covers.

At first she thought he wasn't going to respond, and when he did, she could hear the bitter anger and tension in his voice. "Good night." He reached for his night lamp and switched it off with brusque movements.

She lay on her side listening for sounds that he had fallen asleep, but she heard nothing but her own even breathing and she closed her tired eyes on rising tears. Despite her feelings of unease, she eventually fell into a deep, troubled sleep.

Callie rolled over on her back, then gazed around. The sliding glass door to the patio had been slid partly open, and the drapery was drawn back. She blinked as she realized what she had heard. Chandler was stroking the length of the pool, and the water was hitting the sides as his powerful body created ripples and turbulence. It took Callie a few minutes to digest what she was seeing. The patio was dark, but the pool was lit by two underwater lights, giving an eerie, soft yellow glow to the water.

Glancing at the clock, she saw that it was past midnight. Slowly she sat up in bed, drawn to the sight of Chandler's strong, dark body, covered by a mat of black hair. The muscles of his arms flexed in the golden light of the pool lamps as he moved through the water with the skill of an accomplished swimmer. Transfixed by the sight, Callie opened her eyes fully and stared at her husband.

She would have liked nothing better than to join him there in his midnight frolic, but, as she continued to watch him, she realized that he wasn't swimming for the pleasure of it. When he faced her direction, she saw that his lips were drawn into a tight, determined line. A light breeze fluttered through the open door and gently caressed Callie's face, bringing her fully awake. Reaching up, she massaged her tense shoulder muscles as she continued to watch Chandler.

Suddenly, he pulled himself up out of the water and climbed from the pool. For the first time, Callie saw that he was naked. She wanted to look away, but she couldn't draw her eyes from his lean, bronzed muscular body. She watched with hungry fascination as he picked up a towel and briskly dried his powerful chest, narrow hips, and long, well-defined legs. Propping herself up on her elbows, she felt her breath catch in her throat. She was so much in love with Chandler. She had always been in love with him, from the first time she saw him, it seemed, and she wanted nothing more right at this moment then to run to him and have him enfold her in his dark muscular arms.

She closed her eyes against the tears that filled them. Chandler wanted nothing more than to punish her. He had even admitted that Nadine had consoled him when she had run away. There was no room whatsoever for doubt that Chandler, then and now, was having an affair with Nadine Harris. He had admitted it, and Nadine had confirmed it.

And that fact alone saved her pride. She wouldn't *let* Chandler make love to her, much less ask him to. Rolling over on her side again, she swallowed a betraying sob and brushed at a bold tear as Chandler quietly entered the bedroom and closed the door.

Gently easing himself down onto the bed, he slipped beneath the silk sheet and moved close to Callie. She could hear his irregular breathing in the silence of the room, but she lay very still, daring another tear to fall from her eyes. She felt Chandler's hand on the curve of her hip, and she pretended that it didn't burn through to her very soul, filling her with an even deeper need for him. She heard him sigh deeply as he turned away from her. For a long time she breathed evenly, simulating sleep, and after an eternity, she finally did sleep.

Chandler and Callie were like strangers the next morning as they dressed for the trip to San Francisco. "Take a sweater," he advised. "I told you that when you went to meet my parents, and you didn't listen then. The weather is notoriously changable, but more than two or three very warm days in a row invariably mean that the fog will come in and cool things off. At any rate, summer or winter, the temperature rarely dips below forty degrees or above seventy. Pack accordingly this time."

Callie nodded. "I will."

"Take a couple of special dresses for dining out."

Callie regarded him intently. "I don't think we'll have much time for that sort of thing, Chandler."

His eyes were unfathomable when they met hers. "We won't spend all our time at the hospital." Turning away from her, he began to fill his big brown leather suitcase. Callie fought down the memory of the last time she had seen that suitcase, but she felt her stomach tense all the same.

When the car was loaded with their luggage and a few odds and ends, including some bottles of wine for Chandler's parents, they settled in for the trip. They took Highway 101, and despite the tension that filled the car, Callie marveled at the beautiful scenery along the way. Although they were going to the city for an unhappy occasion, Callie felt an eagerness building within her. She and Chandler hadn't seen much of San Francisco when she had met his parents. Their schedule had been so hectic with the upcoming marriage that they had spent very little time there. She had wanted to honeymoon there, but then Chandler offered to take her to the Bahamas on a cruise ship, and she had liked that idea better. They hadn't gone back to San Francisco in the year they were married because the elder Matthews only spent part of the year there, and Chandler hadn't been able to work his schedule to match theirs.

Callie's thoughts filled with Logan; he was being flown to the city, and she wondered if he had already arrived. She had wanted to call him this morning before she and Chandler left, but had been afraid of disturbing him.

"Want to stop for some coffee?" Chandler asked, breaking into her meditation.

"Yes, that sounds good."

They parked in front of a quaint little restaurant in Morgan Hill, and Callie felt some of the tension drain from her when she had relaxed for a while. The stop had obviously been good for Chandler, too, for when they continued their journey, he began to talk about the number of wineries in California. Callie listened quietly, determined not to make him angry again if she could help it.

As the ribbon of highway unfurled before them, she felt a small stirring of excitement, and when they reached San Francisco, her excitement was full blown. She knew something about the city, and she had had some intimate glimpses from Chandler, who had been born and raised there. Regardless of his desire to live in a less hectic environment, he insisted that no city on the face of the earth was more fascinating than San Francisco. He compared it to a proud, polished woman, and he was particularly annoyed when people referred to it as "Frisco."

Callie sensed Chandler's excitement about the city, and she was pleased when he began to talk about the changes that had taken place since his childhood and pointed out landmarks as they made their way toward his parents' home. Some of the hostility he had shown toward her earlier was gone, and Callie began to enjoy the conversation. When they wound their way around some of the more than forty hills that make up the city, Callie sucked in her breath. The views were magnificent. The fog was just burning off, and while some spots were still covered in the white mist, just over the next hill the sun sparkled brightly. Amazed at the driving skill it took to maneuver the hills, Callie watched as Chandler took his foot off the accelerator at precisely the right moment before topping the rise, thus avoiding shooting wildly over the top or stalling and rolling back downhill. She had never driven here, and she wasn't eager to attempt it.

She smiled, remembering the time they had come here

before: she had been so intimidated at the thought of meeting Chandler's parents, with their money and their sophistication. He had phoned ahead to let them know he was bringing his future bride to meet them, and he had assured Callie that they were thrilled at the prospect. That had only made her more apprehensive, but Mr. and Mrs. Matthews had been wonderful after all. Callie had felt at ease the moment she stepped inside their home.

The smile faded from her lips. Even though Mr. and Mrs. Matthews had been friendly at the reunion party, she didn't know how they would react now that they weren't in the restricting presence of others. She laced her fingers together as she looked out the window at the houses marching up the colorful hillsides.

Chandler made his way up and down hills and the winding streets to an old restored Victorian house, a true San Francisco classic. Callie felt a small thrill course through her veins in spite of her anxiety. She had forgotten how beautiful the house was and how fascinated she had been when Mrs. Matthews had shown her through every foot of it. She gazed up in wonder at the ornate, two-story home, then at the curving stairwell leading to the front door and the underground garage. This was the kind of Victorian house Callie had always loved, and even though she had contentedly settled for Aunt Caroline's old farmhouse, this was her dream house.

To her, the ornamentation and decoration were not at all ostentatious, as some believed. The style was based on a building tradition that began long before the ancient Greeks, and though Callie thought many contemporary styles were magnificent, something about the soaring chimneys, tall narrow windows, oriels and bays, and incised ornaments captured her heart. She thought of the people who lived in such homes as warm and loving, for they obviously cared about tradition and good craftsmanship.

Chandler parked the car in the garage, and Callie drew a deep breath as he came around to her side and opened the door. When he held out his hand to her, she was annoyed that her heart beat faster at his slightest touch. Standing on the sidewalk, she watched as he opened the trunk and took out their suitcases. She was very pleased that Chandler was taking two weeks from his business so that she could spend the time with Logan. The viticulturist, Wesley Joseph, had agreed to take over the tours for the two weeks and to help Roy around the plant. He had laughingly announced that the change of pace would be a treat for him as well as for the tour guests. Chandler had been grateful: the season was picking up momentum, and this was the only time he could spare from the winemaking before the harvest, which was just around the corner.

Carrying the assorted articles Chandler had handed her, Callie kept up with his long strides as he easily balanced their luggage. She smiled with genuine delight as they stepped under the curved archway leading to the front doors, and she gazed lovingly at the beautiful stained-glass panels that comprised the top half of the doors. Her joy turned to apprehension when Chandler set down the suitcases and pulled a key from his pocket to unlock the door.

"Anyone home?" he called out as he ushered Callie inside. "Jiang?"

A tiny, wizened old Chinese woman appeared from nowhere; she bowed politely as she approached Chandler. "Ah, Master Chandler. How good it is to see you," she murmured in a tinkling little voice. "I have lunch prepared."

"Good." Chandler wrapped his arm around the tiny little woman, towering over her delicate frame. "Jiang, you remember my wife, Callie."

"Ah, yes," she murmured, bowing in Callie's direction, her hands hidden in the pockets of her brilliantly flowered

Chinese pajamas. Automatically, Callie bowed in return. She glanced at Chandler, knowing that he would be amused that she couldn't seem to stop bowing to the servants. A smile twitched on his lips, but he didn't comment.

"I'll put the suitcases in my old room, Jiang. Callie, go ahead and sit down in the dining room. I'll be along in a minute."

A frown marred Callie's forehead; she would have preferred that Chandler go in with her to see his parents. She was surprised that they hadn't come to the door, and she wondered if they intended to ignore her arrival. Glancing briefly at the smooth gold of a saber-legged Greek couch that graced the hallway, she followed Jiang to the lavish dining room. She remembered its splendor from her previous visit, but she was too nervous to appreciate it at the moment. She tried to compose herself internally and put a smile on her lips as she prepared to meet the elder Matthews, but to her surprise, they weren't seated at the elegant, curved-legged table, which was set for only two.

Looking at the servant, Callie asked, "Aren't Mr. and Mrs. Matthews joining us?"

Jiang shook her head, but said nothing. Puzzled, Callie sat down on a lyre-back chair with scroll arms and saber legs. She gazed around the beautifully appointed room as she waited for Chandler.

Moments later, he sauntered in and sat down across from her. "Are you hungry?" he asked.

"Yes," she replied, her eyes meeting his. "Chandler, are your parents home?" she blurted.

She was sure she saw a sparkle in his blue eyes. "They're in Tahiti for a month. They wanted to leave us alone for our 'second honeymoon.' "

Callie felt a surge of indignation rise inside. "Why didn't you tell me?" she demanded.

He raised his eyebrows, his blue eyes still holding her

fiery brown ones. "Why, Callie? What difference would it make?"

"I—you—" Callie gripped her hands tightly in her lap. What difference would it make? Had she thought to use Chandler's parents as a shield to make herself less vulnerable with him?

"Well?" he prompted.

Callie looked away from him to study a tall china closet. "None," she admitted at last, looking at him from beneath lowered eyelashes. "But you could have told me that they wouldn't be here."

"Why? You would have come regardless, with Logan here in the hospital."

"Yes, of course," she agreed. "It's just—oh, it doesn't matter."

"Just what?"

"I would have been less apprehensive about coming here."

A taunting smile slowly crept over his beautiful lips and his eyes gleamed mischievously. "Then you're looking forward to being completely alone with me? Jiang doesn't live in, you know, and the other servants have been given the month off."

"Yes, I know she doesn't live here," Callie said, feeling herself grow flustered. "But no, I didn't mean—oh, let's eat," she cried frustratedly. She didn't know what she meant. Why was he always able to make her spin in circles? She couldn't think logically when Chandler confused her so thoroughly like that. She certainly hadn't expected to be completely alone with him. Not that it mattered, she told herself, but the time they shared was less tense, less awkward with the distracting presence of others. Their situation was no different, of course. She had no intention of automatically falling into his arms and making love just because she was here in romantic San Francisco in this dream house, entirely alone with the man she had longed for for four years. She smiled at her own thoughts. She need have no fear; Chandler wasn't going to approach her again, she was sure. And she certainly wasn't going to make herself available to him. Why would she be fool enough to humiliate herself, no matter how desirable she still found him to be, or how legal their union was? Why should she spend one bittersweet year in his arms, as though Nadine didn't exist, then pack her suitcase and conveniently vanish again like a thief in the night? Besides, there *was* Nadine to contend with. She *was* still very much part of Chandler's life. No, she told herself, there was no danger being here in the Matthews home alone with him. So why was her silly heart racing so fast and her foolish mind filled with such speculation?

She was glad when Jiang came back with a bowl of rice and thin slices of beef in a rich sauce. Picking up her fork, she began to eat.

When they had finished the meal, Callie told Chandler she wanted to phone Logan. He suggested that they unpack first and then drive to the hospital, assuring her that Logan was probably still tied up with tests and forms. Agreeing, Callie followed Chandler to his room.

Callie's gaze fell immediately on the Renaissance revival-style bed, with its towering headboard topped with crests and the rich gold spread that flowed to the floor. Quickly glancing away, she noted the Duncan Phyfe window bench decorated with a gold leaf; the tall, heavy-looking French Empire chest; and the Belter chair with its smooth gold seat and carved wood back. Like the rest of the house, the room spoke of splendor and elegance. She blushed, recalling the last time she had seen this room and how she had dreamed of sharing the magnificent bed with Chandler. The time still hadn't come when she could fulfill that girlish dream.

Chandler placed their suitcases on his bed, and, as he opened his, Callie fought down the urge to ask why she couldn't have her own room here. They had already gone through that, but here, alone in this house, they had no need to keep up any pretenses. Still, she knew that Chandler intended that she share his room and his bed, and she was already upset over Logan's upcoming surgery: she couldn't cope with fighting with her husband now. She smiled to herself. Did he think that teasing her with his nearness would finally induce her to come to him, seeking his loving? The smile vanished as quickly as it had appeared. The truth was that she did find it hard to lie beside him in the same bed and not be held in those strong arms or kissed by those beautiful lips or to press her body to his . . . She flipped back the lock on her suitcase and began to take her dresses out.

It was midafternoon when they reached the hospital. Logan had been given a large, airy private room. He was in good spirits and filled with boyish enthusiasm at seeing them.

"Well, hello," he called out. "Come on in." He motioned excitedly with his hand. "How was your trip up?"

"Fine. Just fine," Callie replied cheerfully. "And how was yours? That's the important question." Going to his bedside, she took his hand.

"Smooth as glass," he said, patting her hand.

"How do you feel?" Chandler asked.

"Pretty good. I really feel pretty good," Logan responded, a slight smile on his lips. "Maybe a little tired, but not sick. Now, Chandler, about that copper mine of mine—"

Callie smiled as Logan launched into a long monologue about his copper mine and how it could be profitable if only a little money were invested in it. Chandler had truly given him a new lease on life, and Callie was amazed at his renewed enthusiasm. Her husband's talk about the possibility of reopening the copper mine had done more than even the heart surgery could do to restore his zest for life. Logan had a vitality Callie hadn't seen in many long months.

A twinge of fear shot through her as she listened to Logan speak about the future. What if he didn't survive the surgery? She knew it was always risky. Tears glistened in her eyes as she gazed down at him, watching him talk so happily about his darned copper mine. She was so fond of him and she would miss him dreadfully if something should go wrong. Before she could turn away, he squeezed her hand.

"Callie, I'm going to be just fine. You'll see."

Ashamed that he had seen her weakness, she blinked back the tears. She didn't want him to know how worried she was. "Of course you're going to be fine," she said, smiling determinedly. "I just want this all to be over so you can get on with your life—and that fool copper mine." She laughed lightly, but she wasn't able to interject any merriment into it.

"Now, don't you worry," he said firmly. "The surgery's set up for tomorrow, and I'm going to come through it with flying colors. And, honey"—he patted her hand roughly and then extended his hand to Chandler—"I feel so much better about the whole thing now that I know you don't have to put up with me all alone." He looked at Chandler. "I want to thank you for coming to Callie at this bad time in both our lives. I deeply appreciate it."

Chandler grasped his hand warmly and shook it. "I love Callie," he said with such earnestness that she looked at him in surprise. He sounded so convincing—even to her. "I want to see her through all the rough times in her life, and I want to make them easier." He wrapped an arm around her and pulled her to his side.

Callie felt all fluttery and breathless as she stood there, crushed against the hard, warm length of him. She was sure he knew the effect he had on her, and he used every opportunity to stir up her emotions.

"What time is your operation, Logan?" she asked to ease the tension she was experiencing. Managing to step away from Chandler's grasp, she moved closer to Logan's bed.

"Not until eleven. I understand business is booming here."

Chandler smiled. "I'm sure it is, but you may rest assured that you'll get the best treatment here."

Logan smiled. "Yes, I suppose so." His pale face became serious. "I know I have you to thank for being here, Chandler, and I want you to know I'm forever in your debt."

Chandler brushed aside Logan's seriousness. "Think nothing of it. It's not important. I'm just looking out for future business prospects," he teased. "I might get rich off that copper mine of yours."

Callie swallowed a surge of anger. Not important, he had said so carelessly. She was paying for Logan's surgery with a year of her life, and Chandler had dismissed it as not important. She glanced at him swiftly, but he wasn't looking at her. He was asking Logan if the nurses were pretty.

The two men were laughing when the doctor came into the room. He spoke briefly with the three of them, explaining the procedure he would use, and telling them that the bypass usually took several hours. Callie tried not to betray her anxiety in front of Logan, but she had several questions she needed to be reassured on. The doctor was very kind, and he talked with them until they had exhausted their questions. When he left, Callie kissed Logan on the cheek and she and Chandler left, too.

Chandler's attitude had provoked Callie, but when he suggested a brief sightseeing tour, she was grateful to have something to occupy her mind besides Logan's upcoming surgery. She was more concerned about him than she could ever explain to Chandler. Gazing up at her husband as she walked by his side, it suddenly occurred to her to wonder if he would still demand a year of her life if Logan died. She looked down at her hands, which were clasped prayerlike in front of her. She couldn't possibly endure it if he did.

CHAPTER EIGHT

Chandler drove to Union Street, and Callie couldn't hide the glow she felt when he parked the car and led her to the replica of a Victorian shopping sector. The six blocks, complete with sidewalk gaslights, wrought-iron fences, and Victorian facades, enchanted her. It was almost like stepping into a fairyland, and she took infinite delight in losing herself in the fantasy—exploring the shops and going into half-hidden passages that led into flower-filled courtyards with small fountains between the buildings.

Callie began to unwind a little as she and Chandler strolled along the streets and browsed in the quaint shops, looking at beautiful antiques and fascinating handicrafts. They discussed various objects and Chandler talked about the value of some pieces, the prices of which staggered Callie. She couldn't help but think how much like a loving couple she and Chandler must appear to passersby, and it made her heart ache to know that the image wasn't true. She fought to suppress the unhappy thoughts that were surfacing; she didn't want to spoil the day by dwelling on them. This was one of the rare times since her return that she and Chandler had enjoyed their time together, and she treasured each moment.

When they rummaged through the many books in a bookshop, Callie was thrilled to discover an old and rare copy of a favorite classic, and though she protested that the price was outrageous, Chandler insisted on purchasing it for her. She was too excited about the discovery to refuse to accept it, but she wished he had not paid for it.

By the time they gave up their shopping spree, it had begun to grow dark. Callie had bought a few items, but nothing of significance other than the rare book. She was very pleased with the outing and growing a bit weary when Chandler suggested a sandwich and coffee at one of the numerous restaurants and delicatessens they had passed.

When Callie responded enthusiastically, Chandler added, "We'll eat in one of San Francisco's better-known restaurants tomorrow night. This city has the best and most varied restaurants in the world, and I'm not making an idle boast."

"I'm sure you're not," she said with a smile. He was so serious that she didn't dare refute his statement, and she wondered why he had ever moved away from the city, since he obviously loved every inch of it. When they had been seated at an intimate table, Callie ordered a bacon and avocado sandwich with bean sprouts and Chandler ordered a steak sandwich.

"Want to try some steam beer?" he asked, smiling a little mischievously.

"Do they really serve it here in San Francisco?" she asked incredulously. She recalled reading about steam beer in a novel about San Francisco in the late eighteen-hundreds.

"Of course they do. It's a San Francisco specialty, but you probably won't like it. I'll tell you what—you order coffee, and you can take a sip of my beer to see if you want a glass of your own."

"All right."

When the food and beverages arrived, Callie was indeed glad that she hadn't ordered the steam beer. It was much too strong for her taste, but Chandler insisted that the robust flavor was delicious.

It was quite late when they finally returned to the house. Callie curled up on the scarlet English Regency sofa while Chandler put a record on the old-fashioned hand-cranked Victrola. The music was soft and dreamy and Callie found her head nodding as she listened to the soothing sound. She tried to keep her eyes open, and she was vaguely aware of Chandler pouring himself a scotch on the rocks, but she couldn't even seem to find her voice to refuse a drink herself when he offered. Her eyelids were very, very heavy, and soon she could fight sleep no longer. Giving in to the atmosphere and her tiredness, she sighed softly as she closed her eyes and fell into a dreamless sleep.

Callie awakened the next morning with a start. Rolling over on her side, she found Chandler propped up against the bed pillows, watching her.

"Good morning, sleepyhead," he said with a grin. "Did you sleep well?"

"I don't even remember going to bed," she murmured, looking around her.

"You didn't," he drawled. "I carried you up here and put you to bed."

Callie glanced down at her body, seeing that she was dressed in her panties and bra. "Oh," she said distractedly. "I'm sorry I put you to so much trouble."

"No trouble," he said. "I didn't put you into a nightgown because you were sleeping so peacefully, I didn't want to wake you. Besides, you were cuddly and warm and loving. I didn't want to shatter the spell."

"I was?" she questioned hesitantly, hoping that in her sleep she hadn't done what she had tried so desperately to keep from doing in her waking hours. "What did I—do?"

"You didn't do anything, my dear—unfortunately—but curl up in my arms and sleep."

"I see." Reaching for her robe, which was draped on the corner of the footboard, she slid her arms into it and stood up. She didn't want him to see how relieved she was that she hadn't made a fool of herself over him.

"What time is it?" she asked abruptly. "We're not late, are we?" She had been so saturated with sleep, and so flustered at finding herself in bed with her husband, that she had actually forgotten that Logan's operation was today.

"It's a little after eight. We have plenty of time."

"I'll fix breakfast," she said hurriedly, walking swiftly from the room. She didn't wait for Chandler to reply. She had noticed that he was clad in only his pajama bottoms, and she wanted to leave before she found herself cuddling up to him again. She felt the color rush to her cheeks as she remembered what he had said. Well, it could have been worse. After all, she hadn't let him know how much she really did want him to make love to her.

Hunting through the pots and pans in the unfamiliar kitchen, she found an omelette pan at last. She combined diced green peppers, ham, and onions, and mixed them with eggs and had the omelette cooking by the time Chandler came down, dressed in slate gray slacks and a teal blue shirt.

"Smells good," he commented, grinning at her. Callie didn't know why she felt her breath catch in her throat at the sight of him. The scene seemed so intimate to her: she in her robe, and Chandler looking so handsome as he waited for her to prepare his breakfast. It suddenly occurred to her that she had never cooked for him. What was an ordinary part of being married for most people took on some special significance for her since she had never done it before.

"Shall I make the coffee?" Chandler asked.

Callie turned away from the stove to smile at him. "Sure, if you want to," she said lightly.

Chandler came up behind her, and she quickly turned back to the omelette, taking the lid off the pan to see how the eggs were cooking. For a moment, she almost expected Chandler to wrap his arms around her waist and pull her to him, but he walked over to the counter and began to make the coffee. The kitchen soon filled with the rich aroma of coffee brewing.

Callie set the table with delicate flowered china plates, and then served the omelette. As she was buttering the toast, Chandler poured two cups of coffee and then joined her at the table. The blinds were open, and Callie gazed out at the orange trees flanking the stone patio. The sun was just breaking through the morning mist, and despite her anxiety over Logan's surgery, she felt as if she could sit at the table with her husband in this house forever. A warm contentment flowed through her, and she knew it was unreasonable to feel so good today. Nothing at all had changed between her and Chandler, and yet she felt special and cared for this morning. She glanced at him and when she found him gazing at her, she gave him a shy smile. She knew how dangerous it was to let her guard down around him, but she had no defense in her now.

"The omelette is delicious," he told her. "I didn't know you could cook."

Callie laughed spontaneously, and the happy sound filled the room. "I've fooled you," she confessed. "I can't really cook anything but eggs and baked potatoes."

He chuckled, his blue eyes glittering brightly. "Well, I've tried the eggs. When will I sample the baked potatoes?"

"I don't want to exhaust my talents," she said. "The potatoes will have to wait."

"How have you and Logan managed without a cook?"

Her warm smile faded at the mention of Logan's name. "He did the cooking." She looked at Chandler intently. "Perhaps I should get dressed and get over to the hospital now, Chandler. I want to spend some time with him before he goes into surgery."

He nodded, and they finished their breakfast in silence. Callie was dressed in less than half an hour, and they were on their way. Chandler smiled at her when they reached the front steps of the building, and Callie distractedly returned the smile.

"He's going to be fine," he told her, and to her surprise, he bent over and kissed her lightly on the nose.

"Yes, of course he is," she responded with more confidence than she felt as they went inside.

Logan was talking gaily to a nurse when they went into his room, but Callie could tell that he was nervous. He was joking about getting well so that he could get rich from his copper mine, and Callie and Chandler were just in time to hear him offer the nurse some of his riches if she would run away with him today. He looked up sheepishly when he realized that they had overheard him, but he grinned boyishly as he saw their smiles.

"Isn't that right, Chandler?" he called across the room. "Aren't we going to make a bundle from my copper mine?"

"You can bet on it," Chandler confirmed confidently.

"Didn't I tell you so?" Logan asked the nurse. "This is my partner."

Callie laughed lightly, some of the tension draining away because of Logan's optimism. This warm, enthusiastic, flirty man was a Logan she had never known. He had been an unhappy, defeated man when she arrived in Montana, and she hadn't really known him before. She understood all too well now how he could have easily influenced her mother to follow him to Montana with his fever and his big dream. Glancing at Chandler surreptitiously, Callie wondered if there were a side to her husband that she hadn't yet seen—but, then, she had lived with him. She had seen more than enough of his chameleon changes.

Logan held out his hand, and she took it. "Well, you seem fit as a fiddle this morning."

He smiled. "Things are looking up for us, aren't they? Isn't it great that you made up your mind to come back to California?"

She smiled gently at him. "Yes, it is."

"You two will have to leave the room now," the nurse said. "I've got to prepare Mr. Bartholomew for surgery."

Putting an arm around Callie's waist, Chandler guided her back out into the hall. "Now that you've seen him, do you feel better?"

"I can't believe the change in him," she admitted. "I've never seen him like this, and we owe it all to you."

"Not all of it," Chandler said modestly. "But I'm glad I could be of some help. Callie . . ."

She gazed up into his eyes when he spoke her name so seriously. "Yes?"

He smiled vaguely. "Nothing. It can wait."

His comment shook her self-control, and she let a small sigh escape her lips. What had he wanted to say? Would it have been important? Was it about the two of them? It could have been any number of things, and speculating would be futile. She looked back at the door when the nurse came out.

"You can go back in now, but it won't be long until he's wheeled to surgery."

They returned to the room, and it was only a short time later that a groggy Logan was wheeled out. Callie watched him until he had disappeared down the hall, and apprehension flooded through her with renewed vigor. She could only wait and pray that he would pull through, and it was the waiting that was the hardest.

"Why don't we leave for a while?" Chandler suggested.

"Oh, I couldn't," she said quickly. "I want to be here if—if—"

"If what?" he asked softly. "The doctor said the surgery would take most of the day. If you stay here, you'll just spend the time worrying. Let's get away for a few hours. We'll be back in plenty of time before the surgery is over."

She shook her head, even though she knew there was wisdom in what he was saying.

"Callie, you won't accomplish a thing sitting here, wringing your hands. You need to get away for a while. Let's go to Chinatown and wander through the shops. It will take your mind off Logan for a little bit."

She felt tension coiled like a snake in the pit of her stomach. Chandler was so kind and considerate, and though she had no illusions about the reasons for his concern, she was grateful that they were experiencing a truce at this critical time for Logan. She couldn't do anything to help her stepfather now, and she was appreciative that Chandler was making such an effort to help her through this time. Chinatown would be distracting, and it was one of those places she had always wanted to see. "All right," she finally said.

She took long, slow breaths of air, trying to achieve some measure of calm as Chandler worked his way through the congested traffic to Grant Avenue. By the time he found a parking space and carefully turned the car wheels into the curb, she had managed to isolate her frantic thoughts about Logan and was concentrating on the area. They had to walk some distance to their destination, but it was well worth it. After they had gone through a two-level archway guarded by a fierce, symbolic dragon, they entered an ancient Chinese style world of pagodas, colored lanterns, stone lions, snakes, elephants, and gently smiling Buddhas. Callie was enchanted with the Oriental flavor and sights, not to mention the smell of tangy spices and tempting delicacies and the sound of half a dozen Chinese dialects. The gaily colored scheme of reds, greens, and golds lifted her sagging spirits considerably.

Shops were brimful of exciting and exotic displays of firecrackers, joss sticks, fans, figurines, and the much more elegant wares of ivory, teak, and silk. Market windows were filled with eels and octopuses, dried fish and snails, and rows of roast ducks. Vegetable stands offered long, slender string beans, green peas, bean sprouts, and lichee nuts. Callie gazed up at the glass wind chimes hanging in the doorway of a shop, their airy tinkle carried by a slight breeze.

Lured by the musical sound, she and Chandler went into the shop. There were dozens of items that caught Callie's eyes: ivory combs, delicate paintings done on silk, exquisitely made slippers, and the most beautiful silk robes and dresses she had ever seen. Seeing her gaze at a silk evening wrap, Chandler insisted that she try it on. Callie fingered the smooth silk of the gold brocade coat, then shook her head.

"No. It's much too expensive, and besides, I have nowhere to wear it."

"You can wear it to dinner tonight," Chandler told her.

Callie glanced at him, wary of their new found camaraderie. Was it only because they were here in San Francisco, away from Nadine, that Chandler gave her all his attention and consideration? Was it because he felt sorry for her since Logan was having surgery? Was it both? Or, more importantly, was it something else? Dare she be so foolish as to believe that they were reestablishing a relationship? She didn't want to be hurt again, and she didn't want to keep taking gifts from him. Looking down at her blue slacks and matching top, she said lightly, "Nope, it won't go."

Chandler chuckled. "That outfit won't go for dinner, either. You'll have to change. The coat will go with your white dress well. Try it on."

Embarrassed that she had thought the pants outfit would be adequate dress for dinner, she gazed at Chandler. He must really have a special place in mind. She looked at the evening coat again. What could it hurt to try it on? Slipping out of her blue jacket top, she let the smiling Chinese clerk help her into the coat. It was her size, and she had never felt as well-dressed as she did when she stared into the three-way mirror. The gold color set off her honey hair, and the delicately raised peonies in shades of rust and rose looked rich against their lush background. She admired the Chinese style collar and cuffs and the charming frog buttons, and she fell in love with the coat.

"It's quite lovely on you," Chandler commented.

Yes, it was, she told herself, but she couldn't let him give her such an an expensive gift. She shrugged lightly, pretending disinterest. "It is lovely, but I really don't think I want it."

Chandler was clearly disappointed with her reply, but he didn't say anything. The clerk made a small moue. "It is made for you," she insisted. "You should buy."

Callie truly did want it, but, of course, it was a silly longing. She really wouldn't get much wear out of it. "No, thank you," she said firmly, slipping out of the coat.

"You don't like?" the clerk persisted.

"Yes, it's quite beautiful, but it's just too extravagant for me."

"I've never known that to be a valid excuse for any woman," Chandler drawled, obviously annoyed that she wouldn't let him buy it for her.

The comment irritated Callie. "And you've certainly known a lot of women, haven't you?" she asked, a vision of Nadine prominent in her mind.

He frowned at her. "Not nearly as many as you apparently would like to think, Callie."

"It's not what I *like* to think," she retorted. Seeing the clerk's surprised expression, and realizing what a shrew she sounded like, Callie bit her tongue. "I really don't want it, thank you." She quickly handed the coat back to the woman and turned to Chandler. "I'm ready to leave if you are."

When they were out on the street, she felt she must apologize to him for her behavior. It wasn't his fault that she was still in love with him and doubted his every gesture because of his ties with Nadine. He was trying hard today to make things easier for her, and she had no right to be rude. "I'm sorry I spoke so sharply," she murmured.

"You should be," he said tiredly, but without rancor. Taking her arm, he led her into another shop with a charming array of hairbrushes. When her eyes lit up, he said gently, "Buy one. They aren't extravagant, and it will perk you up."

Callie didn't want to refuse him again so soon, and they truly were lovely. She really couldn't resist, and at last she settled on a brush with a painting of an arched bridge over cool, rippling blue water on the back. After they had made the purchase, they decided to have lunch in a small deli. There were only a few tables and chairs in the room, but a huge display case was piled high with tempting selections. Finding a table in an isolated corner, Chandler and Callie ordered tea, ginger beef, rice, and spring rolls. She soon found that the warm, mild tea had a soothing effect on her jangled nerves, and though Logan was ever in her mind, she was able to unwind a little.

Chandler was making light conversation, and Callie found her heart filling with a curious mixture of love and resentment: love because there was no way she could help but love him, especially now, when he was being so concerned and so patient, and resentment, because this was the way their marriage should always have been. It had taken Logan's problem to bring them back to some semblance of the closeness they had once shared. Her mind flooded with a hundred memories of the love they had shared that first summer, and the plans they had made. A gentle smile curved her lips.

Reaching out, Chandler took her hand in his. "What's amusing?"

She wasn't aware that he had seen her smile. "Nothing much," she murmured, realizing that nothing much was amusing now. The summer had ended a long, long time ago, and with it her dreams for the future.

He released her hand as the waiter approached with plates laden with delicious-looking food, and Callie felt a sense of loss at Chandler's withdrawal.

The food was rich and tasty, and they enjoyed a surprisingly relaxed meal. When they had finished, they each were served a fortune cookie. "Yours first," Chandler said with a smile.

Callie broke the crisp cookie in half and pulled out her fortune. "Happiness is yours for the taking," she read aloud.

Chandler's eyes met hers levelly. "And it is, Callie."

She was unable to hold his gaze. "Read yours," she said, looking at the cookie in his hand.

Breaking it, Chandler held up the tiny piece of paper. "Never doubt a loved one," he read. His brows met in a heavy line. "Well, that's mine, for what it's worth."

At least his was more accurate than hers, she thought wryly. "Can we go now?" she asked, wanting to change the subject.

Chandler slid his chair back, suddenly seeming as eager as she to go back to the hospital.

They had to wait in the lobby for some time before the doctor came out to talk with them. Callie realized she had been holding her breath when it hissed through her softly parted lips in a sigh of relief as she learned that Logan had come through the surgery quite well. While stressing that he wasn't totally out of danger, the doctor told them that he expected a full recovery and that Logan should soon be able to resume his normal way of life.

"When can I see him?" Callie asked, her voice strained.

"He's still quite groggy, and he will probably sleep for some time. If there's any change, you will be notified." He smiled reassuringly at her. "Why don't you come back in the morning and I'll let you visit with him for a few minutes. He's in intensive care."

"Thank you." There was nothing more they could do, so she and Chandler returned to the house.

Chandler suggested that she take a nap before dinner, and she was more than willing. Fatigued and tense, she curled up on the bed in his bedroom, and in minutes, she had fallen into a restless sleep.

As he had promised, Chandler took Callie to one of San Francisco's more elegant French restaurants for dinner that night. The dining room was red-flocked and decorated with rich mahogany tables and red velvet furnishings.

Callie smiled at Chandler as a very proper waiter came for their order. "What do you suggest?" she asked, studying the menu uncertainly.

"I'm going to have *cressonnière froid,* a cold watercress soup, and *canard aux figues,* duckling cooked with figs. I find it superb and I think you will think so, too."

"Sounds wonderful," she said. "I'll try it."

Chandler winked at her. "This isn't good for business, but I'll order a French wine to complement the French food."

She laughed when he placed the order quickly, as though betraying the California wine industry.

They fell into easy conversation as they ate, and Callie began to relax, even though she knew Logan still wasn't tightly. She could feel her thin nightgown absorbing water from his body, and she realized that he must have just gotten out of the shower in the other bathroom. She didn't care how wet she got; there wasn't another place in the entire world she wanted to be at this moment, and she took great comfort in her husband's touch. Finally her tears began to abate and Chandler raised her head again.

His fingers stroked her throat. "Are you all right now?" he asked in a deep voice, his blue eyes searching her misty brown ones.

She nodded solemnly, and she saw Chandler's full lips descend to meet hers. Arching her neck, she parted her lips to claim his. His tongue slipped into her mouth to explore its softness. Her arms went around his neck and she pulled him closer to her. He let go of the towel he had been wearing, then slipped her nightgown over her head. She felt herself tremble as he eased her down on her back, his body pressing down on her gently as he found her lips again in a hungry, tantalizing kiss. Raising his head, he looked deep into her eyes as he trailed a fingertip down her body and his hand found the tender skin inside her leg to stroke it provocatively.

Callie moaned softly as Chandler's lips found the taut button of her breast. Wrapping her arms around his back, her fingers spreading out in circles to feel the definition of his muscles, she gloried in the feel of him. She wanted him to take her to the ragged edges of ecstasy now; she couldn't bear it if he were only teasing her.

His tongue traced the outline of her breast, then traveled down to her belly. He scattered kisses and love bites over the sensitive skin as his hands gently massaged her breasts, and at last his lips found hers again and his long body arched over hers. In seconds she knew that he had no intention of teasing or humiliating her, as his hands slipped under her bottom to raise her hips to meet his and he claimed her passionately.

completely out of danger and she couldn't keep him out of her thoughts. They lingered over the meal, and a rich coffee and the dessert that followed. Callie was quite surprised to discover how late it was when they left the restaurant.

Not until they were back in the Matthews house and Callie had bathed and dressed for bed did she realize how frightened she had been for Logan. A deep depression settled over her as she brushed her hair with her new hairbrush. Placing the brush on the vanity without completing her hundred strokes, she went to the bed and slipped under the silk sheet. Unexpectedly, she burst into tears, the sudden sobs causing her slender body to shake.

Wearing only a towel, Chandler came striding into the room, his face moist from a fresh shave. When he reached the bed, he pulled her into his arms. "What's the matter, Callie? Have you had a call from the hospital?"

It was several moments before she could stop crying, but she shook her head.

"Then what is it?" he demanded.

Gasping and hiccoughing, ashamed of her weakness and upsetting Chandler, Callie fought back a fresh flood of traitorous tears as she clung to Chandler's damp body. "I've been so worried, Chandler, and so much has been going on. And now I'm so relieved that the surgery is over and Logan is going to be all right." She looked up at him with tears shimmering in her big brown eyes. "I'm sorry. I'm behaving like a baby, but I can't seem to stop crying." The tears began to flow again in spite of her attempts to stop them, and Chandler tipped her head back so that he could gaze into her eyes.

"You go ahead and cry, sweetheart. You're just letting go after the intense pressure." His long fingers fanned through her hair, and he caressed her tense neck gently as she cried on his shoulder. She couldn't resist his sympathy, and, wrapping her arms around him, Callie held on

For a short time, Callie forgot all about her problems and her fears. She was a woman lost in the glory of her husband's love and that was all that mattered. Each thrust of his hips sent a tremor of ecstasy throughout her body, and her mind climbed higher and higher into the realm of fiery pleasure. And at last Callie experienced the joy she had longed for a thousand times.

For some time afterward, Callie lay very still beside her husband, hardly daring to breathe. Their love had been so wondrous, so perfect, so precious, that she didn't want to spoil it by logic or reality. She sighed softly as she turned her head to gaze at Chandler's profile in the semidarkness of the room.

She was surprised to hear the huskiness of his voice when he spoke. "Callie, I don't believe you left me because I bored you," he said quietly. "Or because you don't love me. I can't let myself believe that, the way you respond to me."

She knew how badly she had wounded him with her careless words, and she knew how devastating the blow had been, and she was ashamed. "Chandler—" she whispered, hardly daring to trust her voice. She wanted so desperately to explain the pain and the shame that had led her to make that rash statement, and yet she didn't want to admit that she knew he had cheated with Nadine.

"Shhh." He placed a finger to her lips, gently silencing her. "I don't want to drag up all the old hurts of the past, Callie. Let's not spoil the moment. We've both changed in the four years of our separation. I love you. I believe you love me. Let's put the past behind us and begin again. We're both older and, hopefully, wiser now. Logan is doing just fine. We're here in the most romantic city in the world. Let's put our mistakes in another time and have a real second honeymoon—a real new beginning."

Callie sucked in her breath. He had said that he loved her, and she really thought that he sounded as though he meant it. He had said they both had made mistakes, and it was true, of course. He had said they had changed. Dare she believe that he was referring to Nadine? Dare she believe him at all? Did he really love her? Was she fool enough to trust him again? She had done that once, and—But she loved him so deeply. Too deeply. If she threw away this chance to mend her marriage, there would be no other. She was sure of that. Could she put the past and all that had gone with it behind her? She lowered her eyes when she felt her lower lip quiver with her uncertainty.

"Chandler, I—I—"

His hand found her chin to lift it gently and he stilled her trembling lip with his thumb. "Maybe I've been the fool, Callie. It takes two to make or break a marriage," he said softly. He shrugged his broad shoulders. "I only know that we did have something solid and special once, and I want to recapture that something we shared again. Besides"—his solemn voice became lightly teasing—"I need some help at the winery. When I branch out into the copper business, I'll need a partner at the plant to keep Roy in line."

She laughed softly, and the gentle sound echoed in the large room. "I don't know as much as Roy does, and you know it." She suddenly caught his hand and held it to her lips, afraid to give in to his demands. Could he oust Nadine from his heart? From his mind? From his bed? "Oh, Chandler, I do love you," she murmured tremulously, "but I'm so afraid to try again."

"Baby," he whispered in a husky voice, "I've been burned, too. Chances not taken are opportunities thrown away. Don't throw our love away, Callie."

She propped her chin on his broad chest and looked searchingly into his moody blue eyes. "There must be no other woman but me," she said, stiffening at having to make the demand.

He gripped the hair at the nape of her neck, forcing her

lips up to his to claim them in a branding kiss. "There's never been anyone but you, Callie," he murmured hoarsely.

A bitterness surged swiftly up inside her, and for a single moment Callie felt like slapping Chandler's face and drawing away from him. Did he take her for a complete fool? He was lying already. Would he be cheating the moment they returned to the Salinas Valley? She pressed her lips into a thin line and barely kept from uttering what was on her mind. Had he meant that she was the only woman he had ever loved? Had his heart remained true to her while he gave his body to Nadine? It was terribly difficult for her to understand how men could take sex so lightly. To her the act of love was meant only for those in love, but she knew that all people didn't think in such Victorian ways as she did. She lived in the real world, and she knew that affairs were as common as smiles. She drew a deep breath and made herself look into his eyes. She would not tolerate his affair with Nadine if he truly intended to make their marriage work this time, but she couldn't toss her marriage away without trying once more.

"I mean it, Chandler," she said firmly. "I'm willing to wipe the past away and try again, but only if we both can remain faithful—heart and body. We *both* have changed, and we deserve each other's honesty and respect."

"Of course," he agreed, reaching out to stroke her cheek. "This time it will work."

She hoped with all her heart that this time it would work, but she was so afraid to believe it. She had learned a bitter lesson four years ago with this man, but truly she had changed. She would be able to cope this time, surely. She wouldn't fall apart if he did betray her faith in him. She knew all about lies and deceit and heartache. Even as she told herself those words, she doubted that they were true. Chandler would break her heart again if he continued his affair with Nadine, and her heart was so fragile and wounded already.

Chandler gathered her against his body and his full lips found hers again. Yes, she would try again. She loved her husband too much not to—regardless of the cost to her heart.

CHAPTER NINE

Callie awakened the next morning unexpectedly optimistic. Opening her eyes, she gazed around the room trying to remember what accounted for her new feelings of hope. When she looked beside her, she saw the rumpled sheets and the pillow where Chandler had lain. He had already gotten up, but not even his absence could taint the lightness of spirit she felt this morning. Stretching languidly, she relived the sweetness of last night, and she tasted the glorious promise of new life with him. Had it really happened, or had it been a dream so impossible that it was sure to vanish with the daylight? She wouldn't let it be a dream; this second chance was too precious to her. Forcing down the thoughts that told her she should proceed carefully and not too sanguinely in light of Chandler's previous behavior, she tossed the sheet aside and started to get up.

Chandler walked into the room with a tray in his hands, and Callie quickly reached for the sheet to cover herself.

"Don't hide from me, you beautiful creature," he said. "I've been too long without the sight of you."

Smiling shyly at him, she scooted back under the covers. Their closeness was too new for her to feel comfortable around him when she was nude. She glanced at the tray. "What's on there?" she asked, although the rich aroma of coffee made its own announcement. She rested against the pillows, fluffing them behind her back as she held onto the sheet with one hand.

Chandler set the tray down in the middle of the bed and climbed in on the side opposite Callie. "Breakfast, my dear, and don't complain about it. I can't cook very well myself."

Callie smiled again and tried not to keep staring at his scantily clad body. The brief pajama bottoms made him look more appealing than usual after the night of love. "As badly as I cook, I never complain about anyone else's cooking," she said lightly.

Chandler lifted a white linen napkin from the tray and Callie saw two steaming cups of fresh hot coffee, whole wheat toast brimming with blackberry preserves, and four hard-boiled eggs. "It looks wonderful," she said with great enthusiasm.

"So do you," he replied, his voice suddenly husky as he watched her intently. Reaching out a large hand, he turned her head so that his lips could claim hers. Callie's fingers wound into his hair, pulling him more closely to her as her mouth parted eagerly under the pressure of his. She couldn't seem to get enough of his touch. As he moved nearer to her, the tray tipped precariously and coffee sloshed out on the bed.

"Be careful!" she cried, pulling away from him. "You're spilling breakfast."

Chandler steadied the tray and handed her a cup of coffee. Slipping under the sheet, he moved closer to her.

Callie drank a little of the hot beverage and her eyes met his over her coffee cup as he raised his cup to his mouth. Replacing the coffee on the tray, she took a bite of a piece of toast. Chandler had been entirely too generous with the preserves, and when Callie bit down on the bread, the sweet, sticky blackberries spilled down on her chest. She looked at Chandler helplessly as the glob of preserves clung to the soft swell of one breast, visible above the sheet that covered her.

Chandler set his cup back down and took the messy toast from Callie's hand to lay it on the tray. When he had put the tray on the floor, he told her, "I'll clean you up."

A smile still playing on her lips, Callie expected him to get a wet cloth, but she found that he abruptly pulled the sheet away from her body, scooped up part of the preserves with his index finger, then tasted the gooey substance.

"Mmm," he murmured, his eyes glowing mischievously. Callie watched expectantly as he lowered his head to her breast. His tongue snaked out to lick the sticky preserves from her skin and she giggled as he looked up at her and licked her lips. His tongue moved against her skin again in a slow, languid caress, and she felt her delight turn to desire as Chandler sensually licked the firm globe until the nipple stood taut and hard under the onslaught of his tongue. He gazed up at her again and she knew her own desire was reflected in his eyes. His head lowered once more, and his mouth moved down until it trapped the nipple of first one breast and then the other, suckling gently and taking small love bites.

Callie felt a hot heat race throughout her loins as Chandler raised his head and sought her willing lips. She could still taste the rich, distinctive flavor of blackberries on his lips and her tongue searched for his to sample more of the sweetness.

She moaned softly as he pulled her down on the pillows

and stretched out over her body. "Forget about breakfast," he murmured in a husky voice. "I'm not hungry for food." His lips found hers and she pressed against him eagerly, giving no thought to tomorrow. He was much too exciting and her love for him was much too strong not to relish the times in his arms. She felt her pulse quicken with excitement as he arched against her, his questing maleness seeking the passage to desire and fulfillment. Callie gasped with pleasure when Chandler claimed her, his powerful hips stroking and thrusting against hers. She, too, forgot all about breakfast as the fire inside her grew hotter and hotter and her fever drove out all thoughts but those of passion and exquisite pleasure in this man's arms.

"Hey, lazybones, let's get dressed and go buy some breakfast," Chandler said, breaking into Callie's meditations. "All that time I spent cooking for you was wasted." He glanced down at the now cold coffee and hard toast with its black, dried out preserves, and shook his head.

Callie glanced up at him, wanting to tell him that she didn't care if she never ate again if she could lie like this in his arms forever, but she nodded and smiled.

Chandler pulled out of her arms and sat up. "I'm starving," he said. "Besides, we should get up to the hospital and visit with Logan."

Callie's expression changed at the mention of her stepfather. He reminded her of reality, and she knew there was no way she could hold on to these precious moments with Chandler. "Do you think we can spend some time with him?"

"We'll find out. We can get some breakfast along the way." He touched her forehead lightly with his lips, and, as eager as she was to see Logan, she ached to snuggle back down into Chandler's arms. She was afraid that the magic between them would vanish once they began to indulge in routine events, and she wanted to prolong the joy she had known with him last night and this morning—the joy she had been sure she would never know again. He hugged her once more, then got up.

Callie gazed at his tall, muscled form as he walked to the closet, and she hoped desperately that Chandler meant the words he had said to her last night. It would be so cruel and devastating to return to the Salinas Valley and find that his faithfulness and promises had lasted only as long as Nadine was out of his sight.

Chandler took a robe off a hanger and turned around to face her. "Come on. Get some life into that shapely body," he coaxed. "The whole world is waiting."

Seeing her reluctance to venture from the bed and mistaking it for modesty, he dragged her robe from the closet and took it to her. Mustering a smile, she murmured, "The whole world isn't waiting—only Logan. When do you think he will be well enough to leave the hospital, Chandler?"

He shrugged as he stepped into some slacks and untied the belt of his short robe. "I don't know. Two weeks—maybe three."

Callie slipped into her robe and walked toward the bathroom. "I'll be ready in five minutes," she called over her shoulder. Turning around to look at Chandler, she amended, "Make that ten."

"At least," he teased as she hurried into the bathroom.

When she had bathed and dressed in a pair of brown slacks and a white smock top, she met Chandler in the living room.

"Good. You did hurry," he said. "I know a little café where we can get a good cup of coffee, an omelette, and quick service."

The food in the small café was as good as Chandler had said, and after they had hastily eaten, they were once again on their way. Callie was suddenly desperately eager to see Logan and to know that all was well. She hurried down the corridor when they reached the hospital, walking so rapidly that Chandler had difficulty keeping up with her. When they had been admitted to his room, she quietly approached Logan's bed. He was very white and still, and her heart almost stopped beating as she gazed worriedly at his pale face. She hadn't anticipated him looking so very ill. She glanced at the nurse, who was writing something down on a chart.

"Is he awake?" she whispered in a shaky voice.

Logan's gray eyes opened and he smiled weakly at her. When she saw him nod his head, she bent down and lightly kissed his cheek.

"How are you feeling?" she whispered. It wasn't until Chandler spoke in a normal voice that she realized she was whispering. They were only allowed a few minutes with Logan, but just seeing that he was all right was a tremendous relief for Callie. And still she didn't breathe easily until she was out in the corridor. "He looked all right, didn't he?" she asked Chandler apprehensively.

"He looked just fine. He's doing very well to have gone through such a serious operation. And he's going to be better than he has been for some time. You'll see."

"I hope so," Callie murmured fervently. "I certainly hope so."

Chandler slipped an arm around her waist. "What do you want to do today?"

She knew he was trying to keep her mind off Logan, and she was pleased that he was so considerate. She shook her head. "I don't know. This is your city. What do you suggest?"

Rubbing his chin thoughtfully, Chandler looked at her with gleaming eyes. "That's not a fair question to ask me. What I suggest is going home and making love to you again; however, you really must see more of this fantastic place." His brows met in a pensive frown. "I have an idea. They have a wine museum here. Let's take a quick tour of that. You do want to know all about your husband's business, don't you?" he asked with a teasing laugh.

Callie's eyes were serious as they met the glittering blue of his. "I want to know everything about what interests you, Chandler. I want our marriage to work this time."

Chandler gave her a mock tap on the chin. "Of course it's going to work." Then he changed the topic. "Okay, the wine museum it is this morning. After that, we'll have lunch at Fisherman's Wharf. How does that sound?"

Callie tried to match his light-hearted mood, but she felt a fluttering in her heart because he had dismissed her seriousness and their marriage so easily. "That sounds grand," she agreed.

When they reached the wine museum, Callie was glad Chandler had wanted her to see it. A large, airy room that somehow produced the atmosphere and illusion of a wine cellar, it was filled with fascinating artifacts. Callie enjoyed seeing the early wine-making displays and noting the progress to present-day technology, and she was intrigued with the information on the history of grapevines, but she was most interested in the collection of drinking glasses that spanned two thousand years. She was so caught up in the museum and the little tidbits of information that Chandler added as they went along that she didn't realize the morning had faded into afternoon until Chandler mentioned Fisherman's Wharf.

"Are you ready to go now?" he asked. "A crab cocktail sounds delicious."

"Yes, it does." She discovered that she was, indeed, beginning to feel hungry, and she was eager to see the famous area.

Chandler escorted her to the car and then drove to the section along Jefferson Street right on the waterfront—Fisherman's Wharf proper. Chandler explained that the area had originally been called Meigg's Wharf. The current name came from the generations of fishermen who had sailed from there.

Thrilled with the festive atmosphere and gaiety, today Callie dared to forget her troubles and uncertainties and revel in the carefree moment. She was amazed at the number of restaurants flourishing on the street and the number of sidewalk stalls filled with steaming caldrons of fresh crab and shrimp. She and Chandler arrived just as the boats were returning for the day with their catches, and they were able to buy papercups of delicious crab cocktail. Chandler suggested that they eat as they strolled about, and Callie loved the notion.

There were lots of natives and tourists, and Callie and Chandler joined a group of people who had stopped to watch a couple of street artists perform a mime. Having throughly enjoyed the performance, they clapped heartily when the show was over, then worked their way past the many street sellers peddling beautiful jewelry and leather goods to the nearby numerous shops and galleries housed in what once had been a cannery.

Callie fell in love with the red-brick cannery and its myriad shops, restaurants, markets, sidewalk stalls, and cafés. She and Chandler wandered in and out of shops, looking at art objects, handicrafts, clothes, trinkets, and books. Callie's resistance weakened and she succumbed to Chandler's tempting gift offers; soon she had a shopping bag filled with treasures, and contented with her marvelous day, she was ready to go home. Chandler, however, had another surprise for her. Leading her out of the cannery, he took her to an old chocolate factory that had also been converted into shops. It, too, was charming, with red-brick walls and an endless supply of shops, terraces, theaters, cafés, and restaurants. When Callie finally decided she couldn't look in another shop, Chandler and she ate dinner in a sidewalk café. Then Chandler laughingly guided a happy Callie, her arms filled with packages, back to the car.

Dusk was beginning to fall as Chandler wound around the hills to a part of town Callie hadn't seen before. "Where are we going?" she asked.

"Are you willing to make one more stop?"

Callie nodded expectantly, exuberant with joy and excitement.

"An old friend, who's out of town, owns a gorgeous Victorian house in this neighborhood. I thought you might like to take a look at it before we go home. I know how enchanting you find them."

"I would love it," she said enthusiastically, forgetting all about her tired feet. She felt an almost frantic urge to make this marvelous day stretch as far as she could.

He patted her hand as it lay on the seat between them. "I thought you'd like to. Especially this particular house."

"Oh?" she asked. "Why especially this house?"

"It's really something special," he told her with a wink. "It once belonged to one of the richest men in the city. When he sold it, the next owner gave guided tours. My friend bought it some time ago. Most of the original furniture is still in it, as well as rugs and odds and ends that are quite lovely treasures. I know you will be impressed."

"I'm sure," she agreed, her excitement building at the prospect of touring such a house. When Chandler parked in front of the structure several minutes later, she wasn't disappointed. It was glorious; a cream-colored building magnificent with gables, cupolas, pillars, and incised decorations, it stood proud and stately some distance from the street. Callie gazed at the bay windows and the beautiful stained glass and her breath caught in her throat. This house was even more beautiful than the Matthews' home.

"Well, come on," Chandler coaxed unnecessarily as Callie willingly stepped from the car.

Taking her hand, Chandler produced a key and led her

inside. The parlor, done in yellows and golds, the original Victorian furniture intact and upholstered in a now seldom seen original Windsor pattern, was stunning. "Oh, Chandler, it's exquisite," Callie murmured, clasping her hands together. She stared at the lily sconces on the mantel, then her gaze traveled to the charming rosewood escritoire.

"This way," Chandler said, barely letting her recover from the awe of the parlor before he led her into the library. Here, too, the room was gorgeous. Tall rosewood bookcases lined the walls. The beveled ends provided for a series of triangular shelves and closets, many of which were filled with very old books. Luxurious rosewood sofas, upholstered in tapestry, welcomed visitors to the room and offered tempting accommodations for leisurely reading. Callie was admiring the bronze fireplace fender when Chandler called her from the room.

When he had shown her the dining room and the kitchen, he led her upstairs to the bedrooms. Callie was thrilled with the all-wood bed with a canopy in the first bedroom, and she caught her breath as she looked down at the light-tinted floral carpet that matched the bed coverlet. The home was more lovely than anything she had ever imagined. In all, Chandler showed Callie ten rooms, and they were some of the prettiest she had ever envisioned. She stared expectantly at the door of the last room in the house that she hadn't seen, wondering what other treasures could possibly be left to see. To her surprise, Chandler turned away from that room and started back down the hall.

"Aren't we going to look in that one?" Callie asked.

"Haven't you seen enough?"

She laughed softly. "I don't want to miss anything. This is all so wonderful, Chandler. Your friend is very fortunate."

"Yes," Chandler agreed. Then he dismissed the last

room with a shrug of his shoulders. "That room is nothing special. The furniture in there didn't come with the house and the room is constructed the same as the other bedrooms."

His comment piqued her curiosity. His tone had become serious, and she wondered what difference it could possibly make if she peeped inside. Although she pretended to make light of his refusal, she felt unreasonably slighted by it. "If your friend is hiding something in there, I'm sure it's none of my business," she said.

Chandler gazed at her thoughtfully for a few seconds, causing her to feel uneasy. "It isn't," he said at last.

Suddenly Callie wasn't so sure, and ugly suspicions began to rise in her. She had assumed that the friend who owned the house was a man, but she certainly had no cause to think that. It could very well be a woman. A depressing thought surged into her mind: she knew that Nadine owned property in San Francisco. Could this house possibly be Nadine's? No, she told herself vehemently. Chandler *wouldn't* bring her to Nadine's house!

As Callie followed Chandler down the stairs, the old familiar doubts crowded her mind and a depression descended more heavily over her with each step she took. "Your friend is a very lucky woman to own such a house," she ventured when they had reached the bottom. Almost holding her breath, she waited for Chandler to correct her.

To her disappointment, he nodded. "Yes, I think so. The old house is a rare prize." His eyes searched hers as he turned back to her. "Would you like something like this, Callie?"

"Yes," she answered immediately, "but I don't think there are many of these in the Salinas Valley."

Chandler laughed deeply, her remark seeming to bring him out of his pensive mood. "No," he conceded. "No, I don't think so either. Well, are you ready to return to the house? You've had a full day."

"I surely have," she agreed. Feeling unhappy because Chandler hadn't refuted her statement about a female friend owning the house, Callie walked with him out to the car. She gave the marvelous house one last lingering look as Chandler put the car in gear and drove away.

The next two weeks were filled with pleasure for Callie, and she tried to enjoy each day singularly and not let doubts about the future slip into her mind to spoil this time with Chandler. She and Chandler spent their mornings visiting with Logan, and a real friendship developed between the two men. Chandler was very interested in the copper mine and Callie surprised him with her knowledge of the operation. She had learned a great deal from Logan about copper, and her business sense and tact had been developed by dealing with disgruntled creditors and angry employees short of paychecks.

"I'm wasting your talents," Chandler commented, studying her with new interest. "You've acquired quite a business mind working in the copper field. I can use you in the wine industry."

Callie smiled; she had learned a lot, and she did love the wine industry, but she had her own ideas about a career if she were to work. "If I went into business, I would open a plant shop," she confessed.

Chandler gazed at her speculatively, then changed the subject without further comment.

As the time passed in San Francisco, Callie and Chandler did a lot of sightseeing. Their tours included Alcatraz Island, so named because of the thousands of pelicans that first inhabited the rocky area; the Coit Tower, built by Lillie Hitchcock Coit and resembling the nozzle of a firehose; the multimillion-dollar Japan center; and the beautiful Golden Gate Park.

But it was the evenings, which they spent in each other's arms, making up for the four years they had lost, that were the most precious of all. Each time Chandler took Callie in his arms, she felt more confident of his love for her, and the closeness she felt they had once shared seemed possible again.

Callie's life and future were looking most optimistic. Logan was doing amazingly well, and the doctors talked of releasing him at the end of two weeks. Chandler made arrangements to have him flown back to the valley, and Callie began to look forward to going home.

Going home. This time it sounded so good that she was almost afraid to think about it, for back home there was Nadine. She pushed her hair away from her face with an unsteady hand as the old familiar doubts haunted her. She had to trust Chandler; he had said they would start over, and that there was no woman for him but her. She had to trust in him and believe in him or go insane with the misgivings that plagued her.

Their last night in San Francisco, Chandler planned a marvelous evening at home for just the two of them. Jiang had prepared a delicious meal, then left. The table was set with fresh flowers and a single tall candle.

They had just returned from a bay cruise and were getting ready to eat when Chandler handed Callie a gift. Opening it, she found a silk Chinese lounging outfit in a deep purple berry shade. "Oh, Chandler, you shouldn't have," she murmured, holding up the pants and jacket; but she was terribly thrilled that he had.

"They're being called 'Mao suits' these days," Chandler said, feeling the material of the choengsam. "Try it on," he suggested.

Callie eagerly obeyed. Rushing from the room, she quickly changed into the outfit, slipped her feet into backless heels, and then swept her hair up on one side.

When she returned to the living room, she found Chandler thumbing through a magazine. He looked up and his eyes swept over her appreciatively. He produced another box, and Callie couldn't possibly imagine what would be in it. "Here, this is for you, too."

Lifting the lid off the unwrapped box, she found the gold coat she had so wanted in the shop that first day. "Oh, Chandler, it's beautiful," she murmured, taking it out and trying it on.

"So are you," he said in a husky voice, his gaze roving over her.

"Do you like it?" she asked eagerly.

"I like it very much—so much that now I want you to take it off. Forget about dinner. Let's go make love," he said, his eyes glowing mischievously. "I've never made love to a Chinese lady."

Callie laughed merrily and shook her head. "Dinner first. We don't want to waste all the food Jiang cooked."

Chandler winked at her. "I suppose not."

Callie took off the coat and laid it on the couch. "I'll only be a minute," she said, intending to change.

"Why don't you keep that on?" he suggested, standing up and holding his arm out to her. "You look much too pretty to change, my flower. And the food does smell delicious. I think Jiang has outdone herself this time."

Smiling, Callie let him escort her to the dining room where they sat down to a meal of won ton soup, fried shrimp, rice, and steamed vegetables. She had just sampled the first spoonful of soup when the doorbell rang. "Who could that be?" she wondered aloud, wishing the guest had chosen another time to appear.

"Probably someone looking for my parents." Chandler smiled at her as he got up. "I'll only be a moment."

Callie hoped it was someone to see his parents and that they wouldn't stay. Their two weeks in San Francisco had been wonderful and she wanted to relish them to the last possible moment.

As she listened to Chandler's warm voice, her heart sank. He was inviting someone in, and the sultry feminine voice that responded sounded depressingly familiar. She had known their situation had been too good to last, but she hadn't expected it to end quite so soon. To her dismay, Nadine sauntered into the dining room. Dressed in a chic white suit with side slits in the pencil straight skirt, which clung to her curves, Nadine looked lovely and composed.

"Well, well, what a cozy little meal you two are having," she purred, gazing down at Callie.

"Hello, Nadine," Callie said, forcing herself to be polite. "I didn't know you were in town."

"Otherwise you would have invited me over, hmm?" the woman cooed. She looked back at Chandler. "I am welcome, am I not?"

"Of course you're welcome," he said, smiling broadly. He pulled out a chair for the redhead. "Sit down."

Callie felt sick inside: the special time with Chandler was over. Once again she was aware of her precarious position in his life. All Nadine had had to do was appear, and the wondrous spell was broken. The magic she and Chandler had known vanished like raindrops on the desert floor; the two weeks of love came to an abrupt and shattering end, as she had secretly suspected they would. She had been a fool to dare to dream it could have been otherwise. She couldn't hold Chandler as long as Nadine still wanted him.

"I do hate to break up your intimate little dinner," the woman said insincerely, smiling smugly as she sat down.

"Nonsense," Chandler declared, switching on the light before he seated himself. "There's plenty for one more, and the food is superb, isn't it, Callie?"

"Yes, it is." Callie managed a smile, despite the pain in her heart.

"I'm sure you won't want to miss it, Nadine," Chandler said.

"Well," she murmured, pretending to be uncertain, "if you're sure I'm not interrupting anything." She glanced at

Callie. "It looks like you were having some kind of private little costume party. You look so cute in that getup, Callie. Like a little girl playing Chinese."

Callie would not permit herself to be baited by the redhead. She had promised herself that she would never give Nadine that power over her again. "I'm so pleased that you like it," she replied with a dazzling smile. She glanced briefly at Chandler, determined not to show the betrayal she was feeling. Her eyes returned to Nadine. "I'll get a plate for you."

Holding her head high, she walked to the china cupboard. She fought down the bitter jealousy that unfurled inside. Chandler was still Nadine's, and Callie had only herself to blame for being silly enough to think that two weeks could erase Nadine from his mind.

"I'm visiting June and Kathy for a while, and their housekeeper said Jiang told her you were here," Callie heard Nadine tell Chandler. "I was *so* surprised to hear that."

Callie returned and set a place for Nadine. "Were you surprised, Nadine?" she asked evenly. "Surely the news is all over the community that my stepfather has had heart surgery here in San Francisco. I was sure that Chandler must have told you himself."

If looks had the power to wound, Callie would have been sorely injured when Nadine turned to face her; but the woman's tone was devoid of any venom. "Yes, of course I had heard that he was having surgery, but I didn't expect Chandler to spend two weeks away from the business." She smiled solicitously. "How is your stepfather? We've all been so concerned about him, and we haven't heard a single word."

Callie knew the woman hadn't given Logan a thought if she could possibly avoid it, but she spoke calmly. "How kind of you to care. He's doing very well."

Sitting down, she passed several of the dishes to Nadine,

pretending that everything was fine, as the woman and Chandler chatted about friends they had in the city. Chandler did try to include Callie in the conversation, but while she knew some of the people they were discussing, Nadine seemed determined to direct the conversation to only the people Callie didn't know.

Callie's food grew cold while she toyed with it, and her mood grew colder. Why had she dared to dream that Chandler would disassociate himself from Nadine? In her heart, she knew it was impossible. Their affair had lasted over the years—much longer than Callie and Chandler's marriage.

"How long will you be in the city?" Nadine asked, looking sweetly at Chandler.

"This is our last night."

"No!" Nadine cried. "And you haven't even visited with Aunt Mary? Why, Chandler Matthews, shame on you. She's heard you're in town, of course, and she's been waiting for you to call on her."

Chandler smiled. "I have thought of her, but Callie and I have been so busy sightseeing and keeping Logan company that there just hadn't been time to visit. Two weeks isn't long when you've not seen the city before."

Callie noted ruefully that Chandler hadn't mentioned that he and Callie had been on a second honeymoon, but then that wasn't the kind of thing one would tell his mistress. She glanced unhappily at Nadine when the woman spoke again.

"Chandler, you simply can't leave without seeing Aunt Mary. She would just be too disappointed. She's eighty years old now, you know, and you've always been her favorite person in all the world. Let's finish dinner with coffee at her house."

Chandler looked at Callie. "How about it, Callie? Are you up to visiting tonight? You'll love Aunt Mary. I guarantee it. Everyone does. And she's always wanted to meet you. She's the one who sent us the mantel clock for a wedding present. She's a sweet old gal."

Callie gazed at Nadine, then back at Chandler, and she refused to let either of them see her distress. Of course she knew Aunt Mary—Nadine's great-aunt Mary—and she was sure the three of them didn't want her along, but she wouldn't make it so easy for them. "I'd love to meet her. That's a wonderful idea, Chandler."

Nadine pouted prettily, and it was obvious that she had expected Callie to decline. "Then run along and slip into something presentable, Callie. Why, Chandler couldn't forgive himself if something happened to Aunt Mary and he didn't visit with her before he left."

Callie couldn't keep the anger from flashing in her eyes, but her voice was controlled and calm when she spoke. "I'll go dressed as I am," she said, standing up. "Chandler's very pleased with this outfit."

Nadine glanced at Chandler and a little smile played on her lips.

"You look beautiful," he told Callie, ignoring Nadine's expression. His amused eyes found Nadine's. "I selected the outfit. Don't you approve?"

Nadine's laughter was husky. "Well, I'm sure it has it's place, but is it really appropriate for calling on a *grande dame*?"

"I don't see why not," he replied.

Suddenly wondering if she were going to make a fool of herself, Callie tasted the dryness inside her mouth. Was she inappropriately dressed? Many of the Chinese still wore the charming pants and jacket, but then she wasn't Chinese. Straightening her shoulders, she gazed at Nadine. She couldn't back down now, no matter what Nadine said, but the redhead seemed docile now that Chandler had spoken in defense of the Mao suit.

Callie quickly slid the gold coat around her shoulders as they passed through the living room, and she thought she saw Chandler smile. But then, perhaps he was actually laughing at her. She was too upset to tell.

When they reached Aunt Mary's home, Callie wasn't sorry she had agreed to go. Although it wasn't Victorian in style, it was old and elegant and she made herself concentrate on it, speculating on the furnishings. A butler in a stiff uniform responded to the doorbell. A momentary feeling of unease seized Callie as she glanced down at her berry outfit and gold coat. She should have changed into a dress, but it was too late now. They were escorted into a very formal living room, and they stood for several minutes awaiting Aunt Mary's arrival. The butler took Callie's wrap and disappeared.

Aunt Mary finally came into the room. Dressed in a tan silk flowered dress, the old lady was slim, attractive, and quite erect, but she looked terribly formidable as she peered through a lorgnette held by a hand dripping with diamond rings. She extended the other hand to Chandler, and when Chandler bowed low and kissed it, Callie saw a diamond tiara in the old woman's silver hair. Callie felt uncomfortable when a stern glance was directed her way as Chandler introduced them, but she stood proudly before the scrutiny.

Bidding them sit, Aunt Mary perched on the edge of a regal chair. She studied Callie critically for several moments, letting her eyes sweep over the young woman before she spoke. Callie flushed furiously and looked at Chandler helplessly under the bold study. He seemed ready to come to her aid when Aunt Mary said evenly, "So this is the young beauty who stole Chandler Matthews from my great-niece." She looked at Chandler. "She's charming. Absolutely charming."

"Isn't she though?" Chandler said warmly, smiling at his wife. Callie managed a nervous smile, but she was thoroughly intimidated by Aunt Mary, and she was shocked that the woman would make such a statement. Glancing at Nadine, she saw a sour look on her face.

"Where did you get that lovely outfit, my dear?" Aunt Mary asked, still unsmiling, as she looked at Callie again.

"I—Chandler purchased it for me," Callie admitted a little shyly, feeling more uncomfortable than ever now that the woman had called attention to her clothes.

Abruptly, Aunt Mary stood up. "Come along with me," she said in an imperious tone. Callie looked at Chandler, then at Nadine, who obviously were expected to remain in the living room. She stood up reluctantly and followed Aunt Mary's stiff figure from the room and up to the top of some long, winding stairs where they entered a beautiful bedroom dominated by a fancy brass bed, covered with a scarlet velvet spread.

"How lovely," Callie exclaimed spontaneously.

Aunt Mary looked back at her. "Yes, isn't it beautiful? My late husband, Hubert, bought this house for me, and he selected all the furnishings." A faraway look glazed her eyes and her fierce features softened. "We shared forty-nine years of life together, fighting and loving, like all couples do, and I miss him more than I can ever tell you."

A small sigh escaped her thin lips. "But that's not why I've had you come in here." Bending down over an ancient black trunk at the end of the bed, she raised the lid. Rows of beautiful silk lounging outfits were nestled in the trunk next to an old jewelry box and a silver music box. Callie gazed at the jewelry box, and something about it reminded her of the one Aunt Caroline had. Aunt Caroline's had a false bottom: she had forgotten about that. It looked like the bottom of the jewelry box, but a secret compartment was revealed when the panel was slid forward. She and Aunt Caroline occasionally left each other notes in there: she, when she wished to express affection to her stern aunt, and Aunt Caroline, when she felt it necessary to apologize for some severe act or when she wished to instruct Callie upon some matter that good taste dictated not be discussed. Callie suddenly wondered if the missing letter could be stashed there. The compartment had been her and Aunt Caroline's secret, and the old woman might have thought surely she would inspect the box when all the possessions became hers.

She turned her attention back to Aunt Mary as the woman lifted out a gold lounging suit. "I've always wanted to give these pants and jacket to someone special, and I know that anyone Chandler Matthews married has to be special. Will you accept them, my dear?"

Callie was both flattered and embarrassed. She was a stranger to this woman, and she had no intention of taking advantage of her generosity. Besides, didn't Aunt Mary know how shaky their marriage was? Surely she, too, had heard the story of their separation. "Oh, I couldn't possibly," she murmured. "They must be worth a fortune."

"They are," Aunt Mary replied bluntly. "They once belonged to a Chinese empress, but as you can see, they are in excellent condition." She sighed again. "I'm sorry you don't want them. In fact, I'm terribly disappointed. My niece will only cast them away and never look at them, and when I saw your outfit, I hoped that I had found someone who shared my love of Chinese attire."

Callie couldn't stop her eyes from taking in the old woman's formal dress. Seeing her expression, Aunt Mary smiled for the first time and the smile transposed her features so that her face became almost angelic. "You don't expect me to be able to wear such things at my age, do you, my dear?"

Suddenly, Callie felt very comfortable with the woman. She reminded her of Aunt Caroline in a way; beneath the formal exterior was a soft and romantic inside. "I don't know why not. You're quite beautiful at your age."

Aunt Mary waved a wrinkled, diamond-ringed hand, but she was obviously very pleased. "Not in at least thirty years, child, but you're sweet to be so kind. Will you take my little offering?"

Her little offering, Callie thought incredulously. She knew instantly why Chandler had said that everyone loved Aunt Mary. "I will be honored to take the outfit," she murmured, deeply moved that the woman was willing to give it to her—wanted her to have it.

"I'm glad." Aunt Mary smiled at her again. "Well, we must get back to the others. If I were you, I wouldn't leave my man in Nadine's presence too long. I don't need to tell you, I'm sure, that she's always thought she owned Chandler."

Callie was surprised by the comment at first, then she smiled. Aunt Mary had no idea how right she was, but it was too late for her advice. Chandler was already in Nadine's grasp, and Callie had finally convinced her heart that there was no hope of prying him free. The smile left her lips, and she followed the grand old lady back into the living room.

She pretended not to notice that Nadine and Chandler were sitting close together, whispering, when she walked into the room. Chandler straightened immediately, but Callie refused to let him see the hurt look in her eyes. Averting her face, she listened as Aunt Mary ordered the maid to bring refreshments.

For several hours the four of them shared tea, cookies, and conversation. Aunt Mary made every attempt to include Callie in the discussion, and she succeeded quite well. Callie even managed to forget that her world had been destroyed again by Nadine's appearance, and for the time they shared with Aunt Mary, she almost forgot that she faced a bleak and uncertain future.

It wasn't until Chandler drove them back to the house, then escorted Nadine to her car, that Callie's depression settled in again. Taking the gold outfit in one hand and her gold coat in the other, she made her way to the front door and waited for Chandler to let her in. She looked away from Nadine's car when she heard the slam of the door. Even though Nadine was driving off, Callie knew she would never be rid of the redhead. She had been gullible and naive to think that Chandler would be hers again. A chill settled over her and she shivered.

"Cool, darling?" Chandler asked, stepping up beside her to unlock the door.

"Yes," she murmured, and she quickly rushed inside when he opened the door for her.

"How about a cup of coffee?" he suggested.

She shook her head. "No, I think I'll go on up to bed. I'm very tired and tomorrow will be hectic. Good night."

If Chandler noticed her coolness, he didn't comment. "Good night," he said, then turned toward the bar.

Callie stripped off her clothes, pulled on her gown, and climbed into the bed, hoping she would fall asleep before Chandler came up. Of course, she had no such luck, for her mind was filled with a thousand unhappy thoughts, all of them centering on Nadine and Chandler. How easily and willingly she had tumbled into her husband's arms again, so eager to believe his lies. But Nadine had been right: he had never been Callie's—and he never would be.

When Chandler came into the room and turned on the light to get ready for bed, Callie pretended to be asleep. He eased down on the bed beside her and slipped his arm around her waist. She lay on her side, breathing deeply. After a brief time, Chandler rolled away from her, and Callie sensed his displeasure as he stretched out on his side of the bed. A new bitterness engulfed her as she lay there by her husband's side—so near, yet so far away.

CHAPTER TEN

Chandler and Callie left early the next morning to make sure all the arrangements were made for Logan's departure. Logan had requested that he be installed in Aunt Caroline's house even though Chandler insisted that he would be much more comfortable at his. Logan pleaded that he considered Aunt Caroline's house home and that he was weary of moving to new places, but Callie felt sure that he wanted to give them more time to themselves and not be a burden. In lieu of a private nurse, Molly had been enlisted to stay with Logan, and, of course, Callie would spend much of her time with him, which suited her immensely now that she wanted to avoid Chandler as much as possible. She knew that she was obliged to share the year with him, and their recent intimacy made that year awkward and impossible for her in view of the situation. She was determined not to be his fool a third time.

When they greeted Logan in the hospital, he was eagerly awaiting the ride home. "I'll be glad when I can sleep in that old brass bed again," he told Callie excitedly. "Then, before you know it, I'll be ready to tackle the mine." He looked at Chandler. "How about it, Chandler? Have you done any checking into the mine yet?"

Chandler laughed gently. "Slow down, Logan. Let me get home and that will be number two on my list of priorities—after I check on the winery. Callie and I have been enjoying a second honeymoon while you've been convalescing, so I haven't given business a single thought."

Logan smiled sheepishly. "No, I don't suppose you have," he agreed, looking at Callie's pink cheeks. "Have you enjoyed San Francisco?" he asked.

She nodded. "It's as wonderful as I've always imagined, but now I'm eager to get you home and see you get well."

"Not nearly as eager as I am," he told her. "When will you be leaving?"

She looked at Chandler. "We'll get on the road in about an hour," he said. "Callie wants to get back before you do."

"Drive carefully," Logan instructed. "I wouldn't want to see anything happen to either of you."

Chandler laughed deeply. "Logan, you old son-of-a-gun, you really do want to reopen that copper mine, don't you?"

A slow grin curved Logan's thin lips. "Sure I do, but that's not what I was thinking of. I don't want anything to do wrong between you two now that you're finally getting your marriage patched up." He looked at Callie fondly before his eyes met Chandler's. "I don't mind telling you that this woman has been miserable the four years you've been apart."

Callie wished Logan hadn't shared that information, but it was too late to do anything about it. Turning to Chandler, she asked, "Shouldn't we get started if we're going to get home before Logan does?"

She was surprised to see the questioning look that had entered his eyes. He searched her face briefly as though Logan's comment had surprised him. "Yes, I think so." He extended his hand to Logan. "We'll see you this afternoon."

After shaking Chandler's hand warmly, Logan accepted Callie's kiss on the cheek. "Good-bye. Do be careful," he said, watching them leave.

Callie was quiet as they returned to the house to pack their suitcases and get ready to make the trip home. She caught Chandler looking at her peculiarly, and she avoided his eyes. Striding over to her, he grasped her arm.

"What's wrong?" he asked softly.

Lifting her head, she turned away from him. "Nothing."

"Don't tell me nothing," he insisted. "You're upset, and I want to know why."

Her eyes met his levelly. She would have liked nothing better than to confess her pain and anger and charge him with deception, but her pride was too great. It was an old story—one she had no intention of repeating. It was one thing to have believed him when she had been young and naive, but to have believed him knowing their painful past was inexcusable. She looked down at her clenched fists and stiffened her spine. "I've had a lot on my mind. Logan isn't out of danger yet," she replied tightly, telling the truth, but not admitting the real cause of her unhappiness.

Chandler drew her into his arms and smoothed down her hair. "He's going to be fine. You know he is. He's over the worst of it." Holding her a little way from him, he gazed down into her eyes. "I'll tell you what—when we get back home, I'll make sure things are running well at the winery, then I'll fly to Montana and see what I can learn about that copper mine. That will ensure a speedy recovery for Logan. I can almost guarantee it."

Wanting to appear grateful where Chandler's efforts on Logan's behalf were concerned, Callie mustered a semblance of a smile. "Fine."

He ran his fingers through her hair, then tipped back her chin. His lips lowered to hers and Callie remained passive while he kissed her lingeringly. She would to his intoxicating touch this time. When he head, there was a strange look in his eyes, comment as he released her. Walking back to his suitcase, he shoved in the final items.

"I'm ready when you are," he said coolly.

She went to the bathroom and gathered the last of her toilet articles. Keeping her eyes on her suitcase, she tucked in perfume, bath powder, and a shower cap, then closed the top, careful not to remember how thrilled she had been with the gold coat and the Mao suit buried beneath her other clothes.

The return ride to the Salinas Valley was uneventful. Chandler spoke very little and Callie made her comments light and impersonal. She wouldn't let him know how badly he had hurt her with his lies and his promises, or how gullible she had been—again. She had no one to blame but herself. What hurt most of all was the fact that she had actually believed him this time. No matter how much she had warned her heart against such foolishness, she had really thought that Chandler wanted only her; she had been almost certain that he would give Nadine up. And she had been dreadfully wrong.

Instead of returning to a haven, they found that the house instantly fell into a state of turmoil when they went inside. Sung began to rush around madly, preparing lunch; Roy called from the winery asking Chandler to come over as soon as possible; and Wesley Joseph appeared at the door.

Leaving all the confusion to Chandler, Callie went to her room to unpack. She wished she could just leave her clothes in her suitcase and go back to Aunt Caroline's house to live, but, of course, Chandler would never allow that, even though he had lied to her and hurt her again. She was still bound by her agreement to spend a year with him, and in the initial bargain he had not agreed not to see Nadine again. She sighed wearily as she unpacked the suitcase and hung up her clothes. The pretty Chinese lounging outfit and coat only served to make her more aware of her misery, and she hid them away at the end of the closet. When she had completed her chore, she went back to the living room to find Molly dusting the furniture.

"How's Logan?" the woman asked, wiping a cloth across an already spotless table top.

"He's doing very well. He should be home at any time. I want to go over to the house and change the bed linen and freshen the rooms before he arrives."

"I've already done that. Did it this morning, in fact," Molly announced. "Mr. Matthews phoned ahead to say you were coming. I've taken some of my stuff over there and put it in the bedroom next to the patient's."

"Good," Callie replied just as Chandler walked into the room.

"Sung has lunch ready," he told her.

"All right," she murmured, following him to the dining room.

"I'm going to the winery after lunch," he said as he slid out his chair and sat down. "Would you like to go with me?"

She shook her head. "I want to go over to the house and check on last-minute preparations before Logan gets here."

Chandler nodded knowingly, but a coolness settled over the table and they ate the meal in total silence. As soon as he had finished, Chandler curtly bid Callie good-bye, telling her that he would see her later, and he left the room.

She stayed at the table for a while longer, playing with her dessert. She didn't know what direction her life was taking, but she knew that she was more unhappy than she had ever thought possible. It had been so cruel of Chandler to let her think he really loved her and would be true, just to sleep with her for two weeks. She drew a ragged breath: she should be thankful that he had made it possible for Logan to get well again instead of dwelling on how miserable he had made her. Chandler was entirely responsible for Logan's well-being, but it had hurt so much to know that he had deceived her again in the matter of their marriage. Distracted, she wandered out to the car, only to turn around abruptly when she heard Molly's gruff voice.

"Where're you going, Callie?"

Looking up, she saw Molly step down off the porch. "I'm going to Aunt Caroline's house to await Logan's arrival." She felt the color rise to her cheeks. "I'm sorry, Molly. I have so many things on my mind that I forgot about you."

"I'll just ride along with you," Molly said, not waiting to see if Callie wanted her. "After all, I'll be nursing your stepfather and I haven't even met him. I'll fix him something to eat there. I don't need Sung to cook for me, and I don't want him in my kitchen."

Callie had to laugh; Molly was finally getting a kitchen to herself. She was sure Sung was just as happy to be getting Molly out of his hair for a while.

Callie was searching for Aunt Caroline's old jewelry box and Molly was cooking vegetable soup and cornbread when Logan arrived some time later. He was taken upstairs on a stretcher to save him the climb, even though the doctor had told them that he would soon be able to use the steps. Plastering on her best smile, Callie followed the procession up the stairs. Soon a smiling Logan was safely installed in bed. Callie introduced him to Molly, who was hovering around the bed, watching the patient.

He smiled politely when Molly ordered him to lie still while she went down for the soup and bread. After she had stepped out into the hall, Logan turned to Callie and grimaced. "What was that? The prison warden?"

Giggling, Callie shook her head. "She's really a delightful soul. Don't let her get you down with that brusque voice and military manner. Besides, she's in seventh heaven now. She loves waiting on people—and ordering them around—especially when she has a captive audience like you."

They both laughed and began to talk about all the things Callie and Chandler had seen and done in San Francisco. Logan patted her hand. "I'm so glad you and he are getting along so well, Callie."

She looked away from him, trying in vain to hide her unhappiness.

"Callie?" he questioned gently. "You are getting along, aren't you?"

She looked back at him, forcing a bright demeanor. "Of course we are. Things are going much better than I ever thought they could."

Logan grinned. "I'm glad to hear it, honey. You both deserve the very best, and I think you can find it with each other." His smile broadened. "I am so very pleased that you got back together after all this time."

"You should be," Callie said, making her voice light. "Chandler's leaving soon to check out the copper mine."

Logan's face lit up, and Callie was pleased that she had distracted him so quickly. "When is he going?"

She shrugged. "Right away. Maybe even tomorrow."

A frown creased his brow. "Boy, I sure wish I were going with him. I want to show him the mine and its potential myself." He arched his brows. "Say, Callie, why don't you go with him? You know a lot about the mine."

"Not on your life," she said, shaking her head emphatically. "I'm going to stay right here and watch over you." She didn't mention that she couldn't bear more time with Chandler alone after the fiasco in San Francisco.

"But I have the old battle ax for that," Logan declared with a wicked smile.

Just then Molly came into the room and Logan put a

hand to his forehead as if to say he had narrowly escaped her hearing his comment.

"Here we are, Mr. Bartholomew," she said loudly. "Just what the doctor ordered." When she saw Logan's doubtful look, she said, "Now, don't you worry. Ol' Molly'll fix you right up. I've done far more than my share of nursing in my day, and I've never seen a sick day myself."

"Well, if you two will excuse me," Callie said, winking at Logan mischievously, "I'll run alone. I have things to do."

"Must you go already?" he protested. Callie was sure that he felt he was being abandoned to the enemy, but she knew he would like Molly if only he would give himself a chance.

"Yes," she said. "Eat your soup while it's hot. I know you must be hungry."

He looked at the steaming bowl of soup. "I am at that," he confessed, "and it does look tempting."

"Of course it does," Callie heard Molly say as she walked from the room. Closing the door, she left Logan to the woman's mercy and went back downstairs.

She knew she should return to Chandler's house, but she didn't want to. They were both aware of the wall that was growing between them again, and Callie was sure Chandler knew the reason why. A dozen times she had wondered what he and Nadine were whispering about at Aunt Mary's house, but she answer was certain to be more painful than not knowing.

She cursed herself silently. Had Chandler wanted her so badly that he had deliberately lied to her, or had he honestly hoped they could attempt to rebuild their marriage, then found it impossible the minute he saw Nadine? Worse yet, had he simply felt sorry for her because she had been so upset over Logan, then felt obligated to placate her with words of love and promises once they had made love? She brushed the painful thoughts from her mind. The why didn't matter now, but how was she supposed to live with him day after day as if their situation hadn't changed drastically? She could only take it a day at a time and see what transpired. At least Chandler would be in Montana for a while.

Recalling the scene in Aunt Mary's house, Callie suddenly had a suspicion where Aunt Caroline's jewelry box might be. She went back upstairs, then down the hall, and climbed the steep, narrow steps to the attic. With so much on her mind, she had forgotten that Chandler had said Molly and Sung had stored some things up here. Her eyes searched the musty, crowded little area. All of Aunt Caroline's clothes had been neatly folded and stored in boxes. Her glasses, haircombs, and a worn watch Callie had given her for her sixtieth birthday lay in a plastic tray on top of one box. Callie picked up the watch and gazed at it lovingly. It had been cheap and never kept good time, but Aunt Caroline had claimed that she loved it best of all her possessions. The sight of it tugged at Callie's heartstrings, and she laid it down to rummage through the boxes for the jewelry box.

Her disappointment and frustration rising, she took out all her aunt's possessions, but there was no sign of either the jewelry box or a letter. Glancing around unhappily, she spied an old gold trunk in the shadows. She rushed over to it and unstrapped the leather thongs, but it contained only blankets and one handmade quilt.

Callie sighed wearily. What had become of the jewelry box? It was nearly worthless, even though it was an antique. Her eyes scanned the room again. She had almost despaired of finding the box when she decided to look in an old wicker hamper that held her aunt's old-fashioned black shoes. Carefully taking out several pair, she looked down into the tall wicker basket.

There it was! The jewelry box—at last! Callie had become so obsessed with finding the letter that her fingers trembled as she lifted the box from the basket and sought the catch on the bottom that freed the secret drawer. The anticipation was almost intolerable as she slid the long, narrow drawer forward. It was there! Aunt Caroline *had* put the letter in the jewelry box! Callie's hands shook as she tore open the envelope and pulled out the single sheet of pale yellow paper.

> *Dear Callie,* it read, *I couldn't go to my grave without letting you know how much I have treasured your love. You were the darling child that I never had, and you were a constant source of joy in my last years. I know you must think me simply terrible for never responding to your overtures, but please forgive a silly old fool her pride. I was so embittered at first that I was too blind with disappointment to write, and as the time passed, I was too ashamed. I hope you won't think too badly of me. You were such a blessing to me that I never wanted you to grow up, for I was afraid I would lose you. Please try to remember me as the old woman who loved you, and may God bless you as He did me when He sent you to me. Your loving Aunt Caroline.*

Sitting down heavily on the old trunk, Callie stared at the letter. Aunt Caroline had forgiven her; she had continued to love her until her death. The letter was a godsend, and Callie clasped it lovingly in her hands, the relief she was feeling almost tangible. It was as though a tremendous burden had been physically lifted from her heart. If she suffered nothing else but heartache while she was in the valley, this letter and its precious message were worth returning for. She stayed up in the attic for some time, lost in her thoughts and memories and the sweet-sadness of Aunt Caroline's last words, so very thankful that at last she had found the missing letter. The quiet, private time was a healing period for her, and she treasured each minute as she reread the letter with misty eyes.

When she was again composed, she went down to tell Logan good-bye. She was surprised to find Molly and Logan laughing gaily as she walked into the room.

"Come on in, honey," Logan said, seeing her. "Molly was just telling me about the summer she spent camping in Montana."

Callie arched an eyebrow. Logan definitely appeared to have changed his mind about the "old battle ax" as he smiled warmly at Molly. She could tell that the two of them were going to get on famously, and she felt a little less guilty about leaving Logan for a while. "I just wanted to let you know that I'm going to Chandler's house for the evening. I need to know what his plans are, and, of course, you'll want to know if he's going to Montana."

"You bet I will," Logan murmured with conviction.

Callie smiled at him. She almost told him about the letter in her hand, but he was so preoccupied with Molly that he hadn't even noticed it. She decided that she would tell him another time. "You get some rest, and I'll call you later in the evening. If you need me, let me know. Otherwise, I'll see you in the morning." She lightly touched his forehead with her lips.

A grinning Logan told her good-bye, and immediately picked up where he had left off, telling Molly tales of Montana.

Chandler was sitting in the living room studying a map and making some notes when Callie walked into the room.

"How did he handle the trip?" he asked, gazing up at her.

"Fine. Molly's with him now and I think she will work out beautifully. She's even been to Montana," she said, smiling gently.

Chandler patted a spot on the couch. "Come sit by me, Callie. We need to talk."

Immediately, Callie's stomach tensed as she anticipated the very worst. She, too, knew that they needed to talk, but somehow when the critical moment was at hand, she had the fiercest desire to postpone it. She didn't think she could bear the revelation right now. Would Chandler tell her what they both already knew? Would he admit that their two weeks in San Francisco—their entire reunion—had been a stupid mistake? Would he tell her that Nadine was the only woman he wanted and that he had taken Callie to his bed once more merely to be sure?

She felt an anxious and painful thudding of her foolish heart, but she knew it was absurd to procrastinate; she might as well get the agony over with. The more quickly all the ugliness and shame were behind her, the sooner she could begin to rebuild the shattered shell of her heart. She felt the muscles in her throat constrict and it seemed that she had experienced these same painful feelings with Chandler too many times to be able to endure them yet again. Forcing her eyes to meet his, she settled stiffly beside him on the couch.

"I'm going to Montana for five days. I'll fly myself and take Ron Marvy with me. He knows about copper mining, and he can help me evaluate the worth of Logan's mine. Will you help Roy in the winery? I've told him to rely on you as the final authority. He'll probably have some papers that require the owner's signature."

Callie blinked as she gazed uncomprehendingly at him. He hadn't said a word about Nadine, and he had delegated authority to her as though she were a true wife—a true partner in his life, and although she was flattered, she couldn't understand his reasoning. Their marriage was worse than a sham; consequently, she saw no reason to involve herself in his winery.

"Why?" she sputtered.

"Why?" he repeated, his eyes serious. "I intend for you to be my equal in all matters, Callie. You're my wife."

It all sounded so natural, but she was instantly angered that he was continuing the charade. She had been positive that he intended to bring his affair with Nadine out in the open and put an end to the pretense and games.

"I don't know enough about the winery to run it," she remarked, at a loss for anything else to say.

"Roy will help you," Chandler said equably. "Anyway, I'll only be gone a few days." He studied her face. "Don't you want to do it?"

"Yes, of course," she replied. She was pleased that he considered her mature enough, finally, and responsible enough—and intelligent enough—to be an asset in his business. He never would have considered involving her in such a way four years ago, but the whole situation was ridiculous now.

"Good. Then that's settled." He reached out and drew her to his side, but even though Callie was flattered that he at last had credited her with some business sense, she would not be tricked into his arms again and pulled away.

Noting her withdrawal without comment, Chandler removed his arm and stood up. He tucked his shirt into his trousers and said, "I think I'll go pack. I want to get to bed early tonight so we can take off early in the morning." Without a backward glance, he left the room.

Callie gazed down at her hands as she twisted the wedding band she still wore. Somehow she felt unreasonably cold and cruel, as though she were in the wrong to treat Chandler as she had done. But, of course, there was no justification why *she* should feel guilty. If Chandler thought to make a success with his business, his marriage, and his mistress, he would find Callie totally unobliging. She remained on the couch, lost in her thoughts until Sung announced that dinner was served.

Both she and Chandler barely sampled the roast and vegetables, and Sung shook his head in displeasure as he removed their half-filled plates. They both declined the luscious-looking strawberry shortcake Sung tried to tempt them with and neither of them accepted coffee.

Chandler returned to his notes and map, and Callie forlornly trailed to the pantry to get her spray can and water the plants. When she had done that, she returned the container to the pantry and, finding an owl plant hanger she had started to macrame four years ago, she picked it up and automatically began to work with the strands of jute.

Chandler was up before six the next morning. He had already finished breakfast when Callie went to the table. She had just seated herself when he bent down and kissed her cheek.

"I'll see you in about five days. You take care of yourself, Callie."

Callie stared up into his remote blue eyes, and something about the sadness of their situation made her heart weep. Raising her lips to gently touch his, she murmured, "Good-bye, Chandler." Then she sat very still, watching as he slowly walked from the room, his gait tired and stiff.

The next three days passed in a blur for Callie. She spent her mornings and evenings with Logan, but the bulk of her day was consumed at the winery. She did enjoy the opportunity and the challenge, and she had very little time to dwell on the futility of helping with the business. Roy and she took turns breaking in a new tour guide, and there was work that had piled up while Chandler was in San Francisco. Every minute of Callie's time in the winery seemed to be filled with endless jobs to complete.

When she went to see Logan the evening of the third day, she heard excited chatter from the upstairs room. Briskly closing the front door, Callie walked up the steps to his room, and his incredulous tone caused her to pause in the hallway, lest she interrupt some private conversation.

"Do you mean he didn't even go to Montana?" Logan queried in a quiet voice.

"Oh, no. No!" Molly said quickly. "I don't mean that at all. He went to check on the mine, all right. Don't you worry about that. He's as good as his word, he is, and I'm sure that he'll pour his money into it; but he's spending these last two days in San Francisco at *that* house."

"And Callie didn't even *know* about it?" Logan asked in a surprised voice.

"Not a thing, as far as I can tell," Molly replied.

"Where is the house?" he asked.

When Molly gave the address, Callie's hands flew to her mouth to stifle a gasp. She wanted to turn away and stop eavesdropping, but she was too absorbed in the conversation to leave. The address was that of the house Chandler had claimed belonged to his "friend." She remembered the seven-eleven number, and it pained her to have her suspicions confirmed. That house *had* to belong to Nadine! Why was Chandler finding it necessary to continue his deceit? How dare he slip off to San Francisco while Nadine was still there? And why had he found it necessary to insult her further by boasting about it to Molly?

As she stood outside the door, her fists clenched in anger, her cheeks suffusing with color, she decided that she had had enough. There was no way she would continue this outrage another day. If she and Chandler couldn't be aboveboard in this relationship, there was no excuse to go on with it. If he had made her his wife again only to flaunt Nadine to everyone else, she had enough respect for herself, if he didn't, not to let it happen while she stood by. The first thing in the morning, she would take a trip of her own. She would confront Chandler with his mistress this time, and tell him exactly what she thought of the arrangement. And surely this time, when she saw the two of them in Nadine's home, she would finally be able to eradicate Chandler from her system once and for all. She would tell him that she would repay the money somehow—she did owe him that—but she would not go on with the present arrangement.

Taking a few minutes to rein in her emotions, Callie drew deep breaths and closed her eyes. When she walked into the room, she appeared composed, despite her churning hurt and anger. "Good evening," she said warmly. "How are you two?"

Molly looked at Logan and he looked at her.

"What have you been up to today, Logan?" Callie asked to break the tension in the room.

Apparently deciding that Callie hadn't overheard them, Molly stood up. "We've just been passing the time of day. Have you eaten? I've got some stew simmering. How about joining us for dinner?"

"That sounds wonderful," Callie replied. "When you go down, will you please call Sung and tell him not to cook tonight?"

"Will do," Molly said as she bustled from the room.

Callie wasted no time telling Logan of her plans. "Tomorrow I'm going to San Francisco to see Chandler," she said.

"You know?" Logan exclaimed, his eyes wide.

She took his hand, not wanting him to get upset. "Of course I know," she assured him with a faint smile. "I've known for some time."

"But why didn't you tell me?" he asked, his brow furrowed.

"What was there to tell?" she murmured with a shrug.

"What was there to tell?" he repeated incredulously.

"Yes," she said calmly, in spite of her pounding heart. "This has been common knowledge for four years."

Logan's features were distorted as he puzzled over the matter. "You and I are talking about the same thing, aren't we?"

"The house?" she asked carelessly.

"Then you really do know."

She nodded again. "Chandler showed it to me when we were there."

"You're taking it so nonchalantly," he commented.

She had opened her mouth to respond when Molly came into the room with a tray of food. "Here we are," the woman said, unfolding a stand with one hand. Callie walked over to help and the conversation between her and Logan was forgotten.

Callie slept very little that night, and she left for San Francisco at daylight the next morning. Her stomach was somersaulting and she had been much too upset to make any pretense of eating breakfast. Her mind whirling with disappointment and heartache, she drove mile after dragging mile until at last she reached the city. Her palms were moist and there was a painful tenseness in her stomach at the thought of confronting the man she still loved, but she knew it had to be done. It was hard for her to believe that Chandler was deliberately being so callous and spiteful, but the facts spoke for themselves. Once and for all, she had to abandon any notion that there was hope for them.

As she pursued her course, driving relentlessly toward the lovely cream Victorian house, she feared that she had lost her way. Even though she was quite good with directions, and she and Chandler had covered the city rather thoroughly, she had seen the house only once, and she saw no familiar landmarks.

A stop at a service station confirmed her directions to the prestigious neighborhood, and she drove on. When she spied the house, she parked the car boldly in front of it, climbed out, and made her way up the steps. She had to act quickly for she was fast losing her nerve and questioning the folly of her actions. Perhaps she should have simply gone away again. Logan was in good hands. But no, she wouldn't accomplish any more that way than she had done four years ago. She had to see Chandler with his mistress to teach her heart its painful lesson. With the three of them face to face, there would be no more room for lies or deception. She rang the doorbell and stood back to wait.

A sleepy Chandler, barefoot, dressed only in pajama bottoms, his head an unruly mess of black curls, opened the door. "Callie!" he exclaimed hoarsely, making every attempt to shake the sleep from his mind. "What's wrong? What are you doing here?"

Callie swallowed nervously, suddenly feeling strangely vulnerable here before her husband. A thousand regrets poured into her mind, and she longed for something that could never be. "There's no use to pretend, Chandler," she made herself say. "I know who this house belongs to, and I know you've been spending your time here with her." Her voice faltered. "I—I had to see for myself."

Chandler pushed both hands through his hair and tried to make some sense of her words. "Who? What are you talking about? Is Logan all right?"

She sighed tiredly. Why was he dragging this out, making it awkward and painful for all concerned? "Logan is fine. Oh, Chandler," she cried, exasperated, "I know Nadine is here with you."

"What?"

She repeated the words, finding them no less hateful to herself than the first time. She still loved Chandler, and her heart begged her not to go through with this—not to carry around forever this one last ugly memory of Chandler and Nadine. She suppressed a desire to weep. "I know Nadine is here with you."

Chandler's brows met in a dark, angry line. "Do you think so little of me that you find me capable of such actions?" he asked her in a low voice. "Nadine is certainly not here, Callie. Why would she be?"

"Because she lives here," Callie replied in a strained voice, terribly upset that he still played the game.

"Where on earth did you get such a ridiculous idea?" he demanded, all traces of sleep leaving his face to be replaced by ire.

"I'm not a fool, Chandler," she said coolly, "no matter how much you may think so. When I said a woman owned this house, you didn't deny it. The room you wouldn't show me can only be Nadine's bedroom. And I saw you and Nadine whispering at Aunt Mary's house that night. Even Molly knows about you being here with Nadine. I'm well aware that you probably made plans to meet Nadine here while you were in San Francisco with me. You insult us both if you think I don't know what's been going on. I'm only puzzled as to why you would go to such lengths."

A light flickered in Chandler's eyes. "Is that why you've been so cool since?"

Callie glanced nervously up into his face, but she didn't give him the satisfaction of hearing her say yes.

Chandler laughed without merriment. "Sometimes I think you'll drive me mad. Here I was thinking you were bored again and looking for excuses to get out of the marriage before you even gave it the year. That's one of the reasons I asked you to help me in the winery, and that's why I'm here. I can't lose you again, Callie. I *won't* lose you again. Somehow we're going to work at this marriage until we get it right."

Abruptly grasping her hand, he began to pull her inside the room. "What are you doing?" she gasped.

"You want to know what's in that bedroom, don't you? Well, I'll show you. We'll get to the bottom of this, and then—just maybe—we'll have a base to build from. Do you think Nadine's here with me? Is that what this is all about?"

Callie felt breathless and weak-kneed. Her courage was waning fast. What would she do if Nadine were in there? Her anger had begun to dissipate in the confusion of the confrontation.

With Callie firmly in his grip, Chandler marched up the steps and down the hall to the last bedroom—the one he had neglected to show her before. When he shoved the door open, Callie held her breath, fully expecting to find her husband's mistress in bed. Her mouth flew open when she saw all the furniture that had once been in the bedroom in her and Chandler's home—the furniture she had picked out. "But that's our bedroom furniture!" she cried with dismay. "What's it doing here?"

Chandler forced her head around so that she had to look up into his eyes. "The same thing I am," he said softly. "Waiting for you." His eyes searched her face. "When you left me, I couldn't bear the sight of it. It held too many good memories for me, so I had it shipped here—to this house I'd bought for you. This room was the only one that didn't come complete with furnishings. I had intended to let you choose them. I still intend to. That's what I'm doing here. I'm having this furniture sold today."

Callie gazed at him in disbelief. "You bought this house for me?"

"Yes. Four years ago. This is where I was planning to bring you for a second honeymoon when you ran off."

"I don't believe you!" she cried. It was impossible. It couldn't be true. He was joking. "You don't even like living in San Francisco," she charged.

His fingers tightened along her jaw. "I hadn't intended to live here full time then. I purchased it for a getaway house." His eyes gazed intently into hers. "Callie, I know that the vineyards and the valley are a dull place for a modern young woman to live. I could have understood it if you had told me that you were bored there—with the area—but not with me."

She looked away from his penetrating eyes, even though he still held her chin securely. "But I saw you. I saw you and Nadine in each other's arms that night," she murmured miserably.

Chandler's brows met in a hard line as he again forced her to look at him. "You saw what?"

"I saw you and Nadine in our bedroom. Your bag—and hers—were all packed."

He studied her for a moment as though she had lost her mind. "That wasn't her bag," he said at last. "And if she was in my arms, it meant nothing at all. You've known all along that Nadine and I were close friends—but no more. Even when I teased you about her, I didn't think you really saw her as a threat. She considers herself your friend. She went to a lot of trouble for you then. She spent days buying the clothes you saw in that suitcase so you wouldn't know anything about the second honeymoon or the house I'd bought as a surprise." Suddenly he glowered at her. "You thought Nadine and I were running off together? I can't believe that."

Callie bit down on her lip, shaken by his words and confused by the revelation. She had been so sure—so positive—of what she suspected. "Don't tell me you and Nadine haven't been having an affair right along from the day you and I married."

Chandler shook his head. "Of course not. I won't deny that there once was something between Nadine and me, Callie, but it was many years ago—when we were in high school, in fact. She and I grew up together and we were thrown together at every turn, but there was never a passionate relationship. I love Nadine, I'll readily admit—just as you love Logan. She's the sister I never had. I worry about her, and I hurt for her when she's hurt, but I've never cared for her in the way I care for you."

Callie could only stand there, trembling with disbelief. "She thought there was more," Callie insisted feebly. "Indeed, she *told* me that you would always be hers."

Chandler regarded her for several moments. Finally he

sighed heavily. "I don't know where or when things started to go wrong between us, Callie, but you should have come to me with your problems. I had no idea Nadine thought my friendship with her was something more. I find it incredible to believe that we've wasted these years over misunderstandings that could have been cleared up with a few explanations."

Tears glistened in her eyes when they sought Chandler's. "I tried to talk to you—I wanted to talk to you—" Her words trailed off. "Oh, God, Chandler," she whispered, "for four years I've believed that you were planning to leave me for Nadine." She suddenly covered her face with her hands and began to weep quietly.

Chandler dragged her hands from her white face and drew her into his embrace. "Callie," he murmured hoarsely, "for four years I've searched for you, waited for you, loved you—sure that someday you would settle down—that you would see that you would never find a love like that we had shared. I had no idea why you left me so abruptly without at least giving me a chance to right whatever was wrong. It took all my pride to come to you when you returned to the valley. Didn't you know how desperately I wanted you to be mine again—how passionately I wanted us to have a brand-new start as man and wife?"

She could barely hold his gaze. "There was still Nadine. And I thought you wanted to punish me for leaving you. And—and you wanted Aunt Caroline's land for your vineyards."

He shook his head again. "I would have cast Nadine from my life a thousand times if I had known she really meant to hurt you, and I could have had the land at any time in the past few years. I own West Enterprises, and I foreclosed on your aunt for lack of payments

" the money?" she asked, eyes wide.

He nodded. "Yes, but she didn't know it."

Callie pushed her hands through her golden hair, at a loss for what to say. "What were you and Nadine whispering about at Aunt Mary's house?"

"She wanted to know if I'd shown you the house."

"Chandler, I've been such a fool," she murmured at last. "I don't know how to make up for the years I've thrown away—years that belonged to us both. I've ached to be in your arms, and I've had to force myself not to beg you to love me. I wanted so desperately to pretend that you had no mistress and live with you as your wife. I love you with all my heart, my soul. My life is empty without you."

"God, how I've yearned to hear you say that," he murmured, lowering his head to hers. He kissed her hungrily, and when he raised his lips from hers, he traced the line of her full mouth with his thumb.

"I hear the third time is a charm. Shall we try it? We can live here in San Francisco. No nasty Nadines, no small-town snoops, no restricted living. I've missed the marvelous entertainment and the fabulous restaurants to be found here. This will be a wonderful base for the copper mine. Roy can run the winery. And you can even have that plant shop you spoke of. We'll use the ranch house for the getaway house when we become tired of the hectic pace here."

Callie clung to him, wrapping her arms around him tightly. "I don't care where we live—just as long as it's together. I've never been bored with you, Chandler. I couldn't possibly be. I could live on a deserted island and be in heaven if you were there by my side." She laughed lightly. "Then I would know you wouldn't stray."

His eyes were a solemn blue and his voice was husky when he spoke. "I've loved you since the day I saw you, and I'll die loving you. You never have to worry about me straying." His lips lowered to hers again, and Callie met the fire in his touch. She had truly come home, for wherever Chandler was, that was her home—be it in the sweet, vine-covered Salinas Valley or here in metropolitan San Francisco. Her love for him surged higher inside her, and Chandler drew her more tightly to him as he lifted his lips from hers to whisper to her, "My love, my heart, my wife."

When You Want A Little More Than Romance—

Try A Candlelight Ecstasy!

 Wherever paperback books are sold!

Danielle Steel

AMERICA'S LEADING LADY OF ROMANCE REIGNS OVER ANOTHER BESTSELLER

A Perfect Stranger

A flawless mix of glamour and love by Danielle Steel, the bestselling author of *The Ring*, *Palomino* and *Loving*.

A DELL BOOK $3.50   #17221-7

At your local bookstore or use this handy coupon for ordering:

Dell DELL BOOKS A PERFECT STRANGER $3.50 #17221-7
P.O. BOX 1000, PINE BROOK, N.J. 07058-1000

Please send me the above title. I am enclosing $_____ (please add 75¢ per copy to cover postage and handling). Send check or money order—no cash or C.O.D.'s. Please allow up to 8 weeks for shipment.

Mr./Mrs./Miss _____

Address _____

City _____ State/Zip _____